STOW AWAY

Christopher Wager

This novel is dedicated to my loving and supportive wife

Karen (& collaborator) and son Benjamin

To whom I owe everything. Thanks, with lots of love.

Preface

Stow Away is a young adult action/adventure coming of age novel. The story begins when Benjamin Holt, the 13-year-old main character, takes (unbeknownst to him) the first steps into an adventure that will change his life forever, mistaken for a thief at one of New York City's many fruit markets. Benjamin becomes a stowaway on the tramp steamer the U. S. S. Alexandria bound for the wilds of Africa to escape the Citi's cops hot on his tail.

The young boy must figure out how to survive and make a place for himself among a ship full of rough and tough men of the sea, a treasure hungry sea captain, and a bitter first mate who despises him the moment he comes aboard. Abraham, the ship's cook, and Jacob, the ship's first-officer, friend Ben. Through many tries and failures, Ben discovers he can be more than some streetwise kid. In the end, he must find the strength and will within himself to become the most unlikely hero if he is ever to make it home again.

This is my first full-length work of fiction. It has been a long five years bringing it to the world. To start at the beginning, I wrote this novel for my son Benjamin, who was the model and inspiration. I beg your patience while I tell you a little about my son. Benjamin, having a love of reading, was a great help in the writing and development of the story, offering his help and advice at the rare moments I suffered from writer's block. After many rewrites and revisions, adding, taking away and adding pieces back again, countless hours researching ships, engines, maps, and the time period in which the story takes place, a novel started to form.

Stow Away conveys the message of courage and friendship. Benjamin learns with the help of his friends he can do more and be more than he ever thought possible. Stow Away was written to be enjoyed by all ages, paying particular attention to young adult readers creating situations the readers could relate to.

I decided to write about a boy facing the challenges and insecurities of growing up and coming out the other end, a strong and confident young man. To make the point with a little determination and support, young people can do great things.

I have to admit my two biggest inspirations for the story are Indiana Jones, written by George Lucas in 1973 and the Rudyard Kipling novel, Captains Courageous, written in 1897. One offered a great adventure and the other the story of a great friendship. Since writing the novel, I have a newfound respect and admiration for a writer spending countless hours toiling away at their word processors.

It has been a pleasure writing this work, doing the research, and learning a few things about myself. In some ways, it is a bittersweet goodbye to all the characters I have spent so much time with and have come to love and hate. In the end, I knew the day would come; our children grow up and start a new chapter of their own. Thank you for joining the crew of the tramp steamer U. S. S. Alexandria. Welcome aboard!

Index

Chapter 1

The Departure

"Take that you dirty pirate," Ben said.

"Ah," the pirate said, before collapsing to the deck.

"Behind you," another sailor warned.

The buccaneer swung his sword at Ben. "I have you now captain. You and your ship."

Ben grabbed a rope dangling from the mast rigging and swung across the deck. "Not today, Barnacle Bart."

"Surrender or face death," he commanded to the band of pirates.

"Ben!" a voice said.

"Benjamin Michael Holt! Dinner." Ben's mother's voice rang out again from their second-story apartment window, for the whole neighborhood to hear.

"Ah man," a pirate said, dropping his sword.

"Sorry guys. I have to go."

Ben jumped down from the grandest ship ever to sail the seven seas. Constructed of old tires, pallets, and anything else the gang could scrounge. Docked in the empty lot next to Ben's brownstone apartment building.

"See ya, Ben," a boy said before the pirate captain struck him down.

Ben attempted to brush off his worn trousers before his mother laid eyes on him.

"Benjamin, I called you twice. Didn't you hear me?"

"Sorry, Ma." Ben shoved his wooden sword into the umbrella holder beside the door. Car horns from the street bellowed through the open window of their cramped lower east-side Manhattan apartment. Spontaneous sound filled the room. Ben entered the dingy pale blue kitchen, which hadn't always been blue. Former tenants had taken it upon themselves to paint over the flower-patterned wallpaper; weight of the paint lifted the wallpaper at the edges. Throw rugs cover the kitchen floor put there by his mother to cover the places where the tile is missing.

"What's for dinner?"

"Ham and potatoes," his mother said.

Ben liked ham. Potatoes not so much, it being the third time this week they've had them. He went to the sink, washed his hands, and ran his semi-toothless comb through his short dark hair. While he read the calendar hanging on a nail over the sink. August 2, 1937.

"One, two, three, four," Ben counted off the days.

"What," his mother asked.

"Oh, nothin' Ma."

"Wash that face, too."

He and his mother sat and ate their modest dinner and chitchatted about their day. When Ben had stuck his fork into the last of the ham occupying his plate, his mother cleared the table.

"I heard they're hiring boys to sell peanuts at the Yankee's games on the weekends. What do you think Ma, could I?" Ben wiped his plate clean with the last piece of bread before stuffing it into his mouth.

She looked at him with a warm smile, her blue eyes obscured by her gray hair.

"Land sakes, Ben, there's no need for such a young boy to be worryin' about working. We'll be all right; it'll get better."

"I know Ma, but I want to. I don't mind."

Ben being the honorary man of the house ever since his father passed away. He is embarrassed by his mother's comment as he often tried to act older than he was. He didn't like being reminded that he had yet to fill his father's shoes. Ben sat awaiting his mother's answer, hoping this time; she'd see him for his age and not the seven-year-old she always had.

After what felt like forever, his mother turned to speak. "I guess it would be all right as long as your school comes first."

Ben jumped from his seat and tossed his arms around his mother's wide middle. "Thanks, Ma!"

He ran to the door, his fingers closed around the knob when his mother called to him.

"Hold on their young man. Let me get a look at ya."

Ben annoyed as his mother pushed up his chin and fussed over his shirt collar. "There, that's better."

Ben kissed his mother on her round rosy cheek and sped out into the hallway and down the rickety stairs.

"You stay away from the docks you hear me; that's no place for a young respectable boy to be found messin' around."

"I will Ma."

Ben busted through the double doors of his building and leaped to the sidewalk.

"Hey, watch it!" a man said, when Ben collided with him in midair of his jump, all most knocking the man off his feet. Ben picked up the man's dented bowler hat and handed it back.

"Sorry, sir."

The man with his face red as a beet snatched it from Ben with a huff and grumbled down the sidewalk.

Ben shrugged his shoulders and continued on his way when he stumbled into another person. This time it was a woman only measuring half of Ben's size carrying a tiny white dog. She wore an oversized white and black hat, which now sat sideways on her head.

"Sorry!" Ben said, over the barks of the ill-tempered dog that bounced like a fluffy white rubber ball in the woman's arms. The woman struggled to keep the ferocious beast from attacking him.

Ben stuck his hands in his pockets, smiled, and turned into the wave of people that carried him like a river current to the end of his block. Up ahead a reluctant horse pulling a milk wagon decided he favored a portion of the congested sidewalk versus the honking motorists sandwiched on the street. Panicked pedestrians ran for their lives. To avoid delay by the strange scene unfolding in front of him, Ben turned the nearest corner to find himself at one of the cities' many fruit markets.

"Geez, that was close."

Rows of fruit carts lined the cobblestone streets that lead to the waterfront. Ben liked the market, the sights and smells of all the mouth-watering food. The bananas and fresh pineapples were his favorite. He and his mother would come here once a week and Ben had a wonderful time as he watched his mother win an argument with the merchants over the prices.

Ben strolled along the rows of fruit carts. His nose took in all the sweetness that tempted his appetite when he spotted a freckle-faced boy from school named Larry Suliot leaning against one of the stands. He and Ben hadn't always been best of friends, but Larry would do as a first baseman in a good game of stickball, which Ben is happy to play if he can round up enough pals after his trip to the stadium.

Ben said, waving his arms. "Larry!"

Larry gave him a quick glance and turned away.

Ben began to run. "Larry!"

Before Ben could reach him, Larry darted down the packed street. Out of breath and puzzled by Larry's behavior Ben slowed to a walk.

"Help! Police!" a short fat man wearing a black handlebar mustache and dirty apron said. "Stop him. I've been robbed."

From somewhere in the depths of the crowd a sharply dressed policeman appeared. Making his way to the little man who was now jumping up and down.

"All right, all right, what's the hubbub bud?" The policeman said, in an attempt to be funny. The little man scowled at the policeman before he told him how a young boy hanging around the cart grabbed some fruit and ran off.

The policeman removed his cap and scratched his head. "Well, pop, what did the boy look like?"

"I don't know he's short with dark hair and... over there." The old man's eyes widen at the sight of Ben.

"That's him right there."

Ben overhearing the loud exchange turned to see whom the old man is referring. The policeman startled Ben when he ran and blow his whistle and point at him all at the same time.

It took Benjamin a second before he realized that the policeman was after him. Ben jumps over a stack of crates, dove under a cart and out the other side. The frantic boy rounded a corner of a building on one foot and splashed down the long alley littered with trash; the policeman hot on his heels.

"Stop, in the name of the law!"

Ben knew better than to trust the cops and continued to splash his way along the alley until it led him to the waterfront.

Ben thought to himself, Ma's not going to like this.

He paused for a moment and leaned against an old stack of fish baskets to catch his breath. He wiped the sweat from his forehead on his sleeve. Ben dared to spy around the baskets to see if the policeman was still on his heels.

"No sign." Ben took a long sigh of relief.

"Now I got ya, you little thief."

The startled boy struggled to free himself from the policeman's clutches. In his desperation, he connected his foot with the policeman's shin.

"Why you little..."

Ben's worn collar ripped from the policeman's grip. This was Ben's chance; he ran up the wet and slippery dock; the footsteps of the policeman pounded behind him. He dodged back and forth between rows of crates that line the dock when he spotted a tarp and dashed for cover.

From under the tarp, Ben stood frozen like a statue, watching the black shiny shoes of the policeman. Pace back and forth in front of him through a gap in the tarp's bottom. Sweat trickled down his face, the musty smell of the tarp caused his stomach to churn. Ben talked himself out of getting sick.

"That's the last one. Take it up."

"Take it up?" -Ben wondered- "Take what up?"

Chapter 2

A Night in the Hold

In the minute, it took Ben to contemplate whether he should stay or run. There's a jolt and the tarp-covered pallet rose into the air. Ben latched onto the crates to keep himself from falling. All he could do is watch through the small opening in the tarp's bottom as the dock moved away.

Ben's muscles contracted against the sway of the pallet. Frightened to almost a panic Ben squeezed his eyes shut. Higher and higher, the load climbed. Until in one sweep, the load hurled through the air like a roller-coaster ride at Coney Island. In an instant, a lump lodged in his throat when the load plummeted into a dark cavernous hole. Crates and boy collide with the hard steel floor, clanking chains echoed all around him.

"That's the last of it. Close the hatch," a voice announced, from somewhere beyond Ben's sight.

Ben breathed a sigh of relief as he bit by bit loosened his sweaty grip on the wooden box and poked his head out from under the musty tarp to spy his surroundings. A dark, damp place with a maze of dripping pipes that ran in all directions overhead. The walls, a pale green rust color with hundreds of rivets running their length.

"I must have got tossed on one of the ships. This isn't good."

Short for his age, Benjamin couldn't see over the rows and rows of crates, boxes, and baskets that filled the vast room. All is quiet as he made his way down a long row hunting for some way out. When the silence is broken by the faintest of sounds, which caused the hair on Ben's neck to prickle, he interpreted this to mean he was no longer alone. He caught a glimpse of something out of the corner of his eye.

"Ah, nuts."

Ben turned to step backward up the row his eyes fixed on the small force advancing on him. He searched for something, anything to defend himself against the relentless army's attack. The squeaking battle cries of the army of rats grew louder. His steps quickened down the row, which delivered him to a dead-end.

With the rats only a few feet away, Ben jumped and clutched the top of a large crate. Ben dangled and kicked at the rats clinging to his pant legs. With great effort, he pulled himself over the top of the crate.

"Get off, get off." Ben kicked at the last of the rats.

"I hate rats."

He tried to scare off the remaining rats as he banged his fist on the crate with no success. The rats continued to circle. Ben threw his arms up in frustration. "Great! Now how do I..."

Before he could think about an answer, it threw him forward. Ben grabbed for one of the pipes running overhead, catching himself before plummeting to the floor. In an instant, the hold filled with the rumbling of turbines and clanking metal.

Oh, no. It's moving. I gotta get off the ship.

He inched his way to the edge of the crate and looked over. Ben judged the distance to the next stack and backed up to the far end of the crate. He put himself in a runner's stance, his knees bent, and arms swaying back and forth.

"1. . . 2. . . 3. . ."

He flailed his arms and legs like a long jumper in the attempt to gain maximum distance out of his jump. With a successful landing, the small boy peered through shadowy darkness at a hatch door he hoped would lead to the outside. There it is, he thought. Ben maneuvered across the top of the last boxes. The dim light casting down from the ceiling blanketed the area with an ominous glow.

As he jumped toward the pile of baskets that sat at the end of the row, they gave way under his weight, which sent him crashing to the floor. Ben laid there in surprise of the outcome of his effort for a moment among the clutter, holding a now bleeding elbow. With his dented pride and injured elbow, he picked himself up, and stepped with an effort to the door. Ben grabbed the latch and pulled with anticipation of what awaited him on the other side.

Chapter 3

Discovered

Ben's heart sank when the door didn't open. His disappointment weighed on him like a wet overcoat. His sore elbow made the climb back to the top of a stack of crates a painful endeavor. Ben can only guess what the destination of the ship will be. He's sure they've long left New York Harbor and are bound for anywhere in the world and getting there seems to be taking care of itself.

The getting back part had Ben's mind sifting through thoughts of what lied beyond the locked hatch door. The tired and frightened boy stretched out over the hard wooden boxes and folded his arms under his head for a pillow; he thought about how good his old creaky bed at home would feel.

"Ma!"

Ben darted up and banged his forehead on a pipe. "Ouch."

He rubbed the mountain now rising from his forehead and collapsed.

She's gonna be worried sick. Then she's gonna kill me.

Ben rolled on his side with only the throbs from his elbow and ache from his goose egg for company. He stared at the soft glow of the naked bulb hanging over the hatch door. His eyelids weighed heavy.

"Can't go to sleep. Gotta be ready in case..."

Hours passed like minutes, and day faded into night. The only sound is the murmur of the engine throughout the hold. Ben woke to the rhythm of the ship rocking. He opened his eyes to see he was still in the cold, damp, dark place he was when he drifted off. His stomach complained as he righted himself.

"Don't need a watch to know what time it is. Do ya?" Ben said, to his empty middle.

"I don't think we'll find much down here the rats haven't got to."

His stomach complained again. "Well, let's look anyway."

Ben climbed down the steep wall of crates to the floor. With no sign of the rats, he proceeded up the row in search of nourishment when he heard the hatch door slam.

"Tar nation, every times I need flour or butter down here I got's to go." the voice muttered as its owner made his way down the row.

"Abe, you gits to go get it yourself."

"Gettin' tired of doin' all of it myself is what I'm gettin'."

Ben frozen in his tracks. His eyes raced around for anywhere he could hide.

"There."

Ben squeezed and wiggled, but it was no use. His small frame didn't fit. With one last effort, Ben pushed, causing the crates to let out a horrible squeal.

"Who dat?"

Without as much as a breath, Ben waited. Abe searched out the source of the strange noise, banging his flashlight on a crate to help it come on.

"Always somethin' goin' on. Can't get anything done around here."

"Oh, please, don't come here."

As the tall slender man's shadow grew closer, the man became louder and more upset. Ben tried his best to disappear.

"Noises in the dark, I don't need this in my day."

"Oh, Jesus," the man said, stumbling back against the wall of crates.

"Who, who the hell are you?"

Ben said nothing petrified in the small crevice of the crates.

The man's flashlight shook so radically he could barely keep the light on his target.

"I gotta gun, now you come outta they're nice and peaceful like, you here."

The boy squinted against the bright light as he climbed his way out into the row.

"Land sakes, you're just a boy. What're you doin' down here?"

"I got stuck in here by mistake," Ben replied, with his voice raspy, his tongue like a piece of shoe leather. "I didn't mean to. Honest."

"You don't say."

"What's your name little fish?"

"Ben... Ben Holt, sir."

"Sir?"

"I'm no sir. I'm just the cook on this here fine ship of fortune; my name is Abraham B. Washington."

"The B stands for the best cook on the seven seas. My friends call me Abe."

Ben decided he is a little better for his situation for having met Abe. His fear trickled away as he gave him a small smile of approval.

"The one friend you'd always want on a ship is the cook cause you always gotta eat."

"I am a little hungry," Ben admitted.

Abe laughed, "You don't need to tell me that, I got ears. I could hear your belly growlin' from way over there."

"Come on. The first thing we's gotta do is go see the captain."

Ben remembered how the stowaway always walked the plank in the five-cent pirate movies. He hesitated to follow Abe to the door.

"What's the matter little fish? Oh, the captain, he's all right."

"I'll wait here, okay?"

Abe gestured him to follow. "If ya wants something to eat, we have to see the captain, he'll know what to do. Now come on."

Ben came up on Abe's side. The steel hatch clanked behind them as the two make their way up the steel steps to the door that led to the deck.

"What day is it?"

Ben realized as the words left his mouth how foolish his question must sound.

"What day is it? Why it's Sunday mornin'."

At the top of the steps, Abe paused for a moment and turned to Ben. "Now listen, little fish, there's gonna be a lot of men out here, but pay them no mind and stay close to me."

With his stomach aching with hunger again, Ben nodded his head in compliance. Abe pushed the hatch door open, and the two stepped onto the deck and into the sunshine. Ben glanced up at the bright warm light letting it wash over him; the salty sea breeze awoke his senses.

Men hustled about in all directions just as Abe said; they paid little attention to him.

Thankful to be out of the hold, Ben finally got a good look at his rescuer. Abe was a tall, slender black man with short brown hair and tattered tan trousers. That hung loosely on his body by a worn black leather belt with matching black shoes missing their laces. A dirty white t-shirt covered his upper body. Ben decided right away he's going to like Abe. Ben smiled to himself.

Waiting across the deck, Abe said, "Well, come on. We don't got all day."

Ben shaded his eyes with his hand. "I'm coming."

Holding his arms out as he tried to steady himself, with every step across the wet wooden deck against the rocking of the ship.

Abe cannot contain his humor at the weird sight. "Boy, you look like an over-sized gooney bird flappin' your arms like that."

Abe's comment gained Ben some unwanted laughter from passing sailors.

A thunderous voice came from overhead, which caused the whole deck to go quiet.

"Abraham? Has anyone seen Abe?"

Abe grabbed Ben from the deck by his arm and pulled him out of sight. "Yes, sir right here, sir."

"Come up here for a minute, would you?"

"Who's that?"

"That's the captain. Captain Salinger," Abe said, starting for the steps to the wheelhouse. "Now you wait here until I give ya the signal to come up. Ya hear?"

"But what's the signal... Abe?"

Abe dashed up the rusty steel steps and out of sight before Ben could finish. It felt like ages before Abe finally reappeared at the top of the steps.

He waved his hand for Ben to join him. "Come on up here, Ben. Let the captain get a look at ya."

Ben climbed the steps. He felt all the eyes of the crew on him now. This made every step he took feel like a billboard announcement. He stopped on the small platform outside the door. The reluctant boy tried to send Abe a message with his eyes, he didn't want to go in alone. However, Abe didn't pay Ben any mind and pushed him in the door, and closed it behind him.

 On entering the small wheelhouse, Ben noticed a peculiar sight. There sat a larger orange fluffy cat atop the window ledge. He glared at Ben through sparkling disapproving green eyes while swinging his tail ever so gently.

Ben's eyes soon discovered the fascinating instruments and maps of distant lands hanging on the wall. Standing in the center of the room is a sailor staffing a large wheel with a brass compass directly in front of the row of windows.

A man who sat on a stool leaning against the wall behind the door just to his left spoke first, "Well, you seem a little young to be a stow away. Aren't you?"

Ben took no notice of the man until he spoke. A tall broad-shouldered man sporting a first officer's cap, which sat cocked on his head of graying brown hair. Ben slipped his hands in his pockets. "I'm not a stow away. It was an accident. I didn't mean to be here."

"That's what they all say. What did you do? Run away from home?"

He got up from his stool to confront the boy with the full impact of his intimidation, by standing toe to toe with the frightened boy. Ben had to bend his head back to look at the whiskery man in the face. "No, well, I was running from the cops, but...."

"So, that's it. You're wanted by the cops."

"No, I didn't do anything. They thought..."

"That's enough." came from a large man who sat at a table in the corner of the room.

"It doesn't matter; you're here now. You got a name, boy?"

"Yes, sir. Benjamin Holt."

"Well, Mr. Holt, I'm Captain Salinger. Captain Seymour Salinger and that's my first officer, Jacob Stilman." Seymour gave Jacob a wink.

Jacob took the captain's cue to take his turn with Ben interrogation. "How old are you, boy?"

"I'm 13, fourteen next month."

With Ben's answer, Seymour took another turn in the round of questioning. "How d'you manage to get on board, anyway?"

"Um, I was hiding under a tarp, it got lifted up, and then dropped in the hold with rats, and I couldn't get out."

"You know what ship this is boy?"

Ben shook his head no in the direction of the first officer.

"Well, Mr. Holt, you're aboard the tramp steamer for hire The U. S. S. Alexandria."

"She's not much to look at, but she'll do ten knots on a good day," the captain added with a quick smile on his face. The captain got up and joined his first officer in front of Ben.

"The question is what to do with you?"

Ben looked back and forth between the two. "Well, could you maybe take me home?"

"Ha, no, no. We can't do that," the captain answered. "Not even if you were the King of Spain."

"But why?" the desperate boy blurted out forgetting his place and manners.

"Because boy, we have a schedule to keep, besides it costs money to run a ship," the captain said, in a thunderous voice, "Do you have the money to pay for a trip back to New York?"

The last ounce of hope left his body with disappointment and emptiness to taking its place again.

"No, sir."

The first officer leaned into Seymour's ear. "Skipper."

The two deliberated, occasionally glancing in Ben's direction between whispers, until the pair finally decided. Sure, he's going to walk the plank. Ben thought of his mother and how upset she'd be when she heard what happen to him. Moreover, how sorry these guys are going to be when she does. The distraction of the captain's cat broke Ben's train of thought who decided to give Ben his approval by rubbing against his leg. Ben held out his hand and gave the cat a gentle stroke. The porky cat purred.

There are lots of cats in Ben's neighborhood, mostly wild scavengers. Ben hadn't ever seen anyone try to keep one as a pet before. His building doesn't allow pets. The puffy orange fur is soft to touch and his whiskers are long, curly, and tickled Ben's hand.

"Captain, engine room," came out of a funny-looking box hanging on the wall, the voice sounding small and far away.

"Hold on, Jacob," the captain said, turning to the strange box and pushed the button on the black corded mouthpiece. "Captain here. What is it, Daniel?"

"Captain, we're showing fluctuations in boiler pressure down here."

"Did you check the lines for pressure leaks?"

"Yes, they're all good. I don't understand it. We must slow down a bit."

"Well, do the best you can. Captain out."

"Do you want me to go see?" Jacob asked in a concerned voice.

"No, no. It's all right."

The two men conclude their discussion, and the captain returned to his table, sat down, crossed his legs and lit his pipe. The horrible smell of pipe tobacco filled the small room. Ben's face turned a pale shade green as he began to sweat. His stomach turned over again.

"You don't look so good kid. Come on, you need some fresh air," the first officer said, taking notice to Ben's change in color.

The captain said, "I see you've met Admiral Tibbs."

Ben looked back with an expression of misunderstanding on his face.

"Admiral Tibbs, my cat. That's funny he rarely likes strangers."

"What do you mean strangers? He still doesn't like me," Jacob said.

"Go on, you old sea dog."

Jacob held Ben by the shoulder as he guided him back out the door to find Abe fidgeting with an old broom trying to look busy.

"Well, what did he say Jacob?" Abe asked as the two brushed by.

"Don't you worry about it Abe. It's all under control."

"Under control? What's that mean?"

"The captain said, 'put him in the brig until he decides what to do with him. '" Jacob said over his shoulder.

Abe cut Jacob off mid-sentence in protest. His long spider-like fingers perched firmly on his bony hips. "The brig? You're gonna put a boy in the brig for being stuck on the ship?"

"Look," Jacob said, his hand moving back and forth with every word unaware Ben is still firmly in his grip, sending Ben in all directions.

"I know what you're thinking Abe, but it'll be all right."

Abe with his eyes wide and his nostrils flared, said, "But he's just a boy."

"If that's not good enough for you go see the captain about it. "Come Ben," Jacob directed Ben down the step and onto the deck.

Abe watching the two, said, "I'll fetch ya some food, Ben."

"Go ask the captain about it. I'll go all right. Never tell ol' Abe nothin' sepin' when they're hungry, then they know old Abe."

Ben's confidence about his situation wavered with Jacob's words. They wouldn't really make a boy walk the plank, would they? Ben thought to himself.

"Don't worry we're not making you walk the plank or anything. I have to put you in lockup for a while."

Jacob caught Ben off guard with his uncanny ability to know what he was thinking. Although his stomach was still tied up in knots, Ben enjoyed being outdoors again if only for a brief time. The two cut through the crowd of sailors who gathered to watch the exchange between Jacob and Abe, on their way toward the hatch that led below. Ben can't help but feel one man staring at him harder and longer than the others, as if the man's eyes are like daggers piercing the back of his head. Ben turned to grab a glimpse of the man, a short stocky fellow with thick gray hair and leathery dark skin. Like prey hypnotized by the stare of the cobra, Ben stood motionless as the man glared back at him.

Jacob pulled Ben by the arm to get him to follow. "Come on now, Ben. Let's go."

Ben didn't look away from the man until his steps carried him out of sight. The clanking from the over-sized key ring banged against the door as Jacob worked the lock. The door opened with a creek, and they entered the little room. A small table and chair in one corner and an unmade cot in the other. The makeshift cell sported only one porthole in which to view the outside. Old newspapers littered the floor from the last occupant.

"Here we are, make yourself at home." after an uncomfortable moment of silence, Jacob continued.

"I'll check with Abe about your food. Meanwhile, there's water there, I'm not sayin' the glass is clean though." Jacob rubbed Ben's dark head of hair and turned to leave.

Ben caught him at the door. "Jacob, who was the man on deck?"

"Which one?"

"You know the short gray-haired man staring at me."

"Oh," Jacob said, "That's old Edgar. He's the ship's first mate, not too friendly that one."

"Why?"

Ben sat down on the flat, lumpy cot. "It's nothing,"

"You'll be all right in here, Ben. I'm not going to lock you in if you promise not to wander around."

"Don't worry, I promise."

"Good boy. I'll check on you later."

Ben untied his boots and kicked them to the floor where they land with a dull thud. He laid down on the lumpy cot. The rocking of the ship made his unsettled middle bounce around even worse. For the first time since being discovered, Ben is alone with his thoughts that caused more confusion by the minute.

"Maybe some water would help." Ben moved to the dirty sink in the corner of the room and picked up the glass to see a little black hairy spider has taken up residence in the bottom. He abandoned his quest for water and gazed at the blue sky out the porthole window. It is quiet and Ben thought of his mother and how she'll properly go to the police about him missing.

What a needless bother, Ben thought to himself, if I could just get word to her.

Knowing it's impossible at least for a while, Ben wished Abe would hurry with his food to remedy the empty sick feeling in the pit of his stomach.

Some chicken would be nice or maybe some meatloaf. Meatloaf, right, on a ship.

I am the meatloaf for getting stuck here in the first place.

Chapter 4

Into a New World

Jacob made his way out of the hatch of the makeshift cell and down the corridor to the galley where he heard the chatter of the crew about their newest member. Entering the room, he is bombarded with questions fired at him from all directions.

"Where did the boy come from?"

"What's the captain going to do with him?"

He did his best to ignore the crew's queries and continued to the back of the kitchen were Abe prepared Ben's tray of food.

"What've you got there, Abe?"

"Hello, Jacob. I fixed Ben a fine tray of fish and beans with some buttered bread."

Hoping to see Ben again, Abe said, "If you like, I could take it up to him."

"No, that's all right. I can do it," Jacob answered, stuffing an apple in his pocket as he picked up the tray.

"Jacob," Abe called out, "He's a good boy you know."

Jacob smiled back at Abe and said, "I know Abe. I know." before he pushed through the swinging doors.

After saying a few hellos and goodbyes on his way back to the brig, Jacob is stopped by a thick gray-haired man with dark leathery skin sitting by the door leading to the corridor.

"Taking that to the boy?"

Jacob ignoring Edgar's question continued. "How's the deck chores going Edgar?"

"That boy's gonna bring nothin' but bad luck to the ship; it's no place for a child. Besides, I don't like the looks of that one."

"Looks like the weather's changing, maybe you should get the hatches closed?" Jacob told Edgar ignoring his comments about Ben.

The first mate moved to comply with Jacob's request, his lips mumbling silent protests along the way.

"Ben? It's Jacob. I have some food for you."

Jacob entered the room, sat the tray on the small table, and looked over his shoulder at Ben, who has now taken on a light shade of green again.

Concerned he moved to Ben for a closer inspection. "What's the matter boy?" Jacob placed his hand on Ben's forehead.

"You're a little warm."

"It's my stomach. Its flip flopping around," Ben said, holding his middle.

"I see, maybe some food to fix you right up."

"No, no food."

Jacob returned from the sink with a cold towel and placed it on Ben's forehead and sat on the edge of his cot.

"How's that boy, better?"

Ben gave Jacob a nod.

"You've never been on a ship before, have you?"

"No," which sounded more like a moan.

"I'm afraid you're a little seasick, the best thing for you now is to rest."

Jacob got up and went to the door. "Now stay there and rest. I have to go back to work, but I'll check on you later."

Ben shook his head to confirm he understood Jacob's orders as he watched him close the door.

The sick boy let out a shallow, slow sigh before he closed his eyes and tried to follow Jacob's advice to rest. Jacob returned to his duties on the bridge. Checking the ships heading and monitoring ship systems while the captain sat at a table studying charts.

Jacob rubbed his hands together, checking the compass. "Burr, the weather's changing; we may be heading into a front."

Patting the sailor on the shoulder, Jacob said, "Very good holding the bearing, Smitty."

Without looking up from the chart, the captain said, "The boy settled in?"

"Yes, but he's seasick some. He'll be alright in the morning I suspect."

Seymour turned to face Jacob. "Turn on the light, would ya?"

"Sure."

"Looks like we're right on course but losing time. If we run into a storm, we'll have to slow even more," the captain said, scratching his head under his hat.

Jacob picked up the measuring wand and stepped off their course on the chart.

He noticed a second line on the chart along the path of their return course. "What's this Captain?"

"Umm, it's nothing."

"Captain, Captain," a man said, from the small radio room sitting to the rear of the bridge.

"What is it? I'm busy here."

"Well, it's... you need to hear this."

Seymour glanced at Jacob and stood up from his chair.

Chapter 5

Destination Unknown

Jacob and the captain squeezed into the cramped radio room, which gave them the appearance of three sardines in a can.

"What is it, Billy," Jacob asked.

"I intercepted a message. I'm not sure what they're sayin' but I know one thing."

"What," the captain asked.

"It's German."

"German, are you sure?"

"I'm sure, sir."

The captain and Jacob nod at each other at the same time as if they read each other's minds.

"Maybe I can get it back. Hold on," Billy told, the captain with one hand holding his headphone to his ear and the other slowly turning the large dial on the radio.

"Shh," Billy said.

"Listen to this," Billy said flipping a switch on the radio.

Out of the speaker came a strange voice, "Bitte schreiben Sie es auf wo? Wann?"

Jacob watched the lights dim and flickered throughout the bridge. "What the heck."

"Oh no, we lost them. The power surge must have scrambled the signal," Billy said.

"Daniel must be having trouble with the batteries too."

"Thanks Billy. If you hear anymore, you know."

The captain returned to his table and turned over the course chart containing the mysterious line.

"You better get some rest Jacob, if you're taking first watch tonight."

"I will. Captain, what do you suppose that was all about? I never heard of any German boats being this far out in these waters before."

Seymour folded his arms, pondering the question a few seconds before he answered.

"I don't know. We'll have to wait and see."

"Goodnight, Captain."

Down the steps and up the corridor Jacob listened for a moment at Ben's door before he continued to his cabin.

He must be asleep by now, he thought to himself.

Jacob switched on the desk lamp, took off his overcoat and threw it over a chair before he sat on his cot. He picked up a frame containing a wrinkled and faded photo.

"Hello, Mary, honey. How are ya?" Jacob rubbed his wife's hair in the photo with his finger.

"It's been a long day. We have a little stow away named Ben. Can you beat that?"

"A good kid, but he's like a fish out of water around here."

"We're gonna have to find something for him to do though. Well, goodnight sweetheart," Jacob said and gave the photo a kiss.

The first officer rested his head on his pillow and faded to sleep.

"No, I don't... Help! The rats, the rats!"

Gasping for air as if he were drowning, Ben sat up drenched in sweat darting his head left and right in the dark. "Ma, Ma," Ben cried out.

He realized after a few moments he was not in his room. The ache in the pit of his stomach returned, this time not from being seasick or even from being hungry but from being homesick. An emotion Ben has never experienced before. He got up and opened the porthole window; the cool night air is refreshing and helped to calm him down. He stood there for a while before he returned to his cot. Somewhere between lingering thoughts of home Ben fell back to sleep.

As dawn broke over the deck of the Alexandria Jacob finished his shift and decided to check on their stow away.

Outside Ben's door, Jacob knocked in hopes Ben may already be awake. "Ben, you up?"

Jacob didn't wait for a reply before he entered, surprised to find Ben sitting at the table with an empty tray in front of him.

"Nice to see you're feeling better."

"Yeah, I feel better."

"Well, enough to eat cold beans, I see."

Something draws Jacob's attention to a picture of a whale and a mermaid; someone scratched into the dirty white paint on the wall next to the hatch door. Jacob took out his own knife and began to add some details to the carving.

"How would you like to see the rest of the ship?"

"Sure."

"Hey, Jacob?"

"Yeah."

"Where are we? I mean, where is the ship going, anyway?"

Jacob waited a long moment before, he answered, "Umm, well, we have cargo to deliver," Jacob said, nervously closing his knife.

"To where?"

"We're going to Africa."

"Africa!" Ben said his eyes as big as dinner plates. "Africa?"

Jacob turned to face Ben, who continued to hold the expression of utter disbelief.

"It's not so bad. Just think of all the new things you'll get to see like elephants and monkeys," Jacob said, in an attempt to make the situation seem better than it is.

"We have animals at the Bronx Zoo."

"I know, come on, and let's not think about that now. It's a nice day out. We'll go up on deck; it'll make you feel better."

The angry and confused boy picked up his boots and followed Jacob topside. Ben's fears were confirmed. They were steaming toward anywhere in the world with no hope of returning home anytime soon. His feet are like bricks as he lagged behind Jacob up the corridor. It took a few moments before Ben, in his zombie-like state of numbness to notice they have reached the middle of the deck.

"Ben, you're going to love this," Jacob said, pointing out the large chains at the front of the ship.

"See that? That's the cargo hold you went into."

The young boy is preoccupied with looking around for the thick gray-haired man with leathery skin.

Ben said, "I remember."

"Jacob," the captain said, from the bridge deck. "Bring the boy up here."

Jacob gave the captain a wave and led Ben up the steps. Ben's palms began to sweat, and he became aware of his own heartbeat as it lifts his shirt off his chest at the sound of the captain's voice.

"Mornin' Jacob. Anything to report from the night watch?" the skipper said, the whole time his eyes fixed squarely on Ben.

"No, nothing."

Ben sensed the captain's eyes on him. The hair on the back of his neck prickled as it did in the hold with the rat army. He tried to repel the captain's glare by looking out the windows, at the floor and petting the captain's cat. Jacob noticed Ben's color washing out of his face again and stepped between the two in an attempt to shield the boy from the captain's view.

Seymour leaned around Jacob from his chair to bring Ben into view again. "Good, good, I've been doing some thinkin' about the boy."

Seymour's comment doesn't draw Ben's eyes to him as he hoped. Ben continued to pet the cat as if he hadn't heard him.

"What have you been thinking, captain?"

Seymour spoke in a loud bolstering voice; wanting to be sure Ben heard every word. "He can't spend the whole time locked up. He needs to become useful and help pay his way."

"I see. You mean become a part of the crew of the Alexandria."

"Yes precisely," Seymour said, giving Jacob a quick wink. "Why don't you see what you can find-?"

"Excuse me, sir?"

Annoyed at Ben's interruption, Seymour snapped, "What? Speak up, boy."

"What is it, boy? Come on, I don't have all day."

Ben slipped his hands in his pockets. Making eye contact with the captain for the first time since he came in, Ben asked, "If I'm gonna be working, will I get paid, sir?"

"Paid... you want paid, huh," the captain said.

Not expecting the question, the captain stalled his answer as he took an extra-long time to light his pipe. Finally, with all eyes staring at him, the captain said, "First off, what are you lookin' at? Get back to work." Seymour yelled at the sailor staffing the wheel. This startled Ben into wishing he hadn't asked the question.

"Tell you what, you work hard and follow orders, I'll consider it, fair enough," Seymour extended his hand to Ben.

"Yes sir, thank you, sir," Ben agreed, and shook the captain's hand.

"With that settled, get out of here. I have work to do," Seymour said.

Chapter 6

Sailor Clothes

Jacob and Ben made their way down the steps and onto the deck. "That took a lot guts Ben. Good for you. What do you want with money on a ship, anyway?"

"It's for my ma. I thought maybe I could send it to her when we got somewhere," Ben said, putting his hands in his pockets, pretending to be interested in what a few sailors were doing down the deck. Jacob stepped to the railing and looked out over the vast spread of water sparkling like a blue church window. Ben followed him to within three feet of the railing and stopped.

Taking notice to Ben's place behind him, Jacob said, "That's pretty smart."

"Let's go."

"Where?"

"If you're gonna be part of the crew, you need to look like it."

"What? I don't understand?"

"You'll see. Follow me."

Jacob flipped on the light and led Ben down a series of confined hallways into a room filled with lockers and boxes.

"Here we are," Jacob said.

Ben pulled open one of the boxes and looked inside. "What is this place?"

"This is where we store all the stuff like clothes, hats, coats... you know sea wear."

Jacob pointed to the boxes stacked against the far wall. "Go ahead. Look in those over there."

"What am I looking for?"

"Oh, a shirt, some pants, and hopefully a belt."

After a few minutes of digging in several boxes, Ben found a slightly large white sailor shirt with buttons down the front and blue cuffs. He held it up to his nose and gave it a sniff. The shirt smell reminded Ben of that old tarp from the dock. "How about this, Jacob?"

"That's not bad, try it on."

Ben pulled the shirt over his clothes and turned to face Jacob.

Tossing Ben, a dark blue pair of pants, Jacob said, "Not bad. Now you need some pants. Here, try these."

Ben wiggled his boots through the leg holes and pulled them up. "There. Okay?"

Jacob laughed aloud at the sight of Ben in the ill-fitting sea wear, stumbled backward, and fell into one of the open boxes.

Bent in half with his feet sticking up in the air Jacob called out for Ben's help.

The first officer regained his composure and continued to root around in the boxes, managing to find Ben a couple of more uniforms, non-fitting exactly right.

"Let's go find you somewhere better to bunk. By the way, let's keep me falling in the box to ourselves, all right?"

Ben gave Jacob a smile and a nod.

Chapter 7

Into the Belly of the Beast

Curious what Jacob meant; Ben followed with his arm full of oversized sea wear. The young boy tripped over the dangling sleeves as the unlikely friends made their way down yet another narrow corridor.

Jacob guided Ben by the shoulder into the crew's sleeping quarters consumed by hammocks. "Here we go."

Ben entered the room thick with the smell of burning cigars and mellow harmonica music, coming from the far corner of the room. Ben took in the tired, sea-weathered faces of the ship's crew scattered around the room. Some playing cards at a table hinged to the wall, some lying in their hammocks with their caps pulled over their eyes trying to sleep.

"You're Shang highin' them a little young, aren't ya Jacob?" One of the sailors asked causing laughter to break out throughout the room.

"Just pick any empty hammock and throw your stuff in one of the footlockers. Put your name on it and don't lose the key, they only have one."

Ben looked up from the footlocker on the floor to notice Jacob leaving. "Where you going?"

"I have to get back to the bridge. After you're settled in, come find me. You'll be all right; the crew doesn't bite."

Ben looked around the room for some time before he spotted an empty hammock at the end of a row against the wall. Most of the crew paid little attention to Ben moving around. Some sailors gave Ben a curious tip of their hats. Some glared as if they had never seen a small boy before; and some gave him an unwelcome scowl as he passed by. Ben turned to unload his aching arms of clothes into his hammock. He didn't notice the crowd of men gathering around him. One of the sailors coughed to get Ben's attention.

One of the older cantankerous looking sailors spoke first. "So, where you from boy?"

Ben whispered, "New York."

"What? Speak up boy, can't hear ya."

"New York." Ben said, again with a trace of annoyance in his voice.

"Oh, New York, well we have a city boy here," the man said, poking fun at Ben's expense.

Ben knew all too well, what it means to be out-numbered from his days spent in the New York City School system and kept quiet. A tall, thin sailor with a shiny bald spot leaned over almost touching nose to nose with Ben. "What part?"

"What part of what?"

"What part of New York are you from?" The man insisted again waving his arms in the air with frustration.

"Um... I'm from Manhattan, lower Manhattan."

"Oh yeah." Yet another sailor said from the small circle of men surrounding him.

"My mom lives in Manhattan. She's a right pip; she is-"

"Shut up! No one wants to hear about your ol' mom," the thin, balding sailor shouted.

Finding the exchange between the two amusing, Ben cracked a smile listening to the men continue their bickering all the way back to the small table. A large dark-haired man with a bushy mustache chewing on a smoky cigar who had been watching the exchange, stood up from his chair and joined Ben. The man rubbed Ben's head with his hairy paw and nudged him with his shoulder nearly knocking Ben off his feet.

"You'll be fine kid; it's not so bad once you get on to things. Just don't fall overboard."

With the thickening cigar smoke burning his eyes, Ben was eager to stow his clothes and get back to the bridge where he can look forward to the captain smoking his pipe.

"Where's Jacob or Daniel? Has anyone seen Daniel?" A voice asked, coming through the door.

Without having to turn around, Ben guessed to whom the voice belonged. The one man on the whole ship he just as soon stays away from.

"He's up on the bridge," came from one of the sailors in the room.

"Oh, Phillip, you better make sure those port covers are secure. If water gets into the hold, you'll be bailing it out with a teacup," Edgar said, to the sheepish man with glasses who tried to go unnoticed in his hammock.

Edgar patted his pockets looking for something as he stomped his way over to his footlocker, which rested underneath his hammock by the door. He pulled out a small wooden box and peered about from under his thick gray eyebrows to see if anyone was watching him.

Like a hungry animal guarding its prey, he took something out of the box, stuffed it in his pocket, and re-locked the box before shoving it back underneath his hammock.

After Edgar stormed out of the room, Ben came out from behind his hammock grateful Edgar didn't see him. Something about the way this man looked at him, the way his eyes pierced through to his soul. Ben thought of old man Merz who lived across the hall from him and his mother. every day, he'd watch Ben through his cracked door with the same piercing eyes. Old man Merz despised children. Never once speaking a word or dared to make contact.

Ben remembered how for a long time he feared the old man. Until one day, he decided not to be afraid anymore. From then on Ben would say hello and goodbye to the poor old man. Just like that, one day the hoary man stopped watching. Was Edgar like old man Merz?

Watching and judging him from a distance for reasons unknown? Or is it something else, something more sinister? Ben decided the tactic he used on old man Merz would not do under these circumstances. No, caution would have to replace kindness if Ben has any hope of survival. Ben's thoughts played like a movie in his mind forgetting his task. He absentmindedly stuffed his gear in the footlocker.

"You cheater that was my ace," a sailor said, from the table.

Another sailor countered in his own defense. "Go on, you're a sore loser."

The exchange between the men woke Ben to his surroundings. He finished locking his locker and exited the bunkhouse. On his way up to the bridge, Ben mulled over the prospects of sleeping in the same room with the first mate. The idea of it made Ben consider taking his chances with the rats in the hold.

He thought hard about where he could bunk and still be close to the sleeping quarters but away from Edgar. Somewhere no one would think to look for him.

The question lingered in his mind as he entered the wheelhouse where he found the captain and Jacob bickering over something. The two took notice to Ben's presence and ceased their exchange.

Jacob turned to Ben. "Get settled in Ben?"

"Yeah," Ben said, remaining by the door.

Seeing the captain and Jacob bickering is unnerving, he can't help but think that it may have been about him.

"Jacob, we need to find this boy something to do," Seymour said, in a more agreeable tone than he had been using with Jacob when Ben had come in.

"Yes, sir. I have an idea. Come with me."

Ben watched as the captain took out his spectacles and read over a scrap of paper before he turned to follow Jacob without a word until they had left the wheelhouse.

"Where are we going?"

"You'll see."

"Don't walk so fast," Ben said, to Jacob whose long legs allow him to take one-step to Ben's two. Ben caught up with Jacob as he entered a hatch. The sound of the engines grew more ominous the deeper the pair ventured into the belly of the ship. The corridors are lit by naked bulbs that flickered as the ship's power supply varied, casting retracting shadows over the piping and green paint on the corridor walls.

The noise became alive, vibrating the surrounding air tickling Ben's eardrums. The corridor is getting narrower now. Ben can't see the sign on the door ahead of them over Jacob's shoulder that reads Engine Room.

"Here we are."

Ben held his hand up to his ear trying to listen. "What?"

"I said, here we are."

"What?" Ben asked Jacob again, this time with a smile creeping from the corner of his mouth, causing Jacob to return a smile instantly.

"You're playing with me, aren't you?"

For the first time since he arrived on board, Ben felt like himself again. Entering the room, Ben is hit straight in the face with the aroma of machine oil and coal smoke.

"What are we doing here?"

"This is where you'll be working with Daniel. He runs the engine room."

Not sure if Jacob had done him a favor with this new duty, Ben took the place in. Dark smoke filled the cavern with water and steam leaking from pipes everywhere, a place where demons or dragons would feel right at home.

"Hey, over here," a short dirty-faced man with grease-stained clothes, sporting a slightly worn cap said, from a catwalk, perched over the ship's driveshaft. Jacob gave the man a wave and pushed Ben in the man's direction.

Strange noises came from over-sized tanks, perched on pedestals around the pipe-filled room. "Sounds like the boiler's still giving you trouble," Jacob said.

"I swear this ship is going to be the end of me someday," Daniel said, turning his attention to the small boy looking around the room with fascination.

Daniel wiped his oily hand on his pants and held it out to Ben. "So, this is our new engine hand?"

Not sure if he wants to shake hands with the man, Jacob nudged Ben forward.

"Nice to meet you. I'm Daniel."

"Hi" Ben said, taking his hand back, which has been returned to him less clean than when he gave it.

"Well, I'll talk to you later, Ben. Good luck."

"You're leaving now?" which translated into; please don't leave me here.

"I have duties to attend to. See ya later."

Daniel handed Ben an oilcan and began to show him the duties of keeping the different parts of the engine, and gears oiled. In spite of the hot smelly conditions, Ben learned a great deal and worked hard to do a good job. After hours of greasing and oiling parts, Daniel took the oilcan from Ben and handed him a rag to clean himself up.

 Daniel ordered Ben to get some supper. "Good work, Ben. See ya tomorrow, eight o'clock sharp."

"Thanks, see ya tomorrow."

Tired and dirty, Ben left the engine room and went to the mess hall for a well-earned supper.

On entering, Ben spotted Abe filling the salt and peppershakers at one of the tables. "Lordy, what happen to you?"

Ben picked up a tray and handed it to one of the sailors working behind the food counter. "Don't ask."

"You're gonna have to clean yourself up if you are comin' in here to eat in my kitchen. I can't be spendin' my time cleanin' up after you."

"Sorry, I will. Could I have some more potatoes, please?"

"Don't go and sit on my seats with them pants. You go and sit on a box in the back. Go on now, I'm busy." Abe pushed Ben to hurry his steps.

Growing more tired by the minute, Ben barely finished his dinner when Abe took his fork and ordered him to bed.

Ben tired to his bones took his last step to the bunkhouse door. It's filled with sailors from the day turn, including Edgar, who is swinging in his hammock with the appearance of being asleep. Ben hoped his luck would hold as he tried to pass his hammock without detection.

"Look, what the cat dragged in," one of the sailors said, just as Ben reached Edgar's hammock. Ben grabbed his breath and held it in his chest as he looked over his shoulder hoping, but not expecting to see Edgar asleep.

With the warmth of a grizzly bear, Edgar asked, "What are you doing here, boy?"

"Jacob told me to come and stay here now."

"This place is for the crew of the Alexandria; not stow aways."

Ben shrugged his shoulders and looked at the floor.

"You better watch your step, boy," Edgar warned, before rolling over in his hammock.

"Boy, you can wash up over there, through that door." The big bear of a man told him from his hammock. "But you'd better hurry up; lights out in ten minutes."

"Thanks."

Ben soon discovered ship dirt isn't that easy to get off. With his face a bright red, he arrived at his hammock to find a lumpy pillow and a wool blanket. The room is cool and Ben is grateful.

"Lights out," a man announced.

Ben struggled to find some way to gain entry into his hammock making an excessive amount of noise in the process. Frustrated Ben stood there fuming over his defeat when he received some uninvited assistance. Abruptly, he is picked up off the floor by the scruff of his collar into the air and placed in his hammock.

"There now be quiet and get some shuteye," a large dark figure said, returning to his hammock.

Ben covered up and did his best to get comfortable as his eyes began to adjust to the darkness. He could make out from a distance the face of the ship's first mate as the moonlight from the porthole window washed over it, giving the sunken features of the man's face an even greater foreboding. Ben is unable to tell if Edgar is asleep or staring back at him.

Chapter 8

Escaping with his life

The night wore on, and the bunkhouse filled with the reverberation of snoring sailors. Ben lay in his hammock with his pillow pressed tightly to his ears, still the noise seeped into his head. Unable to take it one more minute, Ben scrambled out of his hammock to the floor, desperate to escape.

 With his pillow and blanket in hand, Ben tiptoed through the catacombs of hammocks out into the moonlight in search of a hidden sanctuary; mindful to stay out of sight of the patrolling sailor on nightly rounds. It's late and Ben has grown tired again, with no luck. Ben resigned to abandon his search and return to his hammock when he stumbled across the perfect place.

Gee, why didn't I see this before?

Across the deck up on blocks along the railing sat the perfect hideaway.

Nobody will think to find me in there.

He checked to be sure that the coast was clear and darted across the span of deck separating him and the boat.

Don't look at the water, and you'll be fine.

With both hands, Ben pulled up the heavy white tarp covering the top of one of the four lifeboats on the ship.

"Perfect."

Once inside Ben reached back for his blanket and pillow and carefully pulled the tarp down. It's dark and smells like musty old clothes and dead fish. However, Ben didn't care. He's happy with his find and set out to get comfortable. Ben slept soundly through the night.

He is woken early the next morning by the sound of waves breaking against the ship's hull. Men passed by on their way to relieve the night shift on the bridge. Careful not to be discovered Ben peaked out the top of the tarp before exiting to the crew's quarters for his boots.

On entering, Ben found the room deserted. The empty hammocks swung with the sway of the ship. Ben retrieved his boots, splashed water on his face, and closed the door behind him before his mission to find some breakfast in Abe's galley.

Ben ate his fill of Abe's powdered egg breakfast. He then met Daniel at the top of the steps leading down to the engine room where he could look forward to another day of messy, smelly, work, oiling the many gears and parts that help drive the ship.

Daniel wearing a perky smile on his whiskery face, still somewhat dirty from the day before, asked, "Ready to get started?"

"Sure," Ben said, looking around for his oilcan.

"What are you lookin' for?"

"The oilcan. I left it right here, yesterday."

"Don't worry about that right now. I have somethin' else for you to do."

Daniel picked up an odd-looking contraption and looked at Ben. "Do you know what this is?"

"Uh, no," Ben mumbled, his attention fixed on the object.

"This here is a grease gun. What you do is put this end on the fitting like this and pump the handle like this until grease comes out."

Daniel demonstrated with vigor, pumping the gun so radically that grease begins spitting everywhere.

Daniel handed the gun to Ben. "Do you think you can do this?"

"I think so, I'll try."

"Good boy, make sure the hose is on tight, and you'll do fine. Just start on this one and work your way around the machine."

Ben set to work fitting and pumping while progressively becoming dirty again. Steadily, he made his way to each fitting on the ship's couplings and machinery.

 Daniel, busy with his own work, took no notice to Ben working dangerously close to the exposed engine parts racing up and down.

One man working with Daniel in the engine room took notice to Ben's absence. "Hey, boss. Where's the kid?"

"What do you mean, where's the kid," Daniel said, standing up and looking around for himself. "He was over there greasing... oh shoot."

The two men raced down the catwalk leading to the empty spot where Ben was supposed to be working.

"Ben!" Daniel called out. "Listen. What's that? Shh, listen."

The sailor spotted Ben a way down the catwalk.

"There, over there." He pointed out Ben's position to Daniel.

Ben is unaware the hungry machine has taken hold of his loose shirtsleeve and began devouring it. The machine pulled angrily at Ben's sleeve wanting more. The sudden jerk caused Ben to drop the grease gun and become aware of the machine's intentions.

Ben tugged on his sleeve with his free hand. "Help!"

Ben slammed his foot against the guardrail to find more leverage, desperate to free himself. With every passing second, his sleeve is pulled deeper into the machine winding it tighter and tighter. Completely panicked Daniel grabbed Ben around the waist to attempt to pull him free.

Daniel could feel the machine pulling Ben away from him. "Pull, Ben. Come on."

With his fingers only inches from being chewed up by the machine Ben's shirt is torn from his body and consumed by the hungry machine, sending the two catapulting backward to the floor.

Sitting there trembling, tears streamed down Ben's face.

"I, I tried to yell, but no one heard me."

Daniel put his arm around Ben's neck in an attempt to calm him down. "You're all right. That's what's important."

Daniel watched Ben's shirt travel through the gears of the machine. Maybe you workin' here isn't such a good idea?"

"I am sure Jacob can find something else for you to do. It's a big ship." Ben still shaking nodded his head and picked himself up off the floor.

"Go get some air and maybe find another shirt. You can't run around like that." Daniel getting to his feet, said, "And how bout we keep this to ourselves, no reason to worry Jacob or the captain; your fine and no harm done. What ya say?"

"I won't say nothin' to nobody."

Daniel watched Ben close the hatch door behind him. Ben understood why Daniel didn't want it to get around what had happened; however, Ben had his own reasons for staying quiet.

 His unshakable sense of always being less than he needed to be had come rushing back from his memory of standing in his mother's kitchen hearing the words, he didn't need to worry about their money problems. Understanding too well, what his mother was really trying to say. The point of understanding almost costing him his life.

Ben entered the corridor leading topside where he hit the damp slippery deck. He instantly started waving his arms like a crazed over-sized bird in the attempt to balance himself with every slippery step. Unexpectedly, the ship broke over a wave, sending Ben racing faster and faster down the sodden planks.

"Look out!"

However, Ben's warning came too late as he collided with the captain, knocking Ben to the deck. The impact deflated Seymour with such force it caused him to spit out his pipe.

"What the-Ben what's all the-what happen to your shirt?"

Ben found his way to his feet again quickly handing the captain back his pipe along with his hat. "Sorry," Ben said, continuing down the deck to the crew quarters to recover another shirt.

Chapter 9

Deception

The next few days aboard were some of the longest so far for Ben. With nothing to do again, he spent his time watching card games, feeding fish scraps to the captain's already overweight cat and learning to shoot dice. Jacob disapproving of Ben's recent education decided it's time to find him something else to do.

Jacob came upon Ben sitting on the last step leading to the wheelhouse. "Whatcha doin'?"

"I don't know. Nothin', I guess," Ben said while picking at the peeling paint on the wall next to the steps.

"You know, Abe could use some help in the kitchen."

Ben stood up; he became excited with the thought of getting to work with one of his favorite people in one of his favorite places. "You think Abe would let me help?"

Jacob turned and adjusted his cap so the beak covered his eyebrows. "Let me see what I can do," he said, before strolling off.

Later that day, Ben chasing the captain's cat up and across the hold covers saw Jacob, with what looked like a rolled-up newspaper under his arm. Ben picked up Tibbs and tried to catch up with Jacob. To Ben's astonishment, he vanished around the corner. Tibbs now working hard to gain freedom from Ben's grip, clawed at his arm.

"Ouch!" Ben dropped Tibbs to the deck.

Grabbing his bleeding arm, he looked up in time to see the orange fluffy ball disappear from sight. Thinking perhaps that Jacob went down to his cabin, Ben made his way to the corridor. He had never seen exactly where Jacob's cabin was. Ben started reading the names on the wooden doors lining the narrow corridor.

The third door Ben came to had another name on it at one time, but the name had been poorly scratched out with a pocketknife, and a new one put in its place. It read Jacob Stilman, First Officer.

Ben stood there for a moment trying to decide whether to knock on the door. When suddenly it opened, Jacob with the roll of paper still under his arm stepped forward without looking and plowed into Ben causing him to drop his papers.

"Ben, you alright? I... didn't even see you there; what are you doing?"

Unable to answer Jacob's question because he didn't have the answer, Ben bent over to help pick up the papers.

"What's this?" Ben asked handing it back.

Ben knew what it was before Jacob answered. He recognized it as a sea chart, like one of the charts from the wheelhouse. Like the one, the captain himself was trying to conceal.

"Oh nothin', just lookin' somethin' over," he said, tucking the chart under his jacket. "Feels like it's cooling off a bit." Jacob leaned against the door. "It stays like this; we'll have to find you a coat."

"I am okay, Jacob. Are we almost to Africa?"

"No, not yet." Jacob stepped over the threshold and closed his door.

"Did you ask Abe about the?" Ben said, bashfully not wanting to sound pushy but wanting to know still.

"About the job, yeah, I did. You start first thing tomorrow morning."

This had been the best news Ben had gotten all week. Even with this good news, Ben couldn't help thinking about, even if just for a moment, whether Jacob had one of the captain's charts. If so, how it found its way into Jacob's hands, and why?

The two enter the wheelhouse to find Billy taking a break from radio listening to look out the window and the sailor at the helm giving them a friendly salute. Jacob took the chart out of his jacket and put it back on the table being sure not to catch the eye of the crew member at the wheel.

"Thanks for talking to Abe, Jacob," Ben said, watching his every move.

"It's alright." Jacob lifted Ben's arm for a closer inspection. "What happened there?"

"Oh. Tibbs got me," Ben said, looking with a disapproving scowl over at the captain's cat, who had found his way back to his perch on the window ledge.

Jacob continued to look at the wound. "Best to keep that clean, so it doesn't get infected. We're a long way from a doctor."

"You know. I heard about what happened in the engine room the other day."

Jacob's words ignited feelings of embarrassment in Ben, who wished he could be anywhere on the ship but there. Unable to look Jacob in the face, Ben shuffled around the room as he pretended not to hear Jacob's words, inching his way to the door.

"Did you hear me, Ben?"

Without turning to look at Jacob, Ben said, "Ugh, yeah."

Keen to Ben's obvious evasion of the subject, Jacob said no more about it. "You ready to try working in the kitchen?"

"Sure, I'm ready. I can work as hard as anyone, you'll see," Ben said, taken back by Jacob's question.

The first officer tapped the crew member at the wheel on the shoulder giving him permission to take a break, to get some coffee while Jacob took the wheel. The radioman joined him as well. This left Ben and Jacob alone on the bridge. Getting the answer, he was hoping for from the boy, Jacob smiled to himself as he turned the over-sized wooden wheel to a new course on the bright brass compass.

"You've never steered a ship before, have ya?"

"No." Ben leaned on the ledge in front of the giant windows running along the front wall overlooking the deck.

"Step over here in front." Jacob placed Ben's hands one by one on the wooden posts of the wheel. "Now, see that there. See that? That's the compass."

"I know what a compass is. I went to school."

"Okay, Mr. Schoolin'. We steer the ship by it. Let's say the captain wants us to do some Easting, what would you do?"

"What's Easting," Ben asked, without answering Jacob's first question.

"Easting is when you steer the boat east."

Ben looked from the bright brass compass to Jacob and back. "Then, I would turn the wheel east, right?"

Jacob turned the wheel with his elbow to return the ship to east while pointing to east on the compass.

"That's right, Ben, you're doin' pretty good for a first-timer."

Pleased with himself, Ben proudly held the wheel checking the compass every few moments.

"Okay, Ben, that's enough Easting. Take us back to North."

"Aye Sir," Ben said, feeling like a real sailor of the Alexandria.

"Come on boy. Pull that wheel. Here let me help."

"No, no, I got it!" His face squished up from his extreme effort to command the wheel.

Jacob took hold of part of the wheel. "Ben, part of growin' up is to know when to ask for help. No one works alone on a ship. We all pitch in," Jacob said. "You got it?"

The young boy humbled by Jacob's words and his pride a little dented, said, "Yes, Sir. I got it."

"You did good, Ben. Thanks for your help. Now go and find some dinner then to bed. It's gettin' late," with Jacob's order, Ben is happy again with the prospect of a hot meal.

"Ben, tell me that wasn't fun."

Ben shook his head yes while stepping out the door into the chilly night air.

42

Chapter 10

Ice cream for Breakfast

Ben rose early the next morning, his excitement uncontainable; the thought of working in one of his favorite places with one of his favorite people on board would hardly leave him alone long enough to get any sleep.

With a watchful eye, careful not to give himself away, he exited his lifeboat to the crew quarters to ready himself for the day ahead. Abe waited impatiently in the galley for Ben, who had somehow managed to be late.

Coming through the door, Ben is struck with an apron. "It's about time you showed up, can't be late with people's food or coffee. They get awful cranky when things ain't ready."

Ben pulled the tent-sized apron around himself; the tie string made two passes around him before he could take up any slack.

"Now come here, the first thing you need to do is sweep the floor."

"Okay," Ben said.

"Do real good under those tables."

Ben retrieved the broom and started his chore, his apron dragging behind him. Abe dropped a large rucksack of flour on the table behind the counter; a cloud of the white powder rose into the air.

"I'm going to get started on the biscuits, and you can help me when you're done."

Abe began to sing. "Oh, what's ya gonna do with a drunken sailor."

"I'm done Abe with the floor."

"Let's see what kind of job you did," Abe joined Ben in the dining room.

He peered around the floor with a sharp eye. "Looks good. Now let's get back to those biscuits. Now you keep mixin' that batter, and I'll start the coffee, after that we'll get to cookin' the eggs."

"Yes, sir."

Proudly, Ben put the batter spoon to his forehead as if to salute flinging biscuit batter all over the kitchen wall. Abe shook his head as he turned to go on with his duties, leaving Ben to clean the batter off the wall. The two continued through the morning with their duties without incident.

Benjamin tired after a full morning of mixing, cleaning, and cooking, covered with flour and batter sat down on a box to catch his breath.

"What's you doing, boy? Get up, they'll be here any minute."

Ben exhaled a long breath and stepped up to the serving counter.

"Remember, they're going to try to get ya to give them way more eggs than they can have." Abe made clear to Ben. "But only use one spoon full or somebody at the end of the line isn't going to get no eggs."

"Here they come."

The crew spilled into the galley, shoving, and grabbing for trays. The sailors grew more hostile with every minute, pushing their trays at Ben faster than he can fill them.

"Wait, wait a minute, hold on you'll get your turn," Ben shouted.

"What's this you little barnacle, I want more eggs, hurry up," a man said, causing the frightened boy to take a few steps back.

The sailor, ignoring etiquette reached over the counter and grabbed the eggs with his bare hand. Abe is quick to correct the sailor with a painful blow to the man's knuckles from his coffee ladle.

"Hey!" The man pulled back his hand. For a moment, the crew paused from their feeding to see what is going to happen next.

The angry cook banged his ladle on the counter. "You all listen," he shouted, over the chatter in the hall. "In here, I'm captain and you best watch yourself iffin' you wants to eat."

Abe turned his attention to Ben, "What cha lookin' at? Get back to work."

Ben stepped back to his pan and finished dishing out the eggs.

"That's all in this pan."

"Well, you best go fetch the other pan out the oven before they decide to eat you, little fish."

Ben gave Abe a half-sarcastic smile out of the corner of his mouth before going to get the fresh pan.

"Ooww, gees, owow," Ben said, in pain, dropping the pan of piping hot eggs sending them flying everywhere.

Jumping up and down, the injured boy bumped into the table causing a tray of biscuits to fall to the floor and spin in all directions. Abe moving to help Ben caught one of the biscuits underfoot, sending him hurling to the floor. In the attempt to save himself, Abe grabbed for the counter but got the five-gallon pale of coffee that followed him down.

Coffee flowed across the floor like a tidal wave, the remaining biscuits majestically floating away on the current. Ben sloshed through the coffee to the sink in an attempt to relieve the burning pain as it climbs up his arm. Struggling to regain his footing, stunned in utter disbelief of the events that have unfolded, Abe joined Ben at the sink.

"Let's see, let's see."

"Oh you're gonna have a blister all right." Abe put Ben's hand back under the water.

He leaned into Ben's ear and whispered, "Don't you let them see you cry boy, just save it up."

"But... but it hurts Abe."

"I knows it do." Abe pulled up his sleeve. "You see that mark right there?" He pointed to a scar with his finger.

"I was workin' here one stormy night and old Abe got thrown against the stove, so I know it hurts all right," He said, pulling down his sleeve.

"Keep that hand in the water, and I'll get the medicine kit."

Abe with his long strides sloshed through the kitchen to a white metal box with a bright-red cross on it hanging on the wall.

"Come on. We're hungry over here," a sailor said.

Abe grabbed the medical kit. "If you wants to eat you're gonna have'ta help out; I gots to take care the boy."

He returned to Ben's side. Two sailors took the soggy cook up on his offer and proceeded to serve; while another took action with a mop and bucket against the wave of coffee drifting back and forth across the kitchen floor, with the heave of the ship.

"Now sit right there and let me see. Uh-this is going to sting a little."

Ben pulled his hand back. "What's that stuff?"

"Don't make me have someone hold you down while I's do this, it's for your own good," Abe said, pulling back Ben's hand.

He shook his head in pity. "I'm sorry Ben. I have to," he said, applying the burn cream to the wound on Ben's left hand.

The brave boy cried out at the top of his lungs in pain. "Stop, stop Abe, I'm sorry about the eggs, please stop."

Ben unable to hold back any longer opened the floodgates and an ocean of tears streamed down his face.

Abe looked up from treating Ben's hand to see him wipe away the tears on the shoulder of his shirt. An involuntary quiver developed in Abe's chin.

In a soft, sympathetic voice, Abe said, "I have to put the bandages on now to keep the dirt out."

Ben continued to wipe away the tears still trickling down his face, sniffling every few seconds.

"No."

"I have to Ben." Abe moved to grab the package of white gauze out of the medicine kit.

"Now look," Abe said, "I have some ice cream in the freezer. I was saving it for a special occasion, but looks like you could use some now."

"There, all done. I'll get ya some of that ice cream now. You wait right here."

Ben inspected his bandaged hand. "That didn't even hurt."

After finishing his second bowl of ice cream, Ben thought to himself, Mama doesn't let me have ice cream for breakfast.

"Thanks Abe."

"You feel better now?"

Ben nodded without taking his eyes off his ice cream bowl.

"I don't think maybe the kitchen is the best place for you to be workin'."

"What? I can still do some work with my good hand see," Ben declared, not wanting to wash out of a second job.

The ship's cook stood by Ben's table, with his arms folded is a formidable opponent who happens to be every bit as stubborn as Ben.

"No, I 'm sorry little fish, but I can't use ya like this, besides, there are too many things for ya to get hurt even worse on now that I think about it."

"It's not fair."

"Go on now, get out of here and let me get back to work. I got supper to get ready for."

"But."

"No buts go rest that hand." Abe pushed Ben by the shoulders out the galley door.

Before turning and unleashing his wrath on the remaining crew members loitering around the dining room.

"Get out of here, breakfast is over. Go on before I call the captain on ya all."

Tired and with his hand throbbing Ben decided to sulk in his lifeboat. The young boy laid there soaking in the warmth of the sun as it illuminates the canvas covering. His thoughts strayed to his mother, how he longed to see her again.

Ben closed his eyes, his mind drifted across hundreds of miles of water to his home and she appeared as if watching a movie. He saw her bustling about their tiny apartment, cooking, and cleaning.

Then other images of his life swept into sight: Christmas, birthdays, the time he fell down his apartment steps and broke his arm. Ben bumped his sore hand against the side of the boat as he rolled over to find a more comfortable spot; his face contorted from the pain.

"No... No let go, let me go," Ben said.

"Ben, wake up you're dreaming."

"Mother?"

"No, Ben it's me, Jacob, wake up boy," Jacob said, shaking him.

"Jacob?"

"I've been looking all over the ship for you, when I heard noise coming from over here that must have been some dream." Jacob helped Ben out of the lifeboat.

Damp with sweat Ben thought to himself, more like a nightmare.

"Why are you sleeping in here? What's wrong with the crew quarters?"

Ben, not wishing to share his true reason for taken up residence in an old lifeboat over a warm hammock, goes for the first thing that pops into his head. "Uh, well... they snore too much, can't sleep."

"Don't tell anyone will ya, please I like sleepin' here."

Jacob looked down at Ben's bandaged hand and scratched his chin reluctantly before he agreed to keep Ben's secret.

"So, Abe tells me you had another exciting day."

Ben shrugged without reply.

Jacob put his arm around Ben's shoulder. "Does it hurt much, your hand?"

"A little."

"You best lay off for a couple of days until that paw heals a bit."

"I'm not good at anything; all I do is screw up."

"You just need to find something you don't screw up at that's all."

Jacob put a humorous smile on his face trying to cheer Ben up.

"That will take forever."

"Why don't you go find that cat and see if he needs fed, I'll catch up with ya later?"

Jacob paused to watch Ben turn the corner by the smokestack before he climbed the steps to the bridge, Poor kid.

On entering, he found Edgar and the captain having what looked to be a deep conversation.

"We'll talk about this later," the captain said.

"Talk about what later?" Jacob's glance shifted between the two.

Edgar ignored his question and started in on him. "That boy is nothin' but trouble, next time he'll get somebody hurt."

"Looks like somebody did get hurt," Jacob snapped back.

Getting up from his chair, Edgar said, "We need to get rid of him before it's too late. A Ship is no place for a boy, especially a clumsy, can't do anything right kid like that."

"If the boy got accidentally left in port, no one would be the wiser." His attempt at intimidation is not quite as effective on Jacob as it is on a young boy.

Jacob's anger ignited. "If anybody's getting left behind, it'll be a first mate."

Jacob rushed to stand toe to toe with Edgar his chest heaving with every breath.

Edgar not backing down, said, "I'd be careful Jacob accidents happen on ships all the time."

Jacob clenched his fists. "Are you threatening me mate?" his voice rising to a yell.

"Alright that's enough you two we have more than our share of problems without you two going at it." The captain got to his feet. "Now shake hands and call it over."

"Go on!"

"I'll see ya later... Jacob," Edgar mumbled, under his breath before he exited the wheelhouse.

"You stay away from the boy," Jacob said, after him.

Seymour returned to his seat. "He's partially right you know."

"Not you too? He's just a boy away from home and never been at sea before."

In his outrage, Jacob kicked a chair sending it flying against the wall and crashing to the floor, before storming out the door ignoring the captain's calls to come back.

Chapter 11

Finding His Way

For the next week, bad weather moved in from the south drenching the ship and her crew making life aboard small, as the crew is forced indoors. Ben's hand healed, but his spirits are as damp as the deck boards.

To make things worse, his lifeboat hideaway is colder and damper than usual, which forced him to have to spend more time in doors as well. Jacob having to tend to his duties left Ben to his own devices to get along with the ship's crew, who grew more restless with each passing hour. Ben entered the crew's quarters from the raging weather.

"Shut that door," a crew member said.

"I'll take two cards," a whiskery face man said, sitting at the table.

"I'm in, raise ya two bits."

"I'm in," another man said, between puffs, lighting his cigar with a flaming match.

Ben returned from a long hot shower, dressed and watched two men throwing dice against the wall, while he dried his hair.

"Ben wipe up that water on the floor would you? Can't have someone slipping." The large bear-like man asked, rocking back and forth with the heave of the ship in his hammock.

Without complaint, Ben wiped up the water with his towel.

The raging tempests worked open the hatch door at the top of the steps of the passageway. Slamming it open and closed allowing its fury to find its way to the lower decks. Ben and the ship's crew alike paused to listen to the eerie sound of the door squeaking on its hinges. The creaking traveled through the room like an ice-cold wind, chilling all it touched.

A tall balding man slowly got to his feet. "What was that?"

Then the crew quarters' door flew open and the wild tempest, with its un-merciless fury, swept through the compartment. The first three fellows who had the unfortunate luck to have their hammocks stationed in front of the door took the worst of the soaking. A figure appeared in the doorway.

"The captain needs five men to secure the hatches and refasten the radio antenna, hurry up!" Edgar screamed, over the blowing wind fighting its way into the room.

Sailors scuffled from their hammocks; seizing their boots and raincoats on their way out the door and into the storm. The noise can only be described as a thousand hammers beating on a steel drum all at once.

"Not you," Edgar said, to Ben who has taken two steps toward the door.

"But I-" Is all that Ben gets out before Edgar slammed the door on his way-out leaving Ben standing in the half-empty quarters.

Frustrated and determined, Ben grabbed a raincoat off the hook by the door and ventured out into the weather, anyway. He is pushed into the wheelhouse by the force of the tempest behind him. "What are you doing here?" Jacob demanded to know.

Ben took off his dripping raincoat; spraying water all over Admiral Tibbs, which sends him scampering.

"When's it supposed to stop raining, anyway?"

The soggy young sailor noticed something was holding Jacob's attention at the table. "What are you lookin' at?"

"Well, because of the wind we have to correct our heading, to remain on course. So that's what I'm doing figuring our course correction."

The first officer seeing another moment to instruct Ben moved to the sailor manning the wheel.

"Sailor, take a break."

"Here Ben hold the wheel on North West."

The wheel had its own ideas. Commanding the boy to left then to the right.

Jacob grabbed the wheel post to keep Ben from being tossed to the floor. "Easy, Ben easy."

"I got it now thanks. Jacob?"

"Yes," he said half-paying attention to the chart on the table.

"Why are we going to Africa, anyway?"

"What? Um, we have to deliver an order for some company. Parts I think."

Ben glanced out the window at the miserable-looking men working on the deck.

"Turn to 160, but not too fast or you'll send the captain right out of his bunk. Do you know where 160□ is on the compass?"

"Sure, got it 160."

Ben positioned his foot up on the wall to help him turn the uncooperative wheel.

Jacob joined him, "So, it's just you and your mom, uh?"

The first officer took out his pocket watch pretending to look at it. He treaded carefully not wanting to appear nosey.

"Yeah, she works in a sewing shop making dresses and stuff."

"Not bad Ben I think we found something you're good at."

Ben looked to Jacob, who is checking the heading on the compass.

"You want to work on the bridge with me?"

"Work here? Sure."

The wheel fought against Ben's intention to hold his course, answering only to the chopping waves wanting to control its rudder. Pushing-pushing then pulling, lastly spinning.

"Good, then that's settled. You can start tomorrow."

"Jacob, the radios are back, but I can't get anything," Billy said, from the small room behind the wheel.

"The boys must have got the antenna up," Jacob said. "Keep trying."

"Here Ben let me have it for a while."

"What do you want me to do now?"

"How about you go see Abe and have him bring me up some coffee then you best hit the sack big day tomorrow."

"Okay."

Ben paused from getting his coat to glance at the chart lying on the table. He placed his finger on the line drawn in pencil to a large circle mid-way along the line.

"Hey Jacob this spot here, is this where we are?"

The first officer looked over his shoulder. "That's right."

"What does this line mean?"

"Go on get my coffee; we'll go over all that later." Jacob gestured Ben to go.

After delivering his message to Abe Ben waited outside the crew quarters' door until lights out, before he navigated the path between the rows of snoring sailors to his dry empty hammock. Damp and tired Ben rested easier with the bit of news he overheard earlier that Edgar would be on night watch.

Seymour entered the wheelhouse. "Captain, a call came up, you're needed in the engine room."

Hearing the news, he pulled up his collar and turned to leave. Seymour is drenched by the time he reached the engine room. Daniel noticed the soggy figure come in, laid down his tools, and wiped off his hands on his way to meet him.

"Daniel, what is it?"

Before answering, Daniel waved the captain into his office, which doubled as a parts storage closet.

The captain followed. "What's wrong?"

"Captain the problems with the boiler are getting worse. We won't be able to keep this pressure; we need to make port for repairs."

Seymour took out his pipe and tapped it on the wooden crate sitting on the floor beside him. "I know; I have been feeling the hesitation in the drive."

"Were halfway or so to making port, if we would have to detour... I can't afford the delay the shipment has to be delivered on schedule." Seymour thoughtfully placed his hand on Daniel's shoulder. "I am sorry you'll have to do the best you can."

"Seymour you're risking everything, the Alexandria's too good of a ship to be treating her this way. She's pulled us out of many scraps without complaint."

"That's final," the captain said, before leaving the room.

Chapter 12

Strange Lights

As dawn broke over the horizon, the weather cleared, and the pounding rain left through the night as quickly as it came. All is quiet and peaceful aboard the Alexandria. The ship cut through the glistening water, conspicuous and deliberate with a school of dolphins leading her way. Ben too excited to eat, readied himself and reported to the bridge to begin his new duties. His hopes are high, and his heart is light.

"Morning." Ben heard coming through the wheelhouse door from Seymour.

"Jacob told me of your new post working as a member of the bridge crew."

Ben hesitated, waiting for any sign of a rebuttal from the captain.

"Oh, it's fine, Ben, work hard, learn what Jacob has to teach ya and you'll do well as a bridge hand."

"By the way, I've been working on the schedule this mornin', and I've decided to try you out on a night watch starting tonight. What do you think?" The captain said, looking up from a scrap of paper.

"Sure," Ben said, having no idea what he is about to get himself into.

"So, you have to be back up here at 8:00 pm sharp, and you'll work until 4:00 am when the other shift comes to relieve ya."

"So, I'll stay up all night?" Ben's palms began to sweat, and his mouth went dry.

"That's right."

The latest Ben was ever been allowed to stay up had been eleven o'clock last New Year's Eve. The thought of staying up all night on the deck is both exciting and frightening at the same time.

"Don't worry you won't be completely alone, there will be crew on the bridge. All ya have to do is make the rounds to see that everything is okay, and no one's up to any funny business. Or that we don't stray too close to any ships passing by. There's a whistle and a flashlight that goes along with the job." Seymour pointed to a board hanging on the wall.

"At the start of your watch sign your name and the date on the roster there on the clipboard and sign out when you're done."

The captain removed his cap to scratch his head of thinning gray hair. "I know it sounds like a lot, but you'll do fine."

Jacob entered the wheelhouse caring a cup of coffee and closed the door with a swift kick without spilling a drop.

"Morning Captain, mornin' Ben. You ready to get started?"

"Um," Ben muttered, not sure how to answer his eyes traveling from Jacob's face to Seymour's.

The captain spoke up taking his cue from Ben's expression. "Ben's going to be on the night- shift tonight."

"I see… is that such a good idea? I mean him being new to all this and all?"

"I have faith in the boy."

"Ben, did the captain go over what you'll need to do?"

Before the boy could answer, Seymour jumped in again. "We covered everything but the walking route. Would ya take the boy around and show him where he needs to go?"

"I'll be glad to, come on Ben."

Jacob grateful for the opportunity to speak to Ben alone and perhaps a chance to get to the bottom of this sudden change in plans. The two set out to walk the route Ben will take alone later that night.

"See that over there?"

"Yeah."

Ben and Jacob made their way to Ben's first stop. "That's a watchmen station, there are ten altogether, just make your rounds to them," Jacob explained as the two walked up the deck.

"After that check-in with the bridge so they know you haven't fallin' overboard," Jacob said, laughing at his own humor.

The pair turned the corner, and Jacob pointed out the next station. "Have any question?"

"No, I don't have questions."

"Ben, I don't know why the captain made this decision to start you on nights, but understand it's a big responsibility. You're in charge of the safety of the ship and the men while on watch." Jacob turned and looked down on Ben, insuring he had his full attention.

"You can't fall asleep, ever. I don't want you to be frightened of it though. If you see anything that looks off, don't wait to blow that whistle."

Jacob's seriousness began to create doubt in Ben's mind if this is such a good idea. Spoiling the crew's breakfast is one thing, risking their lives is another.

"It's nice the weather has cleared that rain was getting on my nerves."

Jacob led Ben below deck and down the corridor toured the officer's cabins.

"What are we doing here?"

"You can stay in my cabin and get some rest the best you can; it's too noisy on deck to use your lifeboat."

"Uh, are you sure?"

"Yes, don't be late for work, leave time enough to get a bite to eat," Jacob said, shutting the door behind him.

"I will."

Ben sat on the bunk and looked around Jacob's cabin at all his photos. Some were of ships, one of him and the captain and one of a woman in a small wooden frame sitting on the table next to him.

He picked up the frame to get a closer look. In the corner of the picture, are the words, 'To my beloved Jacob from your loving wife Sara'. A fair-skinned woman with flowing black hair and light blue eyes; her smile was warm and inviting. Ben studied the woman for a long while before returning it to its resting place on the table.

The room is cozy with a homemade quilt on the bunk and green curtains hanging over the porthole window. Ben's eyes scan the room noticing Jacob's clothes scattered throughout, in the corner, sat a worn wicker rocker. The smell of Old Spice and sea salt lingered throughout the room.

Ben lay back on the bunk. His eyes travel along the ceiling to a shelf hanging over his head. He sat up to investigate; on the shelf, sat a variety of books, books about merit time law, birds and one on baseball. He took the baseball book off the shelf for a closer inspection.

 Flipping through the pages he came across a picture of "The Babe," Ben smiled to himself. "The Babe" being one of Ben's all-time heroes. This is also the only thing familiar to him he has seen since coming aboard. He studied the photo for a moment before he returned the book to its place on the shelf. Ben stood up and turned his attention to the rest of the room.

Within a step, Ben is standing on one of Jacob's shirts lying on the floor. He picked it up and threw it on the rocking chair with the rest of Jacob's clothes. He closed the curtains over the porthole to block out the light, the same light for the last week he waited through the long rainy days to see. The room took on a shade of muted green.

The young boy lay down for the last time appreciating how good a real bed felt. He stared at the picture hanging on the wall of some old ship long after she had sailed her last; he imagined her cutting across the waves with a trail of black smoke.

"Ben, time to get up."

"Get up Ben," a sailor said, from the other side of the door.

Ben is unable to remember falling asleep. The cabin is dark and cool; he rubbed his eyes helping them to focus on the clock sitting next to the picture on the table. In its soft amber glow, Ben could make out seven o'clock.

"I'm up."

Half-asleep Ben put his feet to the frigid steel floor and fumbled for the light switch on the desk lamp. After a poor attempt to adjust his baggy pants, Ben washed his face at the chipped cast iron-sink hanging on the wall, put on his boots, and shut off the light on his way out.

He shivered against the wind cutting across the deck. The moonlight cast an ominous illumination over the surfaces along Ben's path, to the galley for a warm meal before duty.

After getting his fill of Abe's gravy and dried meat, Ben entered the wheelhouse and gave Tibbs a good scratch on the neck.

"Did you get some supper?" Jacob asked.

"Some gravy and dried meat."

"Captain, I'm getting some chatter," Billy said, from the radio room.

"It sounds like a mix of English and Dutch; they're going on about. . . about an escort?" Billy wrote down the message and handed it to the captain.

"I don't know anything about their ever being an escort, are they saying anything else?"

"No that's it; they didn't sound too happy about it either."

"Good work."

Jacob turned to Ben and patted him on the shoulder. "You alright?"

"Cold, but good," Ben said.

As the night settled in, Ben concentrated on his duties, rehearsing each step in his head, trying not to let the nagging memories of recent failures get in the way of his determination.

"Take this coat on your rounds."

"Thanks."

Slipping into the oversized dark-blue wool coat, Ben's hands disappear immediately within the long sleeves. He ruffled them out of the sleeves and took the flashlight and whistle from Seymour.

"Ben, this is Bobby. He's working on the bridge tonight," the captain said.

"Hi," Bobby said, waving from the wheel.

Jacob whispered to the man "Keep an eye on the boy." before he turned to leave.

"Come on Ben. I'll walk you out. How d'you like the cabin?"

"Nice."

Seymour joined them on deck. "Jacob, let's get some supper."

"Sounds good. Night Ben."

Excited and confident Ben started his rounds with flashlight and whistle in hand. The ship blanketed in darkness on one side, moonlight on the other which appeared to be a completely different place, menacing and foreboding. The familiar sites gone. The only sites left are a few doors lit by single bulbs suspended from overhead, like islands in the vast ocean of space.

Ben's flashlight cut the blackness a short distance leaving it to fold back in on him from behind. The first station is less than halfway down the deck. That's one. Ben thought to himself with the flashlight beam leading the way. After hours of walking and checking, Ben had grown tired.

He sat down for a moment by the warm smoke stack and closed his eyes for a second, as he did, Jacob's voice plays in his head.

Remember Ben, we're counting on you.

Ben jumped to his feet looking around expecting to see Jacob standing there.

"Can't fall asleep, can't screw this up."

Ben looked up at the wheelhouse and decided to check-in. When he started to walk away something beckoned him; keeping a safe distance from the railing. He looked out over the black sea glimmering with pale moonlight and saw nothing at first.

Then in the far-off distance, his eyes focused on a light, a faint white light. The wind cut across Ben's face causing his eyes to water. Hastily, he wiped them with his sleeve and looked back, but the light was gone.

I must be tired, now I am seeing things. Ben turned to continue to the wheelhouse.

On entering Ben pointed in the direction, he thought he saw the light. "Bobby, did ya see the light out there?"

"No, I didn't see anything. I've been watching the compass."

"You must be getting tired now you're seeing things. There's some coffee over there."

"It'll keep you warm on your rounds."

The steamy black liquid poured like tar into Ben's cup. The boy raised it to his lips. The aroma found Ben's nose first. "It don't smell that good."

"Just try it, I didn't say I made good coffee," the porky helmsman admitted.

Trying again, Ben opened his mouth and poured the coffee in; regretfully, Ben is now committed to swallowing. The substance reminded him of a mix of road patches and gasoline. If he were to ever have those things.

"Well, what do you think? You like it," Bobby eagerly asked, with a look on his face that reminded Ben of a puppy waiting for a bone.

Ben nodded with approval not wanting to hurt the man's feelings; his face contorted as he swallowed hard. The effects of the coffee took hold of Ben almost immediately.

"I... I'll see you later," Ben stuttered.

Ben is a bit queasy on deck with a gut full of the helmsmen's coffee as he starts his rounds again. To the deck stations then down the steps to the corridors and up the other side, finally to the stern. This would go on throughout the night until at last the dawn broke over the horizon.

A tall, bulky sailor in a dark wool coat met him halfway between the smoke stack and the wheelhouse.

"Ben, I'm your shift replacement."

"How'd it go?"

"Uh, good," Ben said, handing the man his flashlight. Not bothering to tell the sailor about the mysterious light he saw or imagined.

"You'll need to go and sign out before you can leave."

"Oh, yeah, I forgot."

Ben dumped his exhausted body into his lifeboat, pulled the cover closed, and fell unconscious. The tired young sailor slept without a stir late into the morning.

Abe entered the wheelhouse. "Here, captain. I brung ya some coffee, and a fresh made biscuit. Since I didn't see ya at breakfast. I thought ya must have started early."

"Ah thanks, it smells good." the captain obligingly took the steaming biscuit.

"I got one for you too, Jacob."

"Thanks."

On handing Jacob his, Abe couldn't help but throw him a question. "So how's the boy doing?"

"Good, good. He stood his watch last night, Bobby said he did well." Jacob dunked his biscuit in his coffee.

"I'd like to see him, where is he?"

"Oh, probably asleep somewhere."

"Well then I'll catch him later, I best get back anyway."

"Alright. See ya later, Abe."

Jacob waited for him to leave before he sought his moment to approach the captain again about the mysterious path laid out on the chart.

"Captain, I discovered a line that looks like a change in course on the return trip. Is there something I should know about?" Jacob kept his voice to a firm whisper as he glared at the captain awaiting his answer.

Seymour employed every avoidance tactic he knew to delay answering Jacob directly.

"Let's see, this one here?"

"You know full well that's the line; what is it? Were you planning a little detour for on the way back and didn't bother to tell me?"

Seymour realizing Jacob knowing him so well would spot a lie the moment the words left his mouth preceded with caution.

"It's really nothing, nothing to be worried about, anyway. Just some late-night doodling of a tired sea captain."

He did it; he lied. For the first time since Jacob has met Seymour. He lied to him. Seymour unable to look Jacob in the eye turned to light his pipe. Jacob himself turns away realizing in that moment nothing would ever be the same between them again. Throughout the years, crews have come and gone on the Alexandria, but the one person Jacob could always trust was Seymour.

Now over the most trivial of things his trust was broken. He can only guess why this line is so important that Seymour is willing to betray him to protect its secret. One thing was certain, if Seymour's plans involved money, you can be sure Edgar has something to do with it. Approaching him for answers wouldn't go any better than with the captain. Jacob is left waiting with everyone else to discover the truth about what Seymour has in store.

"Well, I'm going for a walk," Seymour said.

Jacob looked out over the deck at the lifeboat which is home for the ship's youngest member when it hits him like a two-ton truck, he finally understood. He understood what Ben must have been feeling on this ship, alone and with no one to trust.

He stood there and stared at the lifeboat for a long time before going to his cabin after the captain's return. He took off his coat and hat then he picked up a pile of papers accumulating in the seat of his wicker chair.

He looked at the paper on top of the stack. Noticing it is a copy of the manifest register Ben filled out after being discovered. Jacob dropped the stack and sat down in his rocker to take a closer inspection of the paper.

"Name: Ben M. Holt, Birthdate: Sept 2, 1923," he read.

Jacob glanced up at his calendar sporting a picture of a blonde-haired woman wearing a bathing suit, hanging behind his door. This time Jacob is actually looking at the dates.

"Wednesday… Let's see."

I can't believe he's been on board that long already.

Grabbing his hat and coat, Jacob raced down the corridor to the steps. Bursting into the galley nearly startling Abraham out of his skin.

"What you doin' runnin' around scarin' folks like that?"

"Know what day it is?" Jacob posed with a grin on his face.

"I don't have time for riddles right now. Some of us have work to do."

"It's Ben's birthday!"

"It's his birthday?"

"What do you think we could do for him?"

Abe stood there with his hand on his chin glancing up at the ceiling. "Tell ya what. You bring him by here in a while, and I'll have something special for him, okay?"

"Thanks, Abe. I'll see you later."

The news of Benjamin's birthday pushed the disappointment with the captain temporarily out of Jacob's head as he rallied to make his birthday special.

"Hello Jacob," Daniel said, coming up next to him on the port side along the railing.

"Today's Ben's birthday."

"It is? How old is he anyway?"

"According to what he wrote down on the manifest log, he's fourteen today." Jacob looked down at his shoes. "Kind of sad though him here and away from his Ma."

"Yeah, that's too bad."

"Oh, Abe's putting something together for him later, and I have an idea. Want in on it?"

"You mean for the boy's birthday?"

"Yeah."

"What did you have in mind?"

"Just go and gather up a few guys and go to the galley; Abe may have something for you to do. I'll take care of the rest."

Chapter 13

The Betrayal

Jacob seized Ben's lifeboat and rocked it back and forth. "Rise and shine sleeping beauty."

The half-asleep young sailor spilled out of the lifeboat onto the deck. "I'm up; I'm up," Ben said, in a less than pleasant voice.

"Hurry up, we have to be in the mess hall," Jacob ordered, doing his best to wear the most serious face.

"For what?"

"Straighten up your shirt there."

"Gee what's the big deal?"

Jacob caught up with his own excitement, failed to notice he's dragging poor Ben down the deck rather than escorting. Arriving at the galley doors, Jacob hesitated for a moment and listened.

"What are you doing?"

Ben reached for the doorknob.

"Nothin'. Go on in."

Ben turned the doorknob and stepped through the doorway. Surprise! Rang out through the galley Benjamin jumped two feet off the floor. Smiling and clapping at Ben is the captain, Daniel, Abe, Bobby, Henry and a couple of other sailors Ben has met but can't remember their names.

"Happy Birthday, Benjamin."

Ben threw his arms around Jacob's waist. Jacob is embarrassed but appreciated it just the same.

"Come on over here birthday boy," Abe shouted, from across the room.

Ben let go of his hold on Jacob and joined the party.

"Now, it's not really cake; it's more like... cornbread birthday muffins with matches. So make a wish and blow them out before we set the room on fire."

On orders, Ben blew out all fourteen burning matches on seven of the corn muffins.

"They look great. Thanks, Abe. Thanks, everyone for bothering with my birthday. I... I... I totally forgot."

"It was Jacob's idea he knew it was your birthday and rooked us in to helpin','" the captain said.

"Just because it's your birthday doesn't mean you get out of work, you be on time for your shift," the captain laughed, taking a drink of beer that all the men at Ben's party are enjoying in Ben's honor.

After eating his fill of muffins and apple cider Ben joined Jacob out on the deck where he's been watching the hot sparks rise into the air from the ship's funnel.

"Ben, how'd you like the party? It wasn't much, but..."

"I liked it. No one has ever given me a birthday party 'cept my Ma before. Thanks again."

Jacob reached into his pocket and pulled out a stack of bills folded over, and hands them to Ben.

"What's this?"

"It's nothing just a little birthday present." Jacob continued to watch the funnel.

"I can pay you back when the captain..."

"No, it's a present. Now take it."

Ben humbled by such a gift stuffed the money in his pocket. "Thanks, Jacob."

Being from a poor inner-city family Ben has never even seen that much money in his house, let alone held it or had any of it for his very own. Ben stood there quietly by Jacob, the best friend he ever had. The two friends turned their attention to the vast stretch of water all around them.

"It just goes on forever. A person could get lost for a lifetime out here."

Jacob and Ben spent the rest of the afternoon together tending to duties, watching the dolphins racing to keep pace with the Alexandria, and some well-earned do nothing time.

 At long last, Jacob put his arms over his head and stretched while making what looked like a painful face. Before imitating a deflating balloon, "Well, kid I'm turnin' in. What are you going to do?"

"Um, I'm not working tonight the captain said cause on account it's my birthday and all," Ben said, to Jacob pretending to stretch as well, "I guess I'll turn in too."

"Goodnight kid. See ya tomorrow."

"Goodnight."

Both man and boy went their separate ways. The next morning Ben is awoken to the bellowing sound of a foghorn, but it isn't the Alexandria's. Ben checked to see if the coast is clear before he slithered out of his lifeboat lair to see where the sound is coming from. Over on the port side sailors gathered to see the ship that has come alongside. Her name read The Red Robin. She is a two-stack passenger ship.

Ben walked up on one of the sailor's standing by. "What's going on?"

"It's the Red Robin. She's on course back to America and asked if we have any mail."

"Mail?"

"Yeah, that's how the mail gets delivered out here boy."

"Ya mean I could send a letter? I have mail."

"Well, you best be getting to the captain, he's putting the bag together right now," the sailor said, pointing to the wheelhouse.

Ben took off in a full run hoping to catch the captain before it was too late. Up across the cargo covers, around the corner and up the steps two at a time Ben ran. Bursting in the door Ben caught his foot on Tibb's tail, sending the cat hissing and scampering to cover.

Ben startled Seymour with his explosive intrusion. "Slow down, Ben. What's your hurry?"

"I, I would like to send a letter too." Out of breath, Ben is barely able to get the words out.

"Okay is it ready?"

"No, I need a piece of paper and an envelope."

Getting up from his chair Seymour rummaged through a drawer which is embedded in the back wall of the radio room.

"Just a minute let me see what I have."

"Edgar, signal the Robin. It will be another few minutes, would ya?"

In his haste, Ben didn't notice that Edgar had been standing just on the other side of the radio room door the whole time. His heart skipped a beat at the sight of him.

"Alright," Edgar said, going over to the large lamp placed on a pole sitting in the corner of the room. Switched it on and began to open and close the shutters mounted on the front of the lamp. Ben is momentarily distracted from his task to watch in spite of the fact Edgar is doing the working. The captain returned with a piece of paper and envelope. Noticing Ben's fascination, Seymour explained the light.

"It's for using Morse code."

Seeing the confusion on Ben's face, the captain tried to focus Ben's understanding.

"The different light signals are letters, and you put them together to make a message."

"Oh, you mean like S. O. S.?"

"That's right."

"You best finish your letter."

"Yeah."

Ben sat down at the wooden table and struggled to find the words to begin to tell his mother what has happened.

"Hurry up Ben," the captain said.

Dear Mom

I am fine I got stuck on a steamer by accident. Be home soon. I love you.

P. S. Don't worry, I made a friend.

Your son, Benjamin.

At that moment, the realization of what could happen struck Ben like a bolt of lightning.

"Why I am I sending a letter? I could go home."

"What did you say Ben?"

Without answering, Ben went to the window and looked out over the deck and then to the Red Robin. Seymour glanced at Ben from the corner of his eye as if he could read Ben's thoughts. "You want to go?"

Ben stared at Seymour, lost for words. He looked out the window again at Jacob waving up at him, at Abe running around giving orders to the sailors, and Daniel, who is trying to have a conversation about swapping spare parts with one of the greasy sailors on the Robin. Finally, Ben looked back at Seymour who waited patiently for his answer.

Ben rubbed his letter in his fingers. "I'll stay."

"Good," the captain said. "You best finish that letter then."

"Right," Ben returned to the table and finished the last words of his letter that told his mother about his situation, how much the crew needed him, and how he loved and missed her.

Pleased with himself Ben folded the letter and stuffed it in the envelope, along with the money Jacob had given him before licking the flap and adding his address.

"Here, it's ready," Ben, said.

Recklessly, Edgar took the letter out of Ben's hand and stuffed it in the mailbag. Down the steps and onto the deck, Edgar circled the corner out of sight and opened the mailbag. Digging deep Edgar pulled out a hand full of letters. Pitching them back one by one until he found what he's hunting for, reading the name Dorothy Holt.

With a dangerous look of deceit on his face, Edgar jammed the letter in his pocket and closed the bag. Ben watched out the window at the Robin, who is beginning to pull away with the mailbag safely aboard.

"Captain, how long will it take for the mail to get back?"

"Oh, I don't know two; three weeks I suppose maybe less. The Robin is a fast ship. She can cut waves better than fourteen knots I hear."

Ben's middle reminded him he had yet to eat that morning. "Captain, I'm going to get some breakfast."

"Be mindful of your duties."

"I will."

More excited than he has been since his party, Ben entered the galley not even looking for Edgar or worrying about it.

He thought to himself; Ma will know what's happened to me.

"Come sit over here, Ben."

Ben looked around until he found the source of the call and picked up his tray to join the balding sailor.

"How you doing boy?" While waiting for Ben's answer the sailor stuffed a fork full of home fries in his mouth.

"Good. I got a letter off to my mother."

"You did? That's good. I got one off to my dear mother in New York too," a sailor said, from across the table.

"Now don't you start with that again!" The skinny balding sailor howled, waving a piece of meat at him dangling from the end of his fork.

"I'm just saying that's all."

"You think we'll be in port soon," Ben asked, trying to distract the men.

"Oh, it's hard to say."

"You have to check our position on the chart first to be able to tell."

The bear-like man with the bushy mustache spoke up. "We lonely ship hands don't get to see the charts much from working in the engine room."

Ben watched him chase grits around his tray with a spoon while he spoke; finally, he resorted to picking them up with his fingers. Finishing his meal, Ben exited the galley for fresher air on deck. Standing a safe distance from the port rail Ben searched the horizon for the mysterious light.

 Carefully, he studied the water, until he spotted something, something small leaving a smoke trail across the distant sky. There you are. After watching the ship for a while, Ben returned to the crew quarters to find sailors busying themselves with various personal endeavors. Some washing their socks, others are shaving and still, others going about the daily business of getting in a good card game.

"I hear tell there's another boat off the port side. Could be a freighter," one of the sailors said.

"It's been shadowing us for better than a week now. There's going to be trouble I tell ya; its pirates."

"Go on, it's probably just a fishin' boat," another sailor said, from the card table to the old man lying in his dirty hammock.

Ben is curious to hear more and positions himself closer to the conversation.

"What about the radio?"

"What about it?"

"When they caught that transmission, it was them Germans."

"So?"

"Something's brewing. I tell ya them Germans are up to no good."

The sailor folded his arms and leaned back in his chair. "And how do you know that?"

"They're roaming these waters far from home."

"Ahh, you're crazy."

The grumpy sailor turned and threw Ben a piercing glare. "What do you want?"

"Nothing."

"Just sitting there being a little spy for the captain, are ya?"

"Oh, leave him alone you old sea dog. Before…"

"Before what?" the man said, getting to his feet.

"Before someone puts ya in your place."

"Oh, and suppose it be the boy?" He said, turning to see an empty space where Ben had been sitting. His eyes roamed around the room until they fell on the door leading out on the deck swinging open.

Ben entertained himself throughout the day by throwing pop bottle caps into the water from high above the deck in the crow's nest. The hours trickled by, and Ben decided it was time to snatch a snack from Abe's apple barrel. After a few choice words from Abe for being caught, he is back on deck about to turn a corner when he hears voices.

"Alright. I'll tend to it."

"You best see that ya do, if we keep losing steam, we'll never make port on time."

Ben recognized the voices to be Daniel and the ever-creepy first mate.

Ben wasted no time seeking safe refuge in his lifeboat. This time, however, someone had been watching. Ben has not escaped the peering eyes of Edgar, who had been lurking behind the smokestack.

Why you sneaky little... that's where you've been hiding, Edgar said, to himself through clenched yellow teeth with a sense of adulation.

Unaware of Edgar's discovery Ben laid quietly, thinking about his letter and how he hoped the money would find its way to his mother safely. His thoughts are interrupted by passing sailors, which he took as his cue to get some sleep before reporting to the captain. Day faded effortlessly into twilight; Ben slept soundly dreaming of home and happier times. From his dream world, Ben doesn't hear the approaching footsteps.

Chapter 14

Murderer Aboard

In the darkness, a hand reached out and started to pull back the canvass cover. Deeper and deeper the hand plunged into the blackness of the lifeboat searching for the boy who slumbered within. Clutching Ben by the shoulder the hand shook him violently, startling him awake.

"Ahh. Let go, let go," Ben screamed.

Nevertheless, the hand would not release him. Ben pulled at the hand for his freedom.

"Ben, it's Jacob. Wake up. You have to go on duty soon."

"Oh, Jacob. Sorry, you… you scared the puddin' out of me. I'm up."

Ben pulled himself out of the lifeboat and spilled out into the darkness of the night.

"What time is it?"

"It's about eight-thirty. You best be getting washed and getting up to the wheelhouse. I'll see you there."

"Okay."

Tucking in his shirt, Ben ran down the deck to the crew quarters, into the bathroom and turned on the water, soaked his face with soap, rinsed and grabbed for the semi-clean towel hanging on a hook. He finished off the job by running his fingers through his hair while running out the door again.

A few minutes later Ben arrived at the foot of the stairs that lead to the wheelhouse. Slightly out of breath, Ben entered the room. Inside he finds Jacob hard at work pouring over figures with the captain at his side.

A sailor whistled a cheerful tune at the wheel and Admiral Tibbs occupying his usual spot. None took immediate notice of him. Putting out his hand, he gave Tibbs a stroke along his pudgy body.

"Don't be nice to him. That rascal has been a bad boy," the captain said.

Ben ignored him and gave Tibbs a scratch on the neck, anyway.

Jacob stood upright, then bent far back trying to take the crook out of his back before sitting on his stool. "Ben, relieve the wheelman and turn 260 degrees, would ya?"

With only the captain, Jacob, and Ben left on the bridge the room is filling with an uncomfortable silence. Tibbs moaned a disturbing meow as he jumped down from his perch and strolled around the room.

"Serves you right, you old cat," the captain said.

"What did he do, Captain?"

The captain got to his feet, stretched out his short, stubby arms as if reaching for something and let out a great bellow of air before he began to explain what Tibbs had done to earn a scolding.

"Why that poor excuse of a cat was down in the cargo hold; for what I'll never know. He hasn't done a day's work since he got here when them rats got the better of him."

Folding his arms the captain continued, "Next thing you know, Abe finds him crying there in the dark up on some boxes all scared. Them rats being too much for the great hunter."

"I think we have more rats now than before you got that cat," Jacob said, adding his two cents worth for a smile out of Ben, at the captain's expense and the captain none the wiser.

"Oh, is that so." the captain taking Jacob's bait.

"What are you saying? That my cat is no good?" The captain now red as a beat in the face not realizing in all his ranting and raving his hat is now sitting at an odd angle on his head, which doesn't give to his credibility.

"I'll have you know he was the best mouser in his building, the man I bought him from said so. It's just the sea life doesn't agree with him. That's all."

With that, the captain walked over and snatched the Admiral up from his spot adjusted his cap and bid a good night before vanishing out the door.

The two remaining bridge members burst out in laughter, which carried on for a long while.

"Okay, Ben. Turn to heading 270 and hold."

"270 and hold, Aye," Ben said, returning the order proudly.

"You know you're becoming a good sailor."

"Thanks," Ben said thinking briefly about his painful experiences in the kitchen and how he nearly lost more than his shirt in the engine room.

"Jacob?"

"Yeah?"

Jacob studied the poorly lit chart by the captain's desk lamp, which left the surrounding area of the room in a shadowy mist of light.

"Did you see a ship out there?"

"Out where?"

"Out there ways off from us?"

"I heard something about it."

"Why do think they are following us?"

"What makes you think they're following us?"

"I don't know. The guys have been saying…"

Jacob cut Ben off. "First stop listening to the crew. Half the time they know very little about anything going on. Second, these waters are filled with trade routes that often bring ships close to each other."

Jacob sat down and looked up at Ben. "It doesn't mean that we're in danger. Just that maybe we're traveling in the same direction that's all. Understand?"

 Ben confirmed, "I understand."

"It's dark tonight. No moon; I can barely see the deck lantern."

"Yes, it's that time of year for these waters. Black as coal, many ships have gone ghost on nights like tonight."

Ben felt a sense of nervousness flushed over him. "Jacob?"

"Yes, Ben."

"What will we do when we get to port?"

Jacob got up from the small wooden table to join Ben at the wheel. "Well, we'll unload our goods, take on some supplies, make repairs, and be on our way home."

He put his hand on Ben's shoulder. "I suppose your Ma will be pretty worried about ya, Ben."

"Yeah, she's a worrier alright. But my letter will put her mind at ease until she thinks of some other way to worry about me."

Not wanting to continue to talk about his mom Ben changed the subject. "Anymore radio calls from the Germans?"

Jacob grabbed the engine power controls and gave them a pull. "No, not for a while."

Ben started again. "Jacob?" This time in a more direct and determined voice. "What was that line you found anyway; you know the one on the chart?"

"Boy, you're full of questions tonight. If I didn't know better, I'd thought I was being interrogated." Jacob said, with laughter.

"Sorry." Ben redirected his attention out the front windows.

Billy came out from the radio room. "Jacob, I'm taking a break for the head."

"Sure, grab us some coffee on your way back would ya?"

"You got it."

"You just wait, Ben. You'll be home before you know it."

Ben glanced over his shoulder at Jacob in time to see the thoughtfulness in his eyes. At the moment that followed, Ben and Jacob heard foots steps of someone approaching, expecting Billy to come through the door with mugs of Abe's fresh coffee. Neither one paid any attention to the racket until the door slammed open against the wall with a crash. Abe appeared in the doorway. His right hand clutched the windowsill; he gasped for air wiping his face with his shirtsleeve. His eyes burned with sweat.

"Ja... Jacob, come quick a bad fight broke out in the crew quarters."

"Damn it," Jacob said, grabbing his coat and hat hanging on a hook.

Spinning back, Jacob fired an order louder than he intended startling Ben to attention. "Ben, hold your course. By the way, no, I haven't found out what the line means yet." Jacob finished with Abe pulling him out the door.

The young helmsmen determined not to let his friend down seen to his duties. He checked and rechecked his heading, looking left and right out the bridge windows into the darkness for any sign of possible ships. Soon Billy returned with mugs of coffee in hands, unaware of what has happened.

"Here boys, I got the... Where's Jacob, Ben?"

"He had to go and break up a fight in the crew's quarters." Ben's voice is dry and raspy as he spoke the words.

"A fight? With who?"

"I don't know."

"When did he leave?"

"Just about fifteen minutes ago, I think."

Setting the coffee cups down on the table Billy took a place at Ben's side.

"Probably just a scuffle over someone cheating at cards again," Billy said, growing worried himself.

"Yeah, Jacob said he'd be right back."

The two said little as the minutes ticked by.

"Captain, report to the crew quarters immediately." Blared over the ship's speaker.

"What was that," Ben asked, more frightened now.

"I don't know?"

"Have you ever heard that before?"

Billy looked out the door of the wheelhouse to see sailors scattering down the deck. "No."

"What's happening?" Ben said.

"I don't know."

"Billy, I want to go see if Jacob needs some help?"

"No remain at your post mister, we need you there. If they need us, they'll let us know," Billy ordered to Ben.

He reluctantly remained at the wheel. The two waited on the bridge for any word on what's been happening with their friends when there's a rattle at the doorknob. Abe entered carrying a long expression on his whiskery, wrinkled face looking as if he had just crossed paths with a spirit.

Abe only glanced at Ben trying not to give Ben a chance to read in his eye's the terrible thing that has happened. Ben stood quietly waiting for Abe to speak the words. The words he needed to hear that would allow him to breathe again.

Abe approached Ben and began to speak in a voice he hardly recognized as his own. "Ben, ya needs to come with me down to Jacob's cabin now. He's asking for ya." Abe's eyes fixed on the floor.

Billy stepped closer. "What's happened Abe? What's wrong?" Abe struggled to put one foot in front of the other towards the door.

"It's best we don't speak of it right now."

Ben's feet are anchored to the spot. "Abe, why's Jacob in his cabin?"

"Is he sick?" Ben said, his words sounding more ridiculous aloud than they did in his head. Knowing Jacob wasn't anymore sick than he was, still he's desperate to make sense of the events unfolding around him. Somehow knowing he is powerless to stop it, something so awful Abe can't speak of it.

"Billy, you take the wheel until the captain sends somebody up here."

All the way down the long dingy corridor to Jacob's cabin fear grew in Ben's gut, afraid to think the unthinkable, unable to speak the unspeakable.

Ben not wanting to accept the truth that maybe Jacob, who has become more than a friend to him is only a fallible human being with his flaws and weaknesses like everyone else. Abe stopped Ben outside Jacob's door where a small crowd is gathered. Finally allowing Ben to see in his eyes the truth about what has happened.

Abe began softly. "Now, let me just tell ya what's going on, so's you're ready."

"There was a fight and one fella pulled a knife when Jacob stepped in to break it up, he got the worst of it."

"What do mean the worst of it, Abe? What do you mean, Abe?" Ben's eyes blurred with tears; his mouth went dry as a piece of sandpaper.

Like when you're about to get your punishment for doing wrong at school by your ma but worse. Abe watched Ben as he clung to every word like a life preserver in a sea of uncertainty and fear.

Abe continued, "He doesn't look too good so don't stare at him too hard."

Abe is interrupted when the captain opened Jacob's cabin door.

"Thanks for getting the boy, Abe. You best come. I feel there's not much time."

Ben more frightened than he has ever been in his life barely has the will to make his legs carry him through the doorway and into Jacob's room. A room he himself has spent time in, a room that made him feel safe almost like home.

 Ben would give anything to be anywhere else in the world. His eyes fell on Jacob's motionless body. He couldn't understand how only few hours ago he was laughing and joking with his friend, and now he was watching him die.

Jacob whispered, "Ben."

Ben moved to Jacob's side, his eyes no longer shining with the glimmer of life Ben had grown accustomed to seeing, chased away by the pain and suffering of his injury.

"Sorry, you have to see me like this."

Ben moved closer in an attempt to comfort his friend; Jacob's own words flutter through Ben's mind, best take care of that. We're a long way from a doctor.

"You'll be fine. You'll see. You can lick this." Ben forced out of his mouth.

The frightened boy stopped talking when tears stream down his pale cheeks once more as he watched his friend fight to conceal the true depth of his hurt.

"We've done all we can, but I don't know if it's enough," the captain told Abe, who stood in the back of the small cabin with his back to the wall.

Jacob's voice became weak and frail. "Ben-"

The frightened boy leaned in over him to hear his whisper.

"Ben I'm proud of you. Now you stay strong for your ma and get home safe you hear."

"What do you mean?"

Jacob reached out his hand in search of Ben's face. "You listen to the captain and Abe."

"Where are you, Ben? Can't see too good, it's so dark in here."

Ben grabbed Jacob's hand tight. "I'm right here Jacob, just hold on."

Jacob smiled as he closed his eyes and exhaled his last breath.

"Jacob! Jacob! Wake up! Don't go! I need you!" Ben shouted, shaking Jacob's arm.

Abe moved forward and pulled Ben away from Jacob's body. "No let me go, Captain, help him... help him."

Ben's pleas went unanswered.

"Ben, you need to let go now. He's gone."

"No, I won't, do something, please."

Ben released Jacob's arm. It fell lifeless on to the bunk. He ran from the room. Abe started after him.

"No. Let him go, Abe. He needs to work this out himself," the captain said while covering Jacob's body with his blanket.

Ben pushed through the crowd of men standing outside Jacob's cabin and down the corridor, up the steps, and out onto the deck to the steps leading up to the bridge. He crawled over the railing onto the ladder that led to the crow's nest high above the ship.

A few minutes later the captain, Daniel, and Edgar appeared on deck inquiring to the sailor if he had seen Ben. The man said nothing and pointed up to the crow's nest. Ben's sobs could be heard all the way to the deck. Abe again moved to aid his young friend, and again the captain stopped him.

"He's alright up there. He'll come down when he's ready," the captain said, before turning to walk away.

"But what if?."

"Let him be Abe. That's an order."

Ben had never come to know death or the pain and emptiness that came with losing someone he loved. His father's passing came before Ben was old enough to understand. His mother never spoke of the details surrounding his father's death only that it happened at work.

Sometimes late at night on special occasions like their anniversary or Ben's birthday, he could hear his mother weeping in the darkness of her room. Ben is alone once again. He longed for the comforting touch and words of his mother believing he may never know them again.

Hours passed, and the evening twilight ushered in the night before Ben descended from his place of solitude high above the Alexandria. He came through the galley doors. The room buzzed with the sound of whispers from a shocked and worried crew.

"What's the captain going to do about the two in the fight?"

"What to do about Jacob's body?"

"Will the Alexandria make port early?"

Ben paid no mind to any of it. He walked over to the sink picked up a glass to get a drink of water. He drank it down and turned to see Abe standing there with the same worried look in his eyes he had often seen in his mothers.

"I'm okay. Could I eat?"

"Certainly, I got potatoes and ham for ya. You sit right over here, and I'll fetch it."

After finishing his second helping, Ben grew weary and said his goodnight to Abe. Out on deck, his mind wandered without cohesion, struggling to piece together the details of it all. Devastated by the speed in which his life is once again changed forever, once again alone, faced with the uncertainty of what lied ahead.

The young boy can hardly face the thought of going on without the help and advice of his friend and mentor, or how nothing will ever be the same. Benjamin grew tired of thinking and walking. He sat down on the cargo cover forward of the smokestack away from prying eyes.

Admiral Tibbs somehow sensed the loss of one of Alexandria's own and joined Ben. Ben glad to see him stroked his yellowish-orange fur until Tibbs began to purr with satisfaction. There the two unlikely shipmates remain long into the night.

The next-day Ben is hanging around the crew quarters when Abe found him.

"Ben, how you doin' boy?"

"Alright, I guess."

"Well you best be getting ready for this afternoon. Go and find a proper shirt and get yourself cleaned up."

"This afternoon? What's this afternoon?"

With Ben's question, came a silence over the room. Abe cleared his throat and spoke softly, "Jacob's funeral services."

"Funeral? How can you have a funeral at…?" The boys unknowing quickly gave way to the logical conclusion to his question. "You're going to dump him in the water?"

Ben's face blushed with anger. "No, that's wrong. You can't dump him overboard like the garbage."

A sailor came to Abe's aid with an explanation. "Look, Ben, we can't leave him on board. It's not safe. Sailors have been burying their dead at sea for hundreds of years. We have no choice."

Ben plopped down on the bench at the card table before conceding to what must be done. "But, there's no grave."

"I know, but Jacob was a sailor, and he knew the life. You'll always have memories of the good times we all had with him," Abe said.

"Now go, get a shirt that fits and put your shoes on with clean socks."

"Alright," Ben grudgingly agreed.

Chapter 15

Burial at Sea

"It's time Ben," the captain said, waiting for the young sailor to join him at the cabin door of the crew quarters.

"Ben?"

Ben felt unable to process the captain's words from the cool dark place in his mind, a place that consumed him in the quiet moments since receiving the news that shattered his world. His thoughts fogged over from being there too long preventing complete consciousness of his surroundings.

 Ben's breath went shallow and quick at the sight of the body sitting at the ship's railing. His grief gave way to suffocating fear, which pulsed through his body like pain from a thousand prickly needles.

The captain led Ben forward by the shoulders. "Come on son. Take your place."

Images flash in Ben's mind of the time he spent with Jacob. His ears rang with the last words his friend spoke to him over and over.

"Order!" a sailor said.

Ben imitated the sailors around him. and saluted the remains of his only true friend in this world. He watched the sailors lower his friend to the water. He sent his heart with it. The service ended, and the sailors began to leave. The heartbroken boy remained; his feet too heavy to move.

 Ben watched Jacob disappear under the glistening ocean waves. He bit his lower lip until he could not hold back his pain and remorse any longer. Silently, tears streamed down his face.

Abe whispered, "Come, boy. There's nothing more to do." pulling Ben by the arm. The young sailor yanked his arm away and held his post wiping his runny nose on his sleeve. Abe grabbed his arm again.

"No, leave me alone. Stop it."

Ben tried to free himself; he punched at Abe. "No leave…"

Abe pulled Ben close. "It's alright boy. It's going to be alright." Ben clutched Abe tightly around his mid-section, his uncontrollable sobs heard by all.

The captain and Daniel witnessed Ben's outburst from the wheelhouse steps.

"The boy is taking it hard. I'll have to get word to his wife," Seymour said.

"Not yet, Seymour. Let's wait until we get back to New York; no need to rush her grief."

"Alright."

"What's going to happen with those two guys in the brig? We can't leave them locked up all the way back to New York," Daniel said.

Seymour took out his pipe, struck his wooden match on the railing and turned out of the wind to light it before answering.

"No, you're right about that," Seymour said, between puffs. "I suppose I'll have to turn them over to the authorities."

"What do you mean, here? Not in the states?"

"It's out of my hands. Jacob was well-liked among the crew I can't say if they were left on board, they'd be safe, anyway."

Seymour pulled his collar up to shield himself against the wind cutting across the deck. "How are the repairs on the boiler going?"

"They're not. We don't have the replacement parts we need and I can't make them. She's holding together by a prayer."

"Well, make do and we'll get what we need in port. We should be there shortly if the tides with us."

Tucked away under a set of steps that lead to the lower deck, Ben heard the captain's voice over the announcement speakers asking him to report to the bridge. Ben came through the bridge door to see the captain scanning the horizon with a large set of binoculars out the window.

"You wanted to see me?"

"Yes, I have something for ya."

Seymour reached into his pants pocket to retrieve a brass key with an anchor on it and handed it to Ben. He took the key and held it up for a better look.

"It's the key to Jacob's cabin. Well... since it's empty, I thought you might get some use out of it."

Not knowing for sure what to think or what to say Ben stuffed the key in his pocket and gave the captain a confirming nod.

"By the way, Ben, with Jacob gone, I'll need to ask a little more from you."

"Sir?"

"We'll all have to do more watch and bridge duties, which will mean more responsibility. Do you think you're ready?"

"I can do it, sir. I've learned a lot." Ben said, to the captain proudly.

"I know you have. Jacob taught you well. These additional duties will mean doing some navigation figuring too."

"Okay."

"We'll get started with some quick lessons on the figuring after lunch."

Chapter 16

German Captors

Gathering the last bit of his stuff from the lifeboat Ben made his way down the narrow corridor leading to Jacob's cabin, unaware he's dropping bits and pieces along the way. With his arms full, Ben had more than a hard time getting the key from his pocket.

Finally succumbing to the difficulty, he dropped his belongings on the floor. He opened the door and picked up the pile of clothes, books, and other odds and ends he managed to gather from the crew and entered the cabin.

Ben again dropped his pile onto the bunk and fished for the lamp cord. Ben looked around the room. He thought he could almost feel Jacob in there with him. He picked up Jacob's Sea cap and put it on.

Abe came into the quarters carrying a handful of white sailor socks in his hand startling Ben. "Hey, boy, you're dropping socks all over the deck."

"Geez, Abe, you scared me to death."

"Sorry. I followed the trail. It led me to you. What are you doin' in here?"

"Uh, the captain said, I could use the cabin."

A smirk crept across Abe's face; he turned pretending to look at a picture hanging on the wall. "That's good. Get you out of that boat, anyway."

Surprised, Ben stared at Abe for a moment, not sure what to say or how Abe could have known about him living in the lifeboat. "You know about that?"

Abe sat down in the rocker and folded his legs. "Boy, I knew you was in there the whole time."

Ben's palms started to sweat. He thought about the idea of others being wise to his secret. Or how they could have known. The only person who knew for sure, Ben trusted never to tell. "Abe, who else knows?"

"Nobody, I don't think. Why?"

"No reason."

Abe remembering, he left bread baking excused himself and Ben is once again alone in Jacob's cabin. He lay on the bunk and looked at the rivets connecting the rusting steel plates together feeling the gentle swaying of the ship on the tide.

For the next few days, Ben filled his hours with watch duties, lessons, and thoughts of home. Daniel and Abe do their best to help Ben deal with Jacob being gone. Ben's new duties have brought him closer to the one person he'd rather avoid altogether.

81

Ben kept a watchful eye out for the one man aboard who had come to despise him. Ben knew given half a chance Edgar would just assume leave him on a deserted island or worse.

"All hands-on deck. Now hear this, all hands-on deck." came blaring across the announcement system. Sailors scrambled from their hammocks and out of hatches from all directions.

Ben struggled to get out of a doorway filled with sailors without being trampled to death. He stumbled, lost his footing, and began to fall. A sailor gripped him by the shirt before he had a chance to collide with the deck boards.

"Be careful there, Ben," the sailor said, releasing him once he found his footing.

"Thanks," Ben said.

It doesn't take the crew gathering on deck long to see what the commotion is about. They're off the port side a mile or so is another much larger ship. Flying the colors of the German fleet, signaling the Alexandria.

The captain watched the ship through his binoculars. "Edgar, best run-up our colors."

"What are they signing," Daniel asked.

"I'm not sure. Best get Billy to read this."

A few moments later Billy arrived.

"Well?" the captain asked impatiently.

"They want us to slow and follow them into the harbor. They're our escort." Billy looked up from his scrap of paper used to scribble the message from the German ship.

In a low voice, Daniel said, "There's the mystery ship you've been seeing, Ben, but it hasn't been following us. It's been on patrol."

With a huff of frustration, the captain ordered Billy to return the message they'd comply.

The German vessel continued to signal the Alexandria to slow to one-third. The news of the unwanted escort raced around the ship causing some of the crew to sacrifice shuteye to get a look for themselves.

"Well, at least they don't want to board, for now," the captain said, to Daniel.

For the next forty–five minutes, the Alexandria crept along at a snail's pace into port under the watchful eye of the larger ship; receiving heading information along the way. The captain returned to the bridge his brow damp with sweat. He wiped it every few minutes with his handkerchief while rummaging through drawers and shelves gathering papers and logbooks.

"Where's the manifest? Has anyone seen a large black book that says manifest on it?"

No one answered, preoccupied with the other ship growing closer.

"Best slow to docking speed and make ready with the tie-downs," Seymour ordered, to Edgar, who had been watching the other ship.

"Aye, Captain."

"Ben, go and tell those men standing out there to get below and out of sight."

"Aye," Ben said.

With the Alexandria safely docked and secured the captain ordered all engines to a full stop.

Seymour placed his stack of books and papers on the table and dropped into his chair. The weary captain removed his cap, placed it on the table, and ran his fingers through his thin gray hair before he retrieved a bottle from a drawer along with a glass and poured himself a shot of rum.

 From the contortion of his face, one would have thought he had drunk a glass of flaming turpentine. A few minutes later Ben returned to the bridge. Daniel who had joined the captain in the wheelhouse passed on Seymour's offer of sharing his rum.

There's a knock at the door and Abe stepped in, hardly having time to announce the German authorities who came aboard when he is pushed aside. Three well-built German uniformed men enter the room. All stood no less than six foot tall polished from head to toe.

Seymour got to his feet immediately and returned his cap to his head and stepped forward to greet the men. As if they hadn't seen his approach, the German soldiers ignored him, for the moment.

They scanned the contents of the bridge and its occupants with a trained eye of a surgeon. For any evidence of something out of place, something that would avail them any excuse to unleash their authority to do as they wish. Edgar took offense to the intrusion and rolled his eyes at the captain who gave him a gesture that would be interpreted as taking it easy.

Ben unable to keep his eyes off the three soldiers stared intensely. When one of them made eye contact, Ben quickly looked away. The only uniforms that Ben has ever seen are ones worn by New York Street cops, and these guys weren't street cops. Seymour began to sweat profusely again either from the unwanted presence of the soldiers or from the twenty-five-year five-year-old rum. He wasn't certain. He took out his handkerchief and wiped his brow again.

"I am Colonel Van Chelsing, I am in command of Port Harcourt."

The Colonel who seemed to be clearly in charge of the group continued. "So, you are the captain of this vessel?"

"Yes, that's right, Captain Seymour Salinger from the United Sta. . ."

"I know where you are from captain. I saw your flag."

"What are you carrying, Captain?" the Colonel asked rudely all the while with his back to Seymour.

"We're carrying drills, equipment, and parts for the Winery Company."

"May I see your paperwork and manifest, captain?"

Without replying, Seymour picked up the stack of papers and books sitting on the table. And handed them to the colonel who passed them off to one of the soldiers.

Edgar grew more impatient with every passing moment, his glare squarely fixed on the colonel who accepted Edgar's silent invitation to speak to him. The Colonel, a tall, pale-faced man with sunken cheeks, stood a half foot over Edgar. The first mate moved to engage him. However, before Edgar had a chance to reach the colonel in what would be an unpleasant exchange. Seymour jumped to intercept.

"Colonel," a soldier said, "I have found something."

Van Chelsing joined the soldier who pointed out entries in the manifest; the two conversed in German over the entries pausing only to look up at the captain and once at Ben.

Finally, Van Chelsing spoke again in English, addressing Seymour. This time the Colonel intentionally diminished the captain's authority, by calling him by his first name in front of his men.

"Seymour, you have entered here that you have one extra crew member, one dead man and two murderers on board."

Seymour not prepared for the colonel's question, tripped over his tongue trying to find the words to answer.

The colonel, impatient with Seymour's delay in answering, gave the two soldiers a command in German before announcing his intentions. The two soldiers moved militarily to the door, their hands on their sidearms.

"I can explain," Seymour said, finally finding his tongue.

"And you will," the colonel said, the words slithering from his mouth.

"Until we settle this matter, I will be taking this Ben Holt and the two murderers back to headquarters."

On hearing the colonel's words, Ben felt as if he had been soaked with ice water.

"Take?" Ben unconsciously said aloud giving himself away and sabotaging any opportunity the crew of the Alexandria had of concealing him.

"What? Just one damn minute here why do you need the boy?" Seymour protested.

"You wrote here yourself captain that he is a stow away, did you not?" all the while remaining unscathed by Seymour's outburst. Seymour realized the colonel is using the evidence from the manifest to put a rope around his neck. He also realized the colonel had left him no choice but to answer, "Yes, but that was before-"

"Enough, I gave the order."

The two soldiers removed their side arms from their holsters. "Now, you will retrieve these three men and meet us on deck, so they may be taken into custody. Is that clear?" The colonel addressed Seymour now as if he were a lonely foot soldier in his army.

Seymour's face red and purplish with anger, answered from deep in his throat with as much contempt and loathing as he could muster. "Yes, sir."

Seymour reached for the radio receiver and gave the order to bring the two murderers up on deck. As he moved to conceal Ben behind him. The colonel reading Seymour's actions ordered his soldiers to retrieve Ben.

"Captain, you can't let them take him? I won't let them." Daniel stepped toward the soldiers. Seymour latched onto his arm before he could take another step.

The captain whispered into Daniel's ear, "This isn't the way."

The soldiers led Benjamin down the steps and out into the chilled night air.

"Captain! Daniel!"

Seymour, Daniel, and Abe followed. Abe mumbled his disapproval with what is transpiring before them. The two sailors responsible for Jacob's death soon join the group on deck.

 For the first time, Ben got a good look at the pair. Hate welled up inside him; he wished more than anything that they had never been on the ship. Then maybe his friend would be alive now when he needed him the most.

"Captain, do not try to leave port without permission, or you will be breaking the law. And we wouldn't want that," Van Chelsing said.

"We will be in further contact on this matter of the manifest." On finishing his speech, the group departed the Alexandria.

Ben turned to look at his friends for any sign of a reprieve, but none came.

"It'll be alright, Ben. We'll see you soon," The captain yelled, after Ben, who is half-way down the dock.

A defeated Seymour returned to his cabin. Daniel followed. Upon entering the captain clicked on the light on his desk, opened a bottle of rum that sat on his nightstand and poured two glasses before collapsing in his leather chair. Daniel drank his poison down in one gulp.

"What was I supposed to do?" Seymour said.

The two sat and drank for a long while then came a bang on the door.

"Alright come in," Seymour grudgingly ordered.

Edgar appeared in the doorway, shaking his head at the two. "What should I do about unloading?"

Without looking at Edgar, Seymour told him to get started.

"We'll get him back. The whole thing will get straightened out in the morning," Seymour said, to Daniel through the effects of the liquor.

Chapter 17

The Great Escape

The African moon is full, the colonel paraded his prizes like a great hunter down the deserted dark dirt street, shadowed by the rows of small brownish grass huts, and sun-bleached clay brick buildings, making it difficult for Ben to see exactly where they are going.

The youngest of the party had to apply greater effort to keep pace with the longer-legged men. Wedged between the two guards and the sailors Ben is unable to decide who smelled worse. While listening to the colonel discuss something in German to his men, the echoing words trailed behind them. Ben's mouth is dry and his hair wet with perspiration. The hot dry air made it difficult to breathe.

With no siblings to spend time with on the long winter nights, Ben discovered at a young age book were a passport to the world. They would keep him in the library poring over National Geographic magazines for hours. Fueling fantasies of epic adventures in a wild and wondrous Africa never once did it mention Germans, Ben is sure of it.

One of the soldiers rested his hand on Ben's shoulder, which sweated through his shirt. Ben squirmed to move away, but the man's hand gripped him tighter making his shoulder ache. As the party approached a two-story structure in the African village, a soldier ran ahead and opened one of the double doors leading inside.

The room smelled of old wood and paper. It's dark with only a single light hanging from the ceiling swaying from a fan running on a stand beside the doors, causing shadows to dance around the room chasing the light. In the center of the floor sat, what must be the colonel's desk with stacks of papers neatly organized. An ink well sat in the center, along with two shiny black telephones off to the left suggesting the colonel must be left-handed, as was Ben.

 In front of the wooden desk are two wooden chairs. Along the far wall are three doors; two of them are open and the third closed. The colonel walked past Ben, removed his cap and hung it on a hall tree behind his desk. He pulled out his chair tucked neatly under his desk as if preparing to sit, paused and gave an order, this time in English, to place the prisoners in the rooms. One soldier escorted the two sailors to the far door and pushed them in. Ben watched them disappear when he felt a nudge in his back and stumbled forward. The soldier pointed to the room of the open door.

The small room also illuminated by a single bulb hanging from the ceiling. In the center of the room sat an armless wooden chair. Ben gathered from the gesture of the soldier; He is to take a seat. From the other room sounds of a scuffle breaking out could be heard. Then it got quiet again except for the clanking from the fan, after that more noise, followed by shouts.

"Excuse me," Ben said, to the soldier distracted by the commotion from the other room.

"Excuse me," Ben said, again. "Hey, can I have some water?"

Ben surmised if he spoke slower somehow the soldier would better understand what he was saying. "I said can I have some w-a-t-e-r."

The soldier ignored Ben and directed his attention back to the exchange growing louder from the other room. Hearing his name being called the soldier became excited, he pointed at Ben gave him an order in German, Ben can only guess to mean stay put.

The soldier then departed to join his comrades when Ben heard the man's footsteps grow fainter he stepped to the doorway and peaked out. Everyone, including the colonel, was occupied with the two hostile sailors who were making it clear; they didn't wish to be interrogated leaving the office completely empty.

Ben knew enough to know that this would be his only chance for freedom. He took off his boots and darted across the room to the double doors, stepped through and closed it behind him.

Okay, get going, He told himself while taking long strides to the other side of the street. His heart trying to beat itself out of his chest, he shoved his dirty feet back in his boots not bothering to tie them.

Ben slipped into the alley struggling to find his way. Which way? Which way did we come?" He mumbled to himself. Ben ran down the dark alley frantically looking for any sign that would lead him to the dock. He crossed winding streets and alleys, the pit of his stomach quivering from panic.

 Tired and out of breath he cupped his hands together to take a drink of water from a wooden barrel on the street corner. Ben slid down the barrel to the hard ground.

No, get up. You can't rest now. Find the ship a voice sounded off in his head. Trying to ignore the pain in his side from running, he obeyed the voice; grabbed for the barrel's edge and pulled himself up.

There at the far end of the street, Ben can make out a ship's mast silhouetted against the full moon. The silence was broken by the sound of his worn boot souls pounding down the street.

As if suspended in time Ben approached the ship in a moment that could be used for a year, his senses on high alert. He made out the name painted on her side The Dory.

Then a frightening and crazy thought occurred to Ben. She couldn't have left already. Could she?

Not ready to accept the idea that she would just abandon him their Ben resumed his search.

After finding another ship with a name he couldn't pronounce and a sinking fishing boat occupied by a flock of seagulls, he found her, the Alexandria, sitting there waiting for him.

Racing up the gangplank to the deck, he is greeted by the calls from the watchmen.

"Stop, who goes there?" The watchmen demanded to know to wave his flashlight and running to intercept him.

Ben collapsed to his knees on the deck all out of energy and breath.

"Ben!" the watchmen said, "What are you doing here?"

"Did they let you go?"

"No... not exactly."

"Here, let me help you." Ben recognized the kind man from the engine room.

The sailor carried Ben into the galley and put him to rest on a bench telling him to stay put, and he'd be right back. Ben waved his hand at the man and closed his eyes. A few minutes later, the man returned with a flock of people following, all trying to question Ben at once.

"Slow down, slow down, now, be quiet all of you. I'm asking the questions here," the captain said, to the over-excited mob. Seymour found it difficult to impose his authority on his nightshirt and boots.

"Ben," the captain said, giving Ben a shake. "What are you doing here?"

Ben's vision is filled with the disturbing sight of five whiskery faces staring back at him with fascination. He pulled himself back with his elbows to put some distance between himself and the men before he started his story. After he finished, Ben downed a glass of water offered by one of his spectators in three surprisingly loud gulps.

Seymour stepped back a few steps scratching his head. "Did anyone see you?"

"No, I don't think so."

Daniel joined Seymour speaking in a whisper hoping his words would escape Ben's ears. "What are we going to do?"

Daniel moved to put his back to Ben. "I've heard stories about these guys; they're pretty ruthless. If they find Ben here, you know what they'll do."

Hearing Daniel's words brought to light what Seymour had already been thinking. Furthermore, he knew Daniel was right.

Seymour leaned into Daniel. "The kid's got guts. You'd hardly think he was the same kid we found looking like a scared rabbit."

Seymour gave Ben a nod when he looked over at the two with a "what are they talking about" look on his face.

"Daniel, see if Edgar is finished unloading would ya?"

Daniel moved to leave, giving the men still interrogating Ben about his heroic escape a jester to join him. Ben watched the men leave as he sat up and faced Seymour.

"I didn't know what else to do, I'm sorry."

"It's alright son," Seymour said.

"That was a brave thing to do Ben, but you've put us all in a predicament. They'll come for you, and this will be the first place they look."

"What's he doing here?" Edgar said, coming through the galley door. "I heard about everything. We have to put him off before he gets us all arrested or worse. I told you having a kid on-board would-be trouble."

Ben got to his feet and moved behind a table out of Edgar's reach; looking around for a possible escape route if Edgar decided to move on him. Seymour seeing Ben is clearly frightened of Edgar placed himself between the two.

"You've finished the unloading?"

"Yeah, it's finished and the supplies are on board too," Edgar said, in a low brooding tone.

"Good, then get to the bridge and quietly and I mean quietly prepare to get underway."

Edgar pulled his face into an expression of shock; his lips tighten over his yellow teeth stuttering to get his words out. "Get underway?"

Seymour is un-wavered by Edgar's display of discontent. "You heard me, mister. I'll be on the bridge in a small while."

Gone are the laugh lines and friendly smile, replaced by a face of stone warn by a man determined to have his orders followed or dish out the consequences. Without a word, Edgar shot Ben a look that spoke volumes before storming out of the room slamming the door. Seymour turned to Ben and asked him to return to his cabin. Ben exited the galley for the steps going below leaving the captain with his thoughts. Out of the darkness, a hand seized Ben by the shirt and pounded his body into the wall with a dull thud. They're standing in front of him was a bitter and angry first mate with a look of murder in his eyes. Ben struggled to free himself from the seaman's clutches; his feet dangling off the deck. "Let me go."

"I'm sick of you boy. It's time you left permanently before you get us all killed; no more Jacob to wipe your nose is there? Just you and me."

Having no options for his defense Ben resorted to his prime mortal instinct, digging his teeth into the hand that held him.

"Aaaah, let go, you little brat!" With his bleeding hand, Edgar dropped Ben. Ben hit the floor, dodged under Edgar's arm, and scrabbled down the steps.

Reaching his cabin, Ben locked the door and backed away, waiting for Edgar to burst through at any moment. Shaking and soaked in sweat the boy dropped onto his bunk wondering what he should do next. If he should tell the captain or maybe tell Abe, about how the first mate tried to off him. Abe's been his friend from the start and he doesn't even like Edgar that much.

But, why would they believe me over Edgar? Ben thought. If they did, Edgar would lie about it. Cold, tired, and hungry Ben pulled his blanket over his shoulders and waited in the dark for some thought to come into his head of what to do next.

Chapter 18

Engine Trouble

The news to depart traveled through the ship, catching up with Daniel on his way back to the galley by way of one of the engine-room hands. Daniel spotted Seymour on deck, who just returned from his cabin after changing out of his nightshirt on his way to the bridge.

"Captain, you can't be serious about leaving?"

"We have to. Right now, I'm sure they've figured out Ben escaped, and they're on their way here."

Daniel followed the captain down the deck. "But we haven't made any repairs yet."

"I know we'll have to make do until we can."

"She won't take the beating of the open sea."

Seymour turned and placed his hand on Daniel's shoulder. "I know, but you're the finest engineer I've ever had. Please do what you do best, make it work. If you can't, they're going to take the boy again."

Daniel took the captain's plea to heart and gave him a confirming nod. Seymour turned to continue up the steps to the bridge.

Daniel yelled after him. "You won't get ten knots. I'll tell you that."

Without turning the captain said, "You just get me some steam, and I'll be happy."

Seymour entered the wheelhouse to see the crewmen have already taken their posts. Billy turned the radios, and the helmsman at the wheel awaited his orders. Seymour walked over to the ship's phone and rang the engine room.

"Engine room, we're ready for steam."

He hung up the phone and waved a signal to the man to cast off the lines at the window.

"Lines off and ready captain," the helmsman announced, after receiving the okay from the sailor on deck.

"Here we go, boys. All head two-thirds if you please."

"Aye," the helmsman said, pulling back, then forward with a clang on the engine controls.

Once again, the ship came to life with the rumbling sound of her screws in the water. The anticipation of making a clean getaway excited the ship's crew and her captain.

Jokingly, Seymour said, to Billy, "There's another place we can't show our faces again."

Billy sitting with one hand on the large radio dial and the other with a pencil and paper shook his head at Seymour and smiled.

"What heading captain?" the helmsman asked.

Seymour turned to the small table covered in papers, dug under the pile, and took out the worn and faded chart containing the mysteries and secrets that Seymour has shared with no one.

"Turn to 285." Seymour said, slipping the chart into his coat pocket away from peering eyes. The helmsmen spun the wooden wheel to the ship's new course that would lead her to the x on the captain's chart.

Chapter 19

The Chase is on

After subduing the two hostile sailors and locking them in detention cells. The reluctant soldier informed the colonel of Ben's escape. The furious colonel ordered a search of the headquarters and surrounding area. After hours of fruitless searching, the soldiers returned to headquarters to inform the colonel the tramp steamer is gone as well.

The colonel slammed his fist on the desk and started pacing the room. "Radio the ship to prepare to get underway," The colonel commanded in a furious voice.

The soldier spoke delicately as possible not wishing to further aggravate the colonel. "But, sir?"

"Don't argue with me. Just do as I say."

"Sir, the cruiser has already headed back out on patrol to the north."

"Then, what's left?" The colonel demanded to know.

"We have a smaller boat. It's slower and..."

"Fine. Hurry, private, inform the lieutenant to watch over the prisoners. We're leaving. No one makes a fool of me. I'll have these Americans and their broken-down ship."

Chapter 20

The Truth Revealed

The next morning Ben woke early, lying in his bunk he stared at the rivets in the ceiling. His brain fuzzy. Yesterday played back in bits and pieces like a bad dream. At last, he lumbered from his bunk, washed his face, put on a clean shirt. The young fugitive set out to satisfy his growling stomach, compelling him to seek out the galley, in spite of the fear of running into Edgar.

Ben came into the galley and picked up a tray and fork. "What's for breakfast, Abe?"

"It's Tuesday, we always have grits on Tuesday."

A sailor yelled from the far end of the room. "We have grits every day." causing sailors to break out in laughter.

Abe pointed his spoon at the sailor flinging grits everywhere, including on Ben, "You best be quiet over there, or you won't get nothin'."

Abe scooped up another spoonful of the hot, white grits and pounded it on to Ben's tray with a loud clank.

"Thanks," Ben said, to Abe, but not meaning thanks, meaning more like take it easy.

The hungry boy settled into his seat and began to eat his buttered toast and grits. He overheard some of the sailors nearby talking about their plans after arriving home. One sailor boasted about drinking all the beer in New York, another about seeing his sweetheart.

Ben couldn't help feeling there is more to what Jacob found, and perhaps the captain had other plans for them. The sailors' words are pushed out of Ben's mind; his thoughts turned to the events of last night. Ben pondered the idea of squealing on Edgar to everyone in the room.

A sailor jumped in the seat next to him. "How about you, Ben?"

"What? Sorry, I was thinking about something."

"Well, don't think too hard, or you'll end up lookin' like that bald guy over there," The sailor said, wishing to be heard by all spoke in a loud and blusterous voice.

The bald sailor across the room taking offense to the man's comment fired a return shot, "Oh yeah, well you look like... like an old fish head."

Ben couldn't help but smile at the two men exchanging insults wishing to bring some humor to him.

"So, how bout it, Ben?" The sailor continued.

"Uh, I don't know? I'll be glad to see my Ma and the fellas in the neighborhood."

"Are you sure you don't want to come with us? We're gonna paint the town red," a sailor said, smiling.

"We could fix you up with a right pretty girl."

Ben's face turned three different shades of red at the mention of girls. "Na, that's okay."

"So, how did ya give them German's the slip, anyway?"

"Ah it was nothin'," he replied, getting up from his seat and exiting the galley. Out on the deck, Ben noticed someone at the back of the boat with a pair of binoculars.

"What are you doing?"

"Oh watching," the man said, continuing to look out over the vast spread of water.

"Watching what?"

"Watching to see if we're being followed."

"Followed? By the crazy Germans?"

"You think they'll come after us?"

"That's what I'm checking, that was a brave thing to do and smart. Escaping like that, who knows what would have happened to you."

"What's wrong?"

"Nothin'. I just didn't think of it that way before, I might have never seen my Ma again." Ben left the sailor to his watching.

"You okay, Ben?"

He doesn't reply to the man's question. The thought of never seeing his mother again made him feel sick. All this time it has never crossed his mind that there was a real possibility of never going home. Sitting in his cabin, Ben thought about how foolish he was.

Taking for granted those around him would take care of him and see him safely home. However, he comes to realize it isn't true; it wasn't their job to take care of him; it was his. Although some of the sailors mean well, they're still here for themselves. One thing is clear he must take responsibility for himself and do his duty to the ship if he is to have any hope of getting home.

In his newly found determination, he jumped to his feet stumbling on an empty wine bottle rolling around on the floor. Ben is sent flying into the bookshelf knocking papers, charts, and books everywhere.

Lying in the middle of the pile with a fresh knot on his head from the last book falling from the shelf Ben saw it. A chart, like the one the captain has been so careful to keep hidden.

Ben rubbed the knot rising on his head and plopped himself on the bunk. He turned on the light to get a better look at his find. Ben placed his finger on the spot where they left port and traveled down the chart, across the vast blue ocean until it reached an area Jacob circled with ink.

Jacob must have copied the captain's chart to this one.

Getting Jacob's magnifying glass out of the nightstand drawer Ben took a closer look.

What have you found Jacob? Ben thought to himself.

The longer Ben studied the chart the clearer the captain's true intentions became.

"We're not going home at all," Ben, whispered. "The captain has been hiding something all along, but what? What could be there?"

Ben knew the only way to be sure is to get another look at the captain's chart, but how? Hoping some, air would help clear his head and figure out away. Ben put the chart under his mattress before he locked his door on his way out. Ben almost stepped on Tibbs, who is sitting outside his door, staring back at him.

"What are you doing down here?"

"Meow, yourself cat. Come on, this is no place for you. What if you wandered into Abe's kitchen?" Ben said, laughing to himself.

Out on deck, Ben can't help but think about all his hope for adventure has disappeared with the last glimpses of the African coastline, leaving nothing to look at again but miles and miles of ocean.

"Ben," the captain said, coming up behind him, "I need you to do bridge duties tonight."

"Yes sir, captain… thanks, you know for everything."

Seymour gave Ben a smile, and a rub on the head.

"Don't be late for work."

Ben divided his time over the next few days between bridge duties and odd jobs for Abe. Picking up the mess in his cabin, washing out his uniforms and packing up Jacob's belongings as the captain asked him to do. His only contact with Edgar had been passing glares between the two. The peace and quiet aboard came as a welcomed relief over the last week.

Ben awoke to find a thick fog had consumed the Alexandria. He peered out his porthole window unable to see the water below. After tying his boots, Ben arrived on the slippery deck where the fog hung low as if trying to come aboard like a slithering sea snake in search of an easy meal. His face is damp with condensation.

Ben is nearly startled out of his skin by the foghorn sounding overhead. He made his way around the corner to the steps. Every surface wet with dew. Another blast from the foghorn caught Ben off guard again.

"I've never seen fog this bad in twenty years," a sailor said, standing at the railing.

"It's a sign; I tell ya. Somethin's not right."

"I'll tell ya what's not right. It's why we're sailing southwest instead of northwest," a sailor said.

Ben passed the men on his way to the bridge when two men coming across the deck out of the fog cut his path short. Then two more, soon there was a whole group of sailors standing in front of him with clubs and pipes. As their faces became clearer, Ben could see that some of the men have a look of anger in their eyes, while others had a look of trepidation.

 The group brushed by with such force it almost knocked him over the cargo covers. The angry mob stopped at the foot of the steps leading to the bridge. The big burly, dark-haired man Ben had met in the crew quarters stepped forward.

"I don't like the looks of this captain," Edgar said, looking out the window of the bridge.

The captain joined him to see the mob of men gathered for himself.

"Better go and see what they want before things get out of hand," Seymour said.

Edgar met the sailors' halfway down the steps. Daniel pushed his way through the mob and joined Edgar.

"You men stop this and get back to work," Edgar said.

"Not until we get some answers of why we're heading southwest instead of northwest," a big burly, dark-haired man said from the mob.

Seymour came to stand with Edgar and Daniel on the steps. Fearing a mutiny, he confessed his plan to the men.

"You're right we're not heading home. We're heading for an island."

"An island? For what?" Daniel said, as surprised as the rest of them.

Seymour pushed past Edgar and Daniel to face the men on the deck.

"An island in the Caribbean Sea, boys, an island said to have a treasure of gold."

A sailor pounded his club in his hand. "We don't believe ya, maybe we'll take the ship and go where we like."

"Tell me, do ya have so much money that a treasure's not worth lookin' for? Of course not, ya squander your wages on liquor and cards only to be broke in a week. Havin' to work like dogs for another month without anything to show for it. Year after year ending up with nothin'."

"How do we know you're on the level?" a man said.

"Yeah, that you won't keep it all for yourself."

"Boys, we're going there together, aren't we?"

"I'll share it all with ya and make you the richest sea dogs that ever sailed."

"Why don't you quit trying to sell and let them make up their own minds about your treasure hunting," Edgar said, from the steps.

The captain surprised at Edgar's intrusion agreed to let them decide for themselves.

He returned to the bridge to await their decision. The men's first unanimous decision is to speak in private. The crew retired to their quarters to discuss their situation and Ben joined them. Crowded in like sardines they wasted no time getting started with the job of arguing and bickering.

 Some trying to out yell their opponents' others poking fun of the way they are carrying on nearly starting a fistfight, others choosing not to participate at all.

"Alright settle down, now we have to decide. Do we trust the captain or do we turn back?" A sailor said, standing on the wooden card table.

"Who made you boss?" another sailor shouted.

"Alright, what do you want to say?"

"Uh, I don't know."

This comment rallied the crew to throw their dirty laundry and tin coffee cups at the poor man. "Listen," a voice said from the back of the room. "The captain has never lied to us before; I say we trust him."

"What if he's wrong and we get nothin'," an anonymous voice said.

"What if? What if there is a treasure, and we just sail right by? We got nothin' to lose."

A balding head peeked out of one of the swinging hammocks. "He's right. We got nothin' to lose, nothin' but our lives that is."

Before anyone could argue the man's point, the crew of the Alexandria is abruptly thrown from their seats into a heaping pile on the floor, followed by the sound of twisting metal and the collision siren from the bridge. Fighting to right themselves the men scramble to their feet and out the door. The Alexandria lists hard to port. The deck still damp from the hazy fog made movement difficult and dangerous.

Ben grasped the clothesline strung across the room for dear life. "It's the Germans, they're attacking us from the fog."

"Do you want me to send out an S. O. S. captain," Billy shouted, from the radio room.

"No, Edgar, go see what hit us. Helmsmen all stop."

On deck, the sailors rushed to their posts, and Daniel headed for the bowels of the ship to check for damage. When the fog began to clear, they see that what they've struck is another ship named Groene Draeck, which is pulling the Alexandria's railing apart caught on her anchor. The Groene Draeck started to slow. Shouts could be heard from her deck.

"Pull away, pull away," the captain said.

Ben stood on the deck and watched in disbelief as the Groene Draeck pulled and tour at the ship's railing, releasing an agonizing wale, cutting through the dense fog to pierce the eardrums of everyone on deck. In one final act of force, the railing let loose from its mountings.

"Look out," Ben shouted, to a sailor standing in the path of the flying railing.

In his attempt to dive for cover, the sailor is struck in the leg. The railing continued its course around the deck finally smashing into the funnel and breaking off. The two behemoths come to a dead stop, deckhands running and shouting on both ships.

 Seymour assessed the damage to both the sailor and his ship. When a voice came from above, it's the captain of the Groene Draeck.

"What's he saying? I don't understand a word."

One of the Draeck sailors interpreted for her captain to Seymour. "Are you alright?"

"We're alright, how about your ship?"

"There's no damage, can you get underway? Are you taking on water?" the voice shouted from the deck of the Groene Draeck, which sat three decks above the Alexandria.

"No water. Just the railing."

"What is the name of your vessel?"

"We're the U. S. S. Alexandria."

"We're going to try and pull away," Seymour said.

Seymour turned and gave the wheelhouse a wave of his cap, and the ship began to move. Running back and forth up and down the deck, Seymour watched as they cleared the other ship.

Satisfied Seymour gave the Dutch ship captain a wave. "All clear captain. All clear."

Again, the captain shouted something in Dutch at Seymour.

"What?"

A sailor again interpreted the Dutch captain's wishes. "Good luck and farewell captain."

"Ben!" the captain said.

"Over here, captain."

"Good, Ben this is very important. I need you to go and check the cargo hold for any leaks and then go and get a report from Daniel, alright?"

"Yes, sir."

On his way down to the hold, Ben bothered to pick up one of the clubs lying on the deck as insurance on his way to get Daniel's report.

However, Ben is more worried than ever about his prospects of getting home. He took his time and checked the hold one piece of steel plate at a time to be sure not to miss even the smallest leak.

"Edgar, go and get more lanterns out on deck, we got lucky this time, may not be so lucky next time."

Edgar complied without argument. Seymour rested his bones in his chair on the bridge. Took out a bottle he kept in a drawer to chase away those cold evenings and poured himself a drink. His hand shook spilling a portion on the table. After two sizable drinks, he told the helmsman to sound the foghorn every five minutes until they're clear.

After tending to their emergency duties, the sailors regrouped to finish their meeting. They continued to argue their points until the words all in favor of chasing treasure say, "Aye." The sailor's voices ring out through the cabin as one. The news of the crew's decision reached the bridge. Seymour pleased with their answer poured himself another drink to celebrate.

"Billy, our luck is changin' for the better. I can feel it."

Seymour shuffled through the papers on his desk for his chart plotting their course to his island.

Ben entered the wheelhouse and took a spot up beside Billy in the doorway of the radio room. He watched Billy tune in and out of different radio hot spots. His cigarette smoke circling his head.

"Ben, I didn't see you come in my boy. Are you ready for an adventure on a mysterious island?" Seymour said, smiling more than Ben had ever seen with partial credit going to the rum.

"I guess so," Ben said, with a half-hearted effort.

"You guess? Why my boy, just think of all the new things you'll see. Don't worry you'll get your share of the treasure fair and square. Don't you worry about that."

Ben's mind isn't on the treasure. It's on the captain. Had he misjudged him? Given him too much benefit of the doubt?

 Only when he was forced to, did he share his secret; the secret he didn't think he could even trust Jacob with. The last thing Ben wanted was one more thing to stand between him and getting home. He decided it's best to play along for now. What choice does he have?

"Then, we go home?" Ben said aloud sorry he wasn't paying enough attention to himself to stop the words from slipping out. Nevertheless, he waited for the captain's response just the same. As did the other members of the bridge, who hadn't had the courage to ask.

"Yes, yes, then straight home for a rest and some long-overdue repairs. This treasure will come in handy fixing up this old tub."

The captain feeling generous let Ben finish his shift early and return to his cabin for some rest. Ben took out the chart he had found from under the mattress and sat in Jacob's old rocking chair.

Well, I know what the circle means now, he thought to himself.

Ben can't help wondering how Jacob would have handled the change in plans. He laid down but is too intrigued with the idea of a strange and mysterious island to sleep. His imagination ran away as it often does with young boys. He thought of how he would play pirates with his buddies for fun, how long ago and silly it seemed now.

 The only time he had ever seen an island was at the Saturday matinee. The movies were all the same. The hero is always left hanging from a vine over a cliff; all the while, the natives are throwing spears at him. Somehow, the next week the hero managed to swing to safety and save the girl.

 This wasn't the movies, and no one was the hero. Knowing this didn't make him feel any better about possibly rubbing elbows with spear chucking natives, wearing bones through their noses cooking up people.

"Where's Tarzan when you need him?" Ben said aloud.

Abe entered the engine room. Its noise and steam seeped from pipes running all around him.

"Daniel," he said, through the cloud of vapor.

"Over here."

"What are you doing down here?"

"I gots to know, did you know anything about what the captain was plannin'?"

Surprised by Abe's question Daniel's jaw dropped open, giving Abraham a strange look of disbelief.

"No, not a thing, chancing treasure. They're crazy. There ain't no treasure," Daniel said, throwing his arms up.

Hoping Daniel will have some wisdom Abe asked his question. "What are we goin' to do?"

"Do? Ain't nothin' we can do; those fools have made up their minds. They have treasure fever now. There's no talking them out of it."

"Where did Seymour get this idea, anyway? It's not like him to be so... reckless," Daniel said.

"I don't know, maybe I'll ask him iffin' I get the chance. He didn't even say the name of this treasure island."

"I have to get back to work Abe. But I'll tell ya one thing this ship isn't going to hold together like this forever."

"What's you mean, Daniel? Like this?"

Daniel didn't answer. Abe looked around the room at the boilers and pipes as if the problem Daniel hinted at would be obvious to him. It wasn't. Abe returned to his work in the kitchen.

It's late and there are a few sailors sitting around drinking coffee before going on duty. Abe paid them no mind and took out his dishrag to wipe crumbs off the tables.

"It's a fool's journey we're on. We'll all be killed I tell ya. I heard stories of cannibals on islands. If we're smart, we'd stop that crazy captain before it's too late."

Abe overhearing the sailor entered the conversation. "You don't ever talk like that around me, not like that ever. You hear me. The captain is a good man."

The sailor taking offense to Abe's comment stood up. "Oh yeah, go back to your dishes before you get hurt you old deck rat."

Before Abe could reply another voice joined in. "You best get to your post mister before someone does get hurt."

Abe turned to see Seymour had come through the galley doors branding the expression of a man angered to his boiling point, cheeks red, and nostrils flaring.

The sailor startled by Seymour's intrusion said nothing more and left the galley, the other sailors sheepishly trailing behind him.

"Captain, I didn't see ya come in. You sit there and I'll get ya some fresh coffee."

Seymour complied and found a seat with his back to the wall enabling him to keep a watchful eye on the doors. Neither man wishing to talk about what had just happened searching for something to change the topic.

Abe set a steaming hot cup in front of Seymour. "Here, ya go."

"Thanks."

Moments passed before someone thought of something to break the silence building up in the room.

"So, captain, you never said how you came to hear about this treasure?"

It was obvious to Abe that Seymour didn't wish to divulge all that he knew, however, after Abe's display of loyalty he felt obliged.

Seymour began his story after a long drink of his coffee and struck a match for his pipe. In a low voice, he began.

"Ya, see it was many years ago, more than I care to remember. I was first mate aboard the U. S. S. Angola under Captain Roads. Well, he had been to this set of islands under circumstances he never did share and saw the temple of the treasure for himself."

Seymour paused to take another drink of his coffee. While Abe worked hard to determine if what Seymour is, telling him is true.

Seymour took a puff on his pipe. "Anyway, as fate would have it, old Captain Roads come down with the fever. I was put in charge of caring for him up to his last day."

"The old captain must have known the end was near, cause that's when he shared with me what he knew. He made me promise never to tell anyone, or it would mean certain death for me. That night Captain Roads died," Seymour said, wearing a vacant look across his face as if the whole memory played back in his head. He wasn't merely telling the story anymore to Abe; he was reliving it.

"Ever since that night, I ain't never told a soul about the island or the treasure, until now."

"It's takin' me all this time to find myself in this part of the world, to finally go and see for myself if that old captain was tellin' me the truth or not. Most importantly to go see it with the right crew; a crew a man could trust not to cut his throat."

When Seymour finished, neither man spoke for a long while. The hour was late and Seymour's words seemed to stir something in Abe. A feeling as if a curse had just been told to him and being the hearer of the curse somehow made him a part of it. Abe is now truly sorry he asked and sorrier that Seymour told him.

The captain stood up and took Abe's hand. "Abe, I trust you with my life. You must keep this to yourself. You can't even tell Ben. You must swear."

"I swears. I swears. I don't ever want to hear that story again." Abe pulled his hand back.

Convinced of Abe's sincerity Seymour sat back down. "Anyway, that's it, the whole story. If all goes well, we'll all be rich men. At worst, we lose a few days' time." Seymour said, trying to reassure an obviously troubled cook.

"We should be making good headway; be on the island soon I suspect. Well, Abe, I have some duties to attend to. Thanks for the coffee." Seymour left Abe alone in the galley.

Abe sat down and thought of all the other adventures, and times that he thought were adventures. However, compared to this, they seemed only to be strange places under strange circumstances. What was supposed to be a routine crossing has turned out to be anything but routine.

"Well, can't stay up all night worrin' about it," Abe said, out loud as he got up, and turned off the light on his way out the galley door.

Ben woke the next morning before dawn, washed up, got dressed and was on deck. The air is crisp, and the seabirds greet him. Sailors are about tending to their duties as they always do. Some give Ben a hello while others pay him no mind. Of course, Tibbs found him, hoping for an early breakfast.

Ben picked up the orange fluffy cat. "Morning Tibbs."

The two enter the wheelhouse where the captain likes to keep Tibbs' food. After dishing up Tibbs' breakfast, Ben sat on the floor.

"Boy, you were hungry."

On the table where the captain sits behind the helmsmen, Ben noticed a chart open. The helmsmen gave Ben a nod as he moved to take a closer look. It's the captain's secret chart leading them to the island. Ben put his finger across the line.

"Two inches, we're only about two inches from the island," Ben said, to the helmsmen.

"That's right Ben, I see the captain's been teaching you a thing or two."

"It won't be long now before we're standing on some dry land again at least for a while."

Billy who had been sitting quietly in the radio room joined the two, with a slip of paper in his hand. "Where's the captain?"

"I think maybe either in the galley or his cabin," the sailor said.

"Thanks."

Ben sat there pondering what Billy could have on the slip of paper when he is interrupted by the breakfast bell.

"Sounds like ya best go and find some food instead of worrying about that cat."

"Yeah." Ben left the wheelhouse for Abe's kitchen.

Ben wasted no time getting his tray loaded with food and sat down. Hungrier than he thought Ben got up from his seat to ask for seconds when the call came out.

"Land!" from somewhere outside the galley.

The room emptied in a matter of minutes and once again, Ben is caught in the way of sailors crowding through the doors.

Chapter 21

Going Ashore

The smoke from the island's volcano could be seen for miles as if to bellow from the sea itself. Blocking out the morning sunlight making day feel like night. With every turn of the ship's propeller, the dark cloud grew larger.

The stretch of coastline of white pearly sand met the clear waters on one side and the green lush jungle of trees, vines, and palms on the other giving way to Rocky Mountains and cliffs piercing the sky like teeth of a giant dragon, with the restless volcano in the center.

Ben and Abe watched from the bow as island birds filled the sky in an aerial display of flight and color. Ben ran from place to place to get a better view of the wondrous creatures. He stopped short of the place where railing used to be and looked out into the water. "Abe, where are the dolphins goin'?"

The one thing Ben could count on was the dolphins always followed the ship, either for an easy meal of scraps or for play.

Abe leaned over the railing for a better look. "I don't know somethin' must have scared them off."

"Isn't something," another sailor said, pointing to the volcano.

"Sounds like thunder."

"No, Ben that ain't thunder; that's the volcano grumbling."

Ben's spirit raced with excitement and anticipation of an adventure in a place of such beauty and splendor.

"Would you look at that," a man said, coming on the pair.

"All stop," the captain said, from the bridge. "Give the word to drop anchor would you, Billy?"

Seymour picked up the ship's phone to call down to the engine to ask Daniel to meet him in his cabin. When the captain finished, he turned to speak to the first mate, who had been scouring the island's coastline for any sign of trouble.

"Edgar, get your best man and meet me in my cabin for a short meeting."

Daniel entered the cabin. "What's this about, captain?"

"Everyone sit down somewhere." Seymour moved some papers and dirty clothes to an empty corner of the cramped room.

"There's a bit more you need to know about this place before we can go ashore. I asked you here because I feel I can trust you."

The captain opened a panel in the wall removed a parchment of paper and carefully unrolled it and handed the map to Edgar. "This, gentleman, is the map of the island, it tells the location of where the treasure is to be."

Seymour then took out a bottle of fifteen-year-old rum and some glasses passing them around the room.

"Toasts to our treasure hunt. May it be a successful one." Seymour downed his share of the rum. The men followed his example making growling noises to the burning in their throats. Ben, who had also been asked to join the captain in his cabin but not in the drinking of rum, watched the faces of his shipmates as the map got passed around.

 Daniel is the last to be given the map. He read the hand-scribed notation at the bottom, describing the occupants of the island who built the tomb which housed the treasure of their dreams.

"There are natives on the island? Natives?"

Edgar sounded his displeasure from deep in his throat. "Seymour, you never said anything about natives or a tribe.

"First, the volcano and now this. What else haven't you told us about this place?" Daniel said, from Seymour's rocking chair.

"I didn't know anything about the volcano," Seymour said, in his defense.

"When were you going to tell us? When they greeted us on the beach?"

Seymour poured himself a bit more rum. "I was going to tell everyone when the time was right."

"You have to tell the crew; they might not want to be boiled in a pot or shot full of arrows." Daniel blurted out getting to his feet, pacing the confined space of the cabin. This only allowed him to take three steps before having to turn around.

"I've heard stories of how they can shrink your head, and even cannibals live on these kinds of islands; cut off from the outside world," a sailor said.

"Cannibals? What's cannibals," Edgar asked.

The sailor turned to face the troubled looking first mate to explain. "Natives that are partial to eating their dead enemies."

Edgar's eyes grew as big as portholes at the thought of being on the island menu.

Seymour proceeds to change the subject, not appreciating the sailor's colorful description, scaring his crew half to death.

"Simmer down, they've probably never seen a white man before; more than likely take off for the hills the second they lay eyes on us."

Edgar crept forward in his chair and folding his fingers together. "What makes you so sure this treasure is worth all this?"

"Boys, this could be the big one. We could be set up for life."

"The crews already jittery about spotting the smoke, they're not going to like this," Daniel said.

"If we're quiet about it, the natives won't even know we're there so there would be nothing to worry about. Besides, we have the guns... right?"

Seymour said, "Edgar, make preparations to go ashore."

" Daniel, we'll need provisions and tools."

The two got up to leave. "I have a bad feeling about this," Daniel said.

Edgar standing behind Daniel, impatiently wishing to leave the cramped room gave him a nudge.

Seymour took out his pipe casually lighting it. "It'll be alright. I've been on a dozen of islands before."

"How many of them were stocked with blood-thirsty natives?" Edgar said.

The two men walking down the corridor heard the captain's voice again. "And boys not a word to the crew, I'll tell them when I'm ready."

Before Seymour left his cabin, he placed the map in his breast pocket, opened the drawer under his bunk and removed a wooden box, which held his. 45 revolver. Seymour took care in his inspection of the gun and placed it in a holster on his belt pulling his coat over it.

 Picking up a pocket watch off the shelf the captain opens it to reveal a compass, closes it and puts it in his pocket. On deck, there's a frenzy of chatter going on among the crew about the dark mysterious island, each tale more fantastic than the last. The captain appeared on deck silencing the crew's gossip.

"Men, I'll need volunteers to go ashore; men who know how to handle a gun, men who are brave at heart." Seymour's eyes moving from one face to another before continuing. "I won't think ill of you if you don't, you'll still get an equal share of the treasure."

After several minutes of no one stepping forward, Seymour sweetens the pot. "And volunteers get a share of rum when we return. Hearing these three of the older sailors' step forward followed by seven more.

"That's the spirit. We'll be taking four boats, leaving before the tide comes in."

"Abe." the captain called looking for the ship's cook.

"He's in the galley I think," Ben said, from behind Seymour.

"Oh, hello Ben, I need you to do a job for me," Seymour handed Ben a brass key from his pocket. "Take this key and go to the cabinet below the bridge steps and get some rifles and ammunition, got it?"

"Yeah, I got it, how many?"

"Sixguns... get six."

Opening the cabinet, Ben looked over the rows of rifles, small arms, and boxes of bullets, stored there. The young sailor had never seen a gun close up. He found them fascinating and complex. He carried them back to the captain two at a time until he had delivered all of them.

"Good boy, Ben."

"Here's your key, captain."

"You men prepare the lifeboats and help with the tools. We'll need shovels and machetes. Someone get the canteens filled."

The captain took out his map and compass. "Ben, you best snag Tibbs from the deck and put him on the bridge before he thinks he's going ashore."

Ben turned to carry out the captain's order when his blood ran cold at the sight of Edgar standing there with his bandaged hand.

Seymour noticed the first mate as well. "Edgar, would you come here for a moment?"

The captain's call brought Ben into Edgar's sights. Trying to disappear without success Ben moved back out of his path waiting for the worse as Edgar approached. Ben is surprised when he passed by him to join the captain without so much as a word. What could this mean? Ben thought. He turned to see the captain pointing out an inlet to Edgar. Has he given up on the idea of getting rid of me or does he have something else in mind?

"Ben, give me a hand," Abe said, from the steps, his arms full of wrapped food. "I got some food ready. Help me put it in the boats."

"Smells like chicken and muffins."

"It is and you stay out of it," Abe said, putting the goods under one of the seats in the lifeboat. Abe pushed a warm muffin into Ben's hand. "Here put this in your mouth."

The hungry boy wasted no time devouring the treat while spying over Abe's shoulder to get a glance at Seymour and Edgar checking the map.

"Is that everything," Daniel asked the men packing the boats.

"Ores? Do ya have the ores?"

"Yes," one of the sailors said.

"Well, I guess we're ready," Daniel said, before calling to the captain.

"Good, Good, lower the boats away."

"All men going to shore make way to board the lifeboats."

"Not you," the captain said, putting his hand in front of Daniel.

"But-"

"I need you here to get as much work done on the ship as you can; in case we need to leave in a hurry, and to watch things. You'll go next time."

"Ben, get in the boat."

"Why do you need the boy," Daniel asked, leaning into Seymour's ear. "Remember, it's not safe."

"Don't worry, I'll watch him."

Seymour patted Ben on the back. "Are ya ready for an adventure boy?"

Chapter 22

The Treasure Hunt

Mid-day approached, and the sailors climbed into the lifeboats and prepared to depart. Ben hesitated, to see which of the boats the first mate would be sitting in. The sea is calm, and the winds are light.

"Cast off," Seymour said.

On his command, the sailors withdrew their ores from the boats and plunge them into the sea. Foot by foot the men row toward the inlet. The captain kept a watchful eye out for any unexpected visitors. The lifeboats dipping and swaying in the water made Ben glad he ate the muffin.

 The sailors who aren't manning the ores load their guns and check their aim out over the water. Ben sitting next to Seymour watched him light his pipe and make small clouds of smoke that are caught on the breeze and travel into his face. Coughing Ben covered his mouth and nose. Nevertheless, his eyes water just the same.

"Sorry, Ben nasty habit I have… smoking."

"It's okay," Ben said, drying his eyes on his shirt.

"About a mile and half or so to go," Seymour said, being struck with a wave, putting out his pipe.

"Captain!" a sailor said, pointing to the water from the forward boat, there're too many reefs. We'll have to go to shore somewhere else."

Without a word, the captain waved his cap in agreement. Seymour took out the map from inside his coat pocket, along with his compass and studied the dark line outlining the island; showing Ben their position in the water.

 After a half-hour or so, the small band of men reached the pearly white sands. Two men sitting in the bow of the boats leap into the water and pull the crafts up on the beach.

"Secure those lines. You, there, start unloading the boats. Each man will be expected to carry his share of supplies."

Seymour got out of the boat and tramped up the soggy beach. Ben joined him carrying the food Abe stowed.

The captain handed him the map and compass. "Ben, I want you to lead us to the tomb."

"It's very important you don't lose that."

"But." is all that Ben could get out of his mouth, surprised at the captain's faith in him to lead the party.

"You'll do fine." Seymour took one of the machetes a sailor is handing him.

"I can't carry the supplies, a gun and look at the map. I need you to do that."

Without a word, Ben took the map and looked up to the jungle.

"Keep your eyes open men. Ben, when you're ready."

Waiting, the men's eyes fell on Ben.

"That way, we need to go up there."

At the edge of the jungle, they paused; Ben took a deep breath and entered the dark shadowy underworld of the Jungle canopy. A sailor cut in front of him, chopping at the green overgrowth.

"Stop that chatter. Do ya want to announce to the whole island that we're here?"

The noise from the landing party is reduced to chopping and whipping of the machetes. The jungle itself echoed with the cries and sounds of the jungle beasts watching the men, from far above from the safety of the jungles canopy.

Ben swatted at the mosquitos that have joined the party in hopes of a free meal. The jungle air is heavy. Ben felt the wetness of his clothes from his perspiration trickling from every pore of his body. The captain paused to peel off his coat and draped it over his shoulder.

"Well, Ben, which way?"

Ben studied the map for a long time, then looked up, and pointed to a hill off in the distance. "Over there. We have to go over there."

"You heard the man."

The noticeable weight in Ben's stomach grew from the fear of making a mistake in reading the map and getting everyone lost or worse. It's only after with great effort to push the sensation down in his stomach again did Ben realized that the captain had called him a man. The captain's words helped to ring out Ben's damped spirits. Even if he knew, the captain had been only humoring him. Ben would take the compliment.

"Give me your hand, I'll pull you up."

"Thanks," Ben said, to one of the many sailors along on the journey whose name he couldn't recall.

"Captain, do you think it's a good idea leaving the map reading to the boy," one of the sailors asked.

Seymour in a low voice, to keep anyone from hearing, said, "You just keep a lookout and leave the rest to me, sailor."

Ben not paying attention to his steps stumbled causing to have a painful impact with the ground; the boy's breath is taken away. Ben struggled to get to his feet. His fall caused one sailor to overrun him and leave a rather large footprint on the back of his shirt.

The captain with his large hand clutched Ben's arm and finished bringing him to his feet. "You alright, boy?"

"Uh, I am okay. I think. Could I have some water?"

"Here drink this."

"Better?"

"Thanks."

"The map said over this hill, there's a path."

With slow and deliberate moves, the party reached the top of the hill, but their satisfaction is short-lived at the sight of what lied in front of them.

"How are we supposed to get across that," Edgar said.

With caution, the captain inched his way to the edge of the drop off and gazed down.

"It's a long way down."

All the men turned their heads from side to side in search of a way cross the ravine, found none.

"Well, if we find a way a cross, then we'll have to make one," the captain said.

"We should turn back." Came from among the sailors all standing to gather well away from the edge.

"We've come too far were not turning back now. See that there tree? Cut it down and make a bridge. That's how we'll get across, hurry, hurry up."

With the men busy at work, Ben sat down in the grass by the edge to study the map. Away from where Edgar was standing.

His heart sank when he discovered the gorge is on the map and he missed it. Ben searched for any other obstacles but found it hard to understand all the writing.

He has discovered they still had ways to go and making it back to the ship before nightfall may not be possible. Ben didn't want to think about spending the night in the jungle.

"Timber! The crashing sound from the tree falling over the gorge traveled through the jungle. The impact shook the ground beneath their feet.

"Well, if that doesn't wake up the neighbors, nothing will," Edgar said.

"Good, let's get going, we've lost enough time already."

"Ben, you're with me," the captain said.

Single file, the men lined up and waited for their turn on the tree bridge. Slowly, they made it to the center. The tree bounced under their weight.

Ben's body quivered under the contractions of every muscle in it. "I don't like this."

"You're doing good, don't look down. Keep your eyes lookin' ahead."

A figure soared by the captain and Ben, freezing Ben in his tracks. His muscles quivered even more under his damp clothes involuntarily; noises come out of his mouth not making sense to anyone.

"Damn it!" the captain yelled at the sailors swinging past them on vines.

"Ben, you must keep moving," the captain said, in a painfully calm voice.

Ben said nothing, his breath is short and shallow, and the effects of hyperventilation took control of him.

"Ben!" the captain said again, "we're all going to die here if you don't move. The tree can't hold all of us at one time, now move."

Ben turned to catch the captain's eyes. His hand shook as he fished for a branch to hold on to. With one foot, Ben shuffled along the tree. At last, his feet find solid ground, and he fell to the ground. His chest ached with pain after being struck by a branch rescuing the map from a fall after it had dislodged itself from inside his shirt where he had placed it for safekeeping.

"Everyone alright," The captain said. "Let's keep moving then, we're burning daylight."

Ben picked his frame off the ground and joined the men on their march. The air again is filled with the sound of hacking machetes. Hours pass without a sign of any temple or anything for that matter. The men grow restless the deeper they penetrated the interior.

"Stop," Edgar said. "Take ten minutes rest.

On Edgar's command, the men collapsed on either side of the path. Their bodies drenched in sweat.

"Ben, give me the map now," Edgar said, snatching it out of Ben's hand.

As much as Ben wanted to, he dared not try to take it back. Edgar studied the map carefully. The captain himself is resting against a tree ahead of the party; Ben left Edgar to his map and moved to join him.

"How... you... holding... up... Ben," the captain asked, between gasps for breath.

"Okay. Are you alright, Captain?"

"Oh yes, have to get my wind that's all. Don't you worry, Ben. We'll soon have the treasure and be safe on board."

Ben wasn't as sure as the captain is fronting to be.

"How much further would you say we have, Ben?" Seymour leaned on Ben's shoulder to get to his feet.

Ben's eyes drop to the ground as the words began to leave his mouth. "Captain, Edgar took the map."

"That's alright Ben. He best not get us lost or he'll be working for Abe peeling taters."

The two had a chuckle looking in Edgar's direction.

Edgar sported a slightly bewildered exasperation on his face. Catching on he's some source of the goings on between the two. "What?"

"On your feet you lazy sea dogs, this isn't no holiday," Seymour said.

"Captain, we best stick to the row of trees for a piece until we come to some kind of marker. We find the marker, and we'll be set on our way to finding it," Edgar said.

"Very well, lead on."

Ben fell in behind a few sailors bringing up the rear of the line.

"My head is going around, and my stomach is jumping up and down," Ben told one of the men.

"Ben," the sailor answered, "Don't look at the ground when you're walking, it'll make ya sick and fall down."

"What?" Ben said, with the contents of his stomach trying to escape his body.

"Look up, Ben. Watch the shoulders of the guys in front of ya and take deep breaths."

"That's better," Ben wiped the sweat from his brow. "Thanks."

A screech from high overhead startled the men.

"It's getting dark in here." was voiced, by one of the many sailors with their eyes focused on the canopy.

"Yeah, and we got no lanterns either."

"Stow it back there," Edgar said, without turning to look at the guilty party.

One of the sailors made a rude face at Edgar, the other laughed, gaining them all a look over Edgar's shoulder.

The captain stopped in his tracks. Edgar closed behind him and turned to wave the men off the path into the overgrowth. Edgar turned back to the captain to see him on his knees, focused on the mound ahead. Edgar gestured the men to squat down like the captain and to be quiet while inching his way closer to Seymour, Edgar whispered, "What is it?"

Without a word, Seymour pointed to a figure of a man standing on the mound. Edgar's heart thumped in his chest, and his mouth went dry.

For in the man's hand, they could make out a slender rod with a sharpened tip.

"What do we do, captain?"

"Nothing, we wait, we can't risk announcing to the whole tribe we're here."

"But I could sneak up there and..."

"Forget it; you wouldn't get within twenty feet. He'd smell ya coming."

On the jungle floor, they sat, waiting for the right moment to continue. The small party spent their time-fighting sleep and the unbelievably large mosquitoes.

The captain checked his watch. "It's been two hours. We'll never get back before dark now."

"Look he's moving," Edgar said.

The men's eyes squinted against the darkness, trying to follow the figure that is disappearing in and out of the shadows. (Snap!) Edgar and the captain look behind to see where the source of the sound came from. The two see Ben staring down at the broken stick. He felt the two men watching him. Edgar made an unpleasant gesture with his fist in Ben's direction.

A sailor whispered sitting behind Edgar. "He's coming this way."

Edgar took out his gun and weaved it through the leaves of a bush planted in front of them, ready to discharge the curious figure.

 Seymour grabbed the barrel of the gun and pushed it down, giving Edgar a glare of disapproval. Edgar without a sound obeyed and withdrew his gun. Looking back to where the figure had been standing Edgar let out a sigh of relief.

Edgar whispered, "He's gone."

The men turned from side to side trying to find any sign of the man that threatened to end their expedition, even their return to the ship. After a long few minutes, the men too were relieved.

"That was too close," Seymour said, taking a moment to look around again to make sure the coast was clear.

"From here on out, we have to be more careful. That was no doubt a lookout."

Edgar moved the map back and forth, trying to have a bit of sunlight piercing the canopy land on it. "We should be getting close to the marker by now."

"What kind of marker," the captain asked.

"I don't know, but we'll know it when we see it."

The men started their trek through the underbrush again, Edgar purposely falling back every few steps making it to the middle of the line. Ben forever watching Edgar took no chances and to fell back to maintain a healthy distance from Edgar.

This went on for some time until Ben ran out of line. Edgar now with-in a few feet of him turned to throw a look at Ben that needed no interpreting. Ben slowed his steps even farther falling out of line and farther down the trail.

"First mate," a sailor said. "The captain needs ya upfront."

After Edgar's departure to the front of the line, Ben rejoined the men to bring up the rear.

"You best keep up, Ben. Don't wanna get lost out here. Hell, we'll never find ya and some big old snake might have ya for breakfast."

"Or dinner." another sailor, in the line added.

"More like a snack as little as he is."

"Yes, captain," Edgar said.

"Is that the marker there ya suppose?" the captain pointed to a vine-covered stone pillar fifteen feet tall and four feet square standing alone in the middle of the jungle.

Pulling back the vines and leaves, Edgar spotted a symbol carved in the blackened stone. He held up the map and smiled at the captain.

"Well, it looks like whoever gave ya this map didn't steer ya wrong. They match."

Pleased with the discovery, the captain asked, "Which way? Are we close?"

Edgar held the map close to his face as if holding it closer would speed up his understanding of the symbol. "Hold on. That's a little harder; give me a second."

"Take your time, but hurry," the captain said.

"Ben, come here, boy."

"Yes," Ben answered, from the middle of the line of tired and hungry sailors.

"Ben, break out some of them rations Abe packed and pass them around while we wait."

Chapter 23

The Temple

Pacing the deck Daniel waited for some sign or signal from the landing party. He stopped every few steps to glance out over the lagoon, hoping to see the captain, Ben, and the rest of the group returning to the boat.

"Here, maybe these will help make them come back quicker," Abe said, to Daniel handing him the captain's binoculars.

Giving Abe a half-sarcastic grin Daniel took the binoculars and began scanning the beach. Slow and easy, he turned toward the open sea. Pulling the binoculars down Daniel looked out with his own eyes as if not trusting what the binoculars were showing him. Taking a few steps to the railing, Daniel looked through them again adjusting the focus on something far out at sea.

"Oh, no."

"What? What is it? What you see out there?" Abe said, looking for himself.

"I don't see nothin'."

"There, right there... here look," Daniel said, handing Abe the binoculars.

"Lord be, we gots to tell the captain." Abe's voice quivering.

"How? We can't use the flare gun, too dangerous."

Black cinder and smoke rose from the funnel into the blue sky.

"Damn it, what are they trying to do? That'll give us 'way for sure," Daniel said.

"I'll go tell 'em to put it out," Abe said, pushing the binoculars back to Daniel.

"No, not out, Abe tell them to use wood, we'll need the fires hot in case we need to leave in a hurry."

Looking back out to sea Daniel can clearly make out the red and black German flag flying at the mast of the distant ship.

"Come on, Seymour, hurry up. We got to get out of here."

"Well, what ya find, Edgar? Or do ya need me to have Ben give ya a hand?" The captain said, to the first mate pouring over the map like the Holy Scriptures.

"No, I got it. It's this way, but we're most likely to run into more locals. There's another building not too far away."

Finishing his words, Edgar rolled up the map and stuck it in his shirt for safekeeping. The captain ordered the men to their feet, and with some hesitation, they complied. The jungle seemed more alive the deeper they went; movement could be felt from the jungle's inhabitants in all directions.

"There through the trees. There's a clearing. That must be it." Edgar pointed.

Without any further conversation, the party fought their way through the trees and bush to find themselves standing in the clearing.

"Would ya look at that?" Seymour said, reaching up to take his hat off and wipe his brow with his sleeve.

Before them stood a giant black stone temple, covered in vines and growth. It climbed out of the jungle floor like the fist of God himself. In the center of the temple is an opening leading to the interior. Above it is a two-foot by two-foot panel covered in ancient symbols. The opening is dark and uninviting; a cool breeze touched their faces as they drew closer.

"We found it!" a sailor shouted, to his mates as he brushes past Edgar, the captain, and Ben.

"No, stop, wait." the captain said, after the man before he disappeared into the doorway.

The men go silent, completely at a loss of what to do next, when the silence is broken by the screams coming from the entryway of the temple. Blood curdling screams, triggering Ben to jump straight up into the air, followed by nothingness again. All eyes are fixed on the opening. A figure of a man appeared from the darkness into the light and then collapsed to the ground. What they saw next struck horror in the men to their souls.

There on the moss-covered ground laid the sailor in a pool of his own blood, growing ever larger, soaking into the ground. His body pierced by hundreds of wooden darts. They penetrated both flesh and bone. The man's eyes still open reflecting the agony he lived for a brief moment before his death.

The party said nothing. Some looked away; some couldn't, all wearing the same expression. This is no longer just another expedition to an island like so many before. No longer did they talk lively about their riches.

Seymour's shoulders wore the load of guilt. He brought them here. He's responsible for the death.

Kneeling over the body, Seymour closed the man's eyes and folded his hands over his chest, before covering the man's face with his coat. Pulling his eyes away, Seymour watched as Edgar stood in front of the doorway.

Edgar stretched to feel the edges of the panel with the tips of his fingers. "I bet that's the mechanism closest, behind that panel."

"Be careful Edgar or..."

"You men give me a hand. Use the shovel to help pry it open."

Ben stood away from the body, which had turned quite pale. This is the second time he has seen someone die since joining the crew. He still has nightmares about Jacob's death. Ben no longer cared for treasure, adventure, or the ship. His only wish is to be back home.

He's brought to the present with the thud of the panel cover striking the ground.

"There, that's got it," Edgar said. "Can't see much though, we need some light."

Tearing a piece of his shirt off Edgar wrapped it around a broken branch and fished in his pocket for his Zippo. The rest stood watching Edgar prepare the torch. He looked from the closet to Ben, then to the captain.

"Seymour, we're going to need someone small enough to fit up in there."

"To fit into there to do what?"

"To either trigger or deactivate the rest of the trap. The boy is the only one of us that can fit," Edgar said, pointing the torch in Ben's direction.

"No, it's too risky I won't allow it."

Ben joined the conversation but holding his spot away from the temple. "No, it's alright. I want to help."

"You don't understand, Ben." Seymour placed his hand on Ben's shoulder. "I can't risk losing you."

"Then you best be heading back now, we can't go in while the place is trapped."

"The closet is not going to be trapped. How else would they be able to set them?"

"No, someone else will have to try."

"Are you sayin' someone else's life is worth less than the boys?"

Seymour knew Edgar 's question painted him into a corner. With all eyes on him Seymour has no choice but to let Ben try or the expedition would be for not.

With a nod, the captain agreed to let Ben try to trigger the rest of the traps in the closet.

"Come here, boy," Edgar said.

Swallowing hard Ben moved within feet of Edgar when he seized Ben by the shoulder to draw him near. Seymour joined them below the closet to hear Edgar's instructions to Ben.

"You ain't afraid of small places are ya? Or the dark?" Edgar's voice riddled with contempt for Ben's boyhood.

"No," Ben's eyes fixed on Edgar's leathery face.

The sailors talked among themselves in whispers. Some wished they'd turn back, others voted for the treasure hunt to continue, while others still talked of mutiny. However, none talked about taking Ben's place.

"Ben," Edgar started. "Look for a handle or lever coming out of the wall."

Ben looked between the two men and gave a nod that he understood his instructions.

He walked to the wall; his eyes followed the vines snaking their way to the opening. A sailor gave him a hand. Ben gripped the ledge and pulled himself up, once in, he turned and reached for the torch.

"Remember, anything looks strange, you get out of there," Seymour said.

Seymour and the group of men watched the light of the torch fade away as Ben descended into the temple; the closet is once again dark. The sound of Ben scuffling on his hands and knees on the damp stone faded seconds later as well.

"He'll be alright, you'll see."

Edgar joined Seymour. "Best have the men look around for any company."

"What? Yeah, right, go ahead then."

Seymour turned back to the opening, watching for any sign of Ben.

"Captain, we should also think about getting the body underground before too long."

"Did you hear that?" Seymour said. "Over there what was...?"

Before Seymour finished speaking, a yellow and red-feathered bird sprang from the shadows of the canopy for the open sky.

Seymour muttered, "I need to relax." He sat down on a log to rest and wait for Ben to return.

"How long has he been in there?"

Edgar assured him it might take some time to find a way to open the door. Nevertheless, the captain unconvinced got up and went to the opening anyway to try to look in.

"Someone needs to go and get him. It's been too long."

"It's only been about fifteen minutes or so, the boy is alright," Edgar said, against what he was hoping. This trip to the island would not be a total loss if it meant getting rid of the kid for good, he thought.

"Besides, who do you want to send? He's the only one that fits, remember."

Knowing Edgar is right Seymour said nothing.

The two leaned against the stone wall and waited. Most of the men busy themselves with the loathsome duty of committing their shipmate to the island forever. The two tired and frustrated men hear a sound from the dark opening at the same time. They turned in anticipation of Ben's return. Moments pass until the sound of a muffled shout flew out of the opening.

"What's that?"

The sound grew louder; with a great noise, vines began snapping and pulling away from the ancient stone door as it moved to open, filling the air with a cloud of dust. In a few moments, the cloud dissipated and Seymour could make out the faint glimpse of a torchlight.

Ben appeared in the stone opening for a second before he jumped to the ground. On his feet, Ben jumped up and down in some weird tribal dance round and round, all the while smacking and knocking away the hairy black spiders who hitched a ride on his shirt on the way out of the temple.

"Ah, get'em off," Ben shouted.

"Hold still Ben," the captain told him trying to knock off the spiders from Ben's back.

"You are alright now, Ben? Did you find the lever okay?"

Still gasping for breath in the heavy jungle air, Ben answered, "It... it was a long way in, but there was a wooden lever like you said..."

"And?" Edgar a bit frustrated with Ben's delay in finishing the story.

"Yeah, I pulled it and there were a lot of moving sounds. Then one big sound."

Ben's skin still tingling from the feel of the eight-legged monsters, he wiped his neck with the captain's handkerchief.

"We best be sure," Edgar said when he picked up a heavy rock and threw it into the blackness of the doorway. The rock made a clanking sound as if falling down a flight of steps then the sound was gone.

"That's good enough for me," Edgar said. "We'll need more torches."

Edgar left the two standing by the doorway to retrieve the rest of the men and to gather more torchwood.

"You really alright, Ben? Have some water. It'll make you feel better," Seymour said.

"Thanks."

Ben took a drink from the canteen. As he lowered it from his lips, he noticed the dead man's body was gone. Seymour watched Ben look around and knew the question he is about to ask.

"They went to bury him in the jungle."

"We're not taking him back to the ship?

"No, Ben we can't. It's too hard we'd have to bury him at sea like…" Speaking more than he wanted to, Seymour stopped himself.

"You mean Jacob? It's okay captain. I understand."

In spite of the conversation, Ben is refreshed by the cool water and smiled at Seymour.

"Alright, come on now you sea dogs get those torches ready. We don't have all day." Edgar said, to the sailors as they all came out of the jungle together.

Ben and the captain say nothing more about the dead man.

"Is it done?" the captain asked Edgar, who has just finished ripping more of his shirt for more torch rapping.

In a low voice, Edgar said, "Yeah, and the men said a few words. We marked a tree, so we'd know where he is."

"The torches are ready first mate," one of the sailors said.

Edgar pulled his gun. "Check your weapons."

"I'll light the torches," the captain said.

The group waited, wet with sweat. The captain looked over the men. They all have the same white-eyed glare of impending doom.

Edgar stepped into the captain's line of sight. "Your orders, captain?"

His hand on his own weapon Seymour inhaled deeply before speaking. "Two men stand post here; any sign of trouble gives out a signal; the rest come with us."

"You two, stand here keep your eyes open," Edgar told his men.

Seymour grabbed Ben by the arm and pulled him closer. "Ben, you stay close to me."

The men entered the dark damp stone entryway their weapons drawn, torches high, and thoughts of the horrible death of their friend still fresh on their minds.

"Watch your step, it's slippery," the captain warned.

Smoke from burning cobwebs rose into the thick air.

The captain pushed Ben back against the wall. "Watch it, there're steps here."

Edgar held his torch out; he looked hard against the nothingness. His image distorted as the torch flames reflected from his face. Murmurs of ghostly sounds circulated through the line of men.

Seymour moved his torch back and forth, burning away the webs. "We've been lucky so far no traps."

The light from the outside disappeared altogether as the last man is consumed in cool darkness. The air is thick with moisture and tastes as old as the tomb itself. Ben's feet slipped on the floor at the bottom of the steps. The ground has gone soft; they sank into glue-like matter. He almost lost his left boot when he tried to pull it free.

"Yuk, what is this stuff? It smells like a manure farm."

Stuck between the captain and Edgar and without a torch of his own he can't see the floor.

"It's guano," Edgar said.

"What's that?"

Seymour turned to answer Ben's question. "It's bat poop."

"Yuk!"

"Be glad you're wearing shoes; half the men aren't which means we just lost our tail. Look." the captain swung around to show Ben the rest of the men are no longer following them.

"What do we do now?" Ben asked.

"We'll pick them up on the way back."

Ben's eyes moved from the back of the captain's coat to the dark ceiling. "Wait, if there's bat poop down here. Where's the bats?"

"Don't worry about them. Keep moving," Edgar said.

Ben continued looking up at the ceiling which seemed to be alive. He detected movement against the flicker of the torches. Ben moved closer to the captain clutching his belt.

The three pass through another archway opening into a chamber. The walls are lined with alcoves filled with carved idols. The ceiling curved to a point meeting in the center. Two rows of coffins sat near each other in the middle of the room. The lids also are covered with carvings.

"The burial chamber of the tribe's kings I suspect," Seymour said.

Ben stretched out his hand. His fingers glided across the surface of one of the coffins. They sense the wood's texture. His hand trembled. He stepped closer; his imagination ran away with him on what could be in the old, dirty box.

"Ben," Seymour said. "Get over here."

Seymour's call startled Ben causing him to drag his fingers into one of the deep curves of the coffin lid giving him a splinter. He pulled his finger back and put it into his mouth.

"We've been in here awhile. We'll be running out of time. We have to find the treasure chamber soon or get out of here before our luck runs out." Edgar said.

He took small steps around the room patting the walls with his hand until he found a soft spot.

"Right here, captain." Edgar pushed on the spot.

He stepped back and waited. Ben and Seymour join him. The wall moved in then to the left, exposing an opening. The three stepped forward. The air filled with the reminiscence of death. The captain threw his torch in the room. This room is unlike any of the others they have seen. The walls are smooth and peppered with indentations of where it was once adorned with jewels.

The floor is white with tile. In the center of the room sat several coffins.

"We need to block open the door before we go in," Edgar said.

Quickly, Ben wedged a piece of rubble into the doorway. Edgar entered the chamber, sat his torch down and began to pry up on one of the coffin lids.

"Seymour, help me move this."

Ben joined Seymour on his corner and began to push. After pushing and grunting, the lid gave way.

"Don't look, Ben. Don't look in."

"Watch out," Edgar warned giving the lid a last push to the floor, shattering it into many pieces.

"Empty! All empty."

The captain sat down on one of the coffins. Ben took Seymour's torch and moved it over the chamber floor. The coffin lid knocked loose one of the floor tiles upon striking. Ben moved the torch over it. With his fingernails, he clutched the edges of the tile pulling it free. On the tile, Ben made out the faint scribe of a symbol.

"Captain, I think I found something."

With effort, Seymour found the strength to get to his feet and join Ben.

"What is it, son?

"I pulled up on this loose tile and found this. It looks like a symbol."

"Pull up another if ya can and let's see."

Ben's fingers once again pried up an edge of a tile and worked it loose.

"Nothing," Ben said, his lips contorted to display his disappointment.

Seymour picked up the tile Ben worked loose and studied it in the light of the torch for anything that might give them a clue to what the symbols meant.

Edgar who has been rummaging around the room for any remaining treasure stumbled on to a bright-red object hidden between the wall and a stone statue of some sun god. He picked up the red object and to his delight, he discovered it to be a jewel. It sparkled brilliantly against the flames.

 The smile washed from his face, like removing a mask to reveal his true self that was concealed beneath. He closed his hand around the jewel, his eyes fixed on the captain and Ben, who are still preoccupied with their tile project. In a second, Edgar stuffed the jewel into his pocket.

"Edgar," the captain said.

"What!"

"What are you doing over there?"

"Nothing, I didn't find nothin'," Edgar said, his voice crosser than usual.

"What? What are you doing?... bring the torch closer."

Edgar complied all the while making grumbling noises to himself. Ben, peeled up another tile, and found another strange symbol beneath. After finding and peeling up the marked tile, the three stepped back to study their findings.

"What does it mean," Ben asked, the captain. His hand wet with the perspiration mixed with the dust on the tile making it hard to read the symbol.

"I don't know? Edgar, what do you think?

Edgar rolled the jewel through his fingers in his pocket answering the captain.

"What it means is we've been down here too long and we're out of time... we have to go."

Seymour put off by Edgar's unexpected answer, looked at Ben, with his eyebrows up.

As Seymour opened his mouth to speak, a strange animal-like sound travels down the dark stone corridor to find the ears of the three.

Without a word, Edgar turned to leave the room Seymour followed. Ben not wishing to be left alone is on Seymour's heels.

"Keep up Ben." The captain's words are cut short by the sound of stone as it grinds against itself producing panic in the small party.

They all knew the sound meant the stone wall was moving, which meant someone or something reactivated the traps within the chamber.

"Go, go, go!" Seymour shouted, at the two.

"The torch," Ben said, "We… the…" Before Ben could take a step to retrieve it. Edgar grabbed his shoulder and tossed him through the doorway, Seymour following close behind them. Dust and rock fell from cracks in the ceiling from the vibrations of the moving doors.

The three stumbled in the dust clouds desperate to escape. Their hands press against the wall as a guide to safety. The sound of rock grinding against rock grew louder. Ben in the lead tripped over a boulder and fell to his knees. Edgar following closely behind Ben tripped over him, catching himself against the wall, all the while continuing to search for an escape.

Ben's eyes watered making impossible to see, called out for help, but Edgar ignored his cries.

Edgar discovering the way out and is the first to exit the temple, leaving the two to rescue themselves.

"Ben, where are you?" Seymour called, out turning in all directions listing for Ben's voice.

"Here over here."

"Come on, we have to hurry."

The two struggled in the thick dust through the poop-filled passage leading to the outside. At the other end of the passage, the sunlight broke through the cloud showing them the way out. The doorway is being wedged open by a sailor fighting to keep a log braced against the closing force of the stone door.

The sailor's arms shuddered from the force of the door wanting to close. "Hurry up, I can't hold it much longer."

Ben and Seymour dove for the opening, rolling together onto the grass. At that moment, the log is used to hold open the doorway snapped in two, sending splintering wood in all directions. The sailor is cast off his feet into the grass, next to the two still gasping for air.

Ben rubbed his eyes to clear the remaining dust and focused on the sailor lying next to him who is grasping his neck. His face washed with the exasperation of terror. His eyes stare blankly into the tree canopy above them. The sailor fought to capture his next breath. Ben watched the trail of blood trickling down the man's neck through his clutched fingers.

Ben pushed himself away from the injured sailor. "Captain!"

Seymour rolled over to see for himself, the horrible sight frightening Ben into controllable trembling. He clutched the man's neck to apply more pressure to stop the gushing blood pouring out of him.

"Hold on Lyle. You hear me."

The man shook uncontrollably before going dead still. Ben wrapped his arms around his legs and began rocking back and forth. Tears streamed down his face, he pressed his lips against his legs muffling his weeping.

Seymour released his hand on his friend's neck. The man's hand also fell away revealing the jagged piece of splintered shard protruding from his neck.

Seymour rolled back to look at Ben, who has buried his face in his lap to quiet his whimpers. The image of the man's face fixed on his closed eyes.

Edgar revealed himself from the growth of the jungle path. "Captain."

Seymour dwelling on thoughts of his friend's death hadn't noticed Edgar's disappearance until he returned.

"What the hell happened to you back there?" The captain demanded to know getting to his feet.

Without answering his question, Edgar replied with his own news. "Never mind that now, we have trouble."

Edgar stepped over Ben to join Seymour. He took out his gun and cocked it telling Seymour what he learned.

"There was a fight after we entered the temple with the natives. The men are making their way to the beach. Seymour, we're losing a lot of them. We have to go."

An arrow whizzed by Seymour 's head, impacting a tree behind him.

"Ben," Seymour said, crouching down in a sitting position, "Come on."

Ben not seeing the arrow narrowly missing Seymour's head paused to wipe his face and recover himself from what happened.

Edgar grabbed Seymour's coat, pulling him to follow. Ben got to his feet.

"What's going on? What's wrong?"

Seymour called back to Ben to get down. The native's calls mixed with the cries of the dying men, reverberated throughout the jungle, sending flocks of island birds into the sky. The three haste to break free of the wilds to witness the battle and the lifeless bodies of both the natives and the sailors riddled with arrows, spears, and bullets.

They could see the arrows flying through the air and the return fire from the sailor's guns. The guns released clouds of gray smoke into the air with every shot. The numbers of arrows far outweighing the bullets driving the sailors toward the beach.

"You stay here. It's safer. I'll be back," Edgar said, before ducking under one of the large green leaves sprouting from the jungle floor and disappearing out of sight.

"Where's he going," Ben asked, from behind Seymour's left ear.

"Edgar is gonna try and sneak up on them and pop a few I suspect."

With his pistol raised, Seymour said, "Come, if the men make for the boats they won't wait for us, so we best be ready."

"But what about the natives?"

"Don't worry about them, natives. All of their attention is on catchin' up with the men, not somebody following from behind."

The two crept their way down to a fallen tree, neither wanting to abandon the safety of the bush for the long stretch of open ground separating them from their ticket off the Island.

"There's another way."

Seymour took a breath, and the two weary shipmates re-entered the thick of the jungle. Unsure of his captain's intentions Benjamin trailed behind, keeping a watchful eye on the rear. The terrain has grown steeper and is taking the last of Ben's strength to keep pace until the pair reached the spot Seymour had been hiking for.

"Did you say you went to the movies," Seymour asked.

Ben is curious about what spending his Saturday afternoons in the movies had to do with anything. "Yes."

Seymour stuffed his revolver back into his pocket and grabbed one of the vines dangling from the high treetops.

"Did ya ever see any Tarzan movies?" Seymour reassured his grip on the vines.

"Yeah?"

"Well, grab on and hold tight, I always wanted to do this." Seymour looked down at the cliffs below before swallowing hard.

Realizing what the captain was getting on to, Ben gripped the captain around the neck with his arms and his waist with his legs.

"Are you sure you know what you're doing?"

Seymour picked up his feet. "No, not really."

The two sailed across the cliff edge over the beach. The vine is insufficient to support their weight released from the treetop, dropping the two screaming goony birds to the ground with a thud.

Ben landed headfirst into a patch of berry-producing bushes, staining his shirt and face with dark purple spots instantly.

"You, okay?"

"Those taste terrible," Ben said, picking himself up off the ground and spitting out the last of the berries that made it into his mouth.

"Let's get going. I don't know how much time we have."

The two move stealthily toward the sound of the fighting, ever closer to what they hoped would be a safe escape. Benjamin couldn't help worry about the friends who were hurt or lost. So close now, they could hear the wiz of arrows flying through the air. After some time of walking bent over, which was making every step a painful way to get around the two made their way down to the pearly white beach and freedom.

"There look." Seymour pointed to the cluster of men racing around.

Some dressed in feathers and bright-colored paint spread all over their bodies and others in blue, gray, and brown ship attire. Seymour once again drew his revolver from his coat pocket and waited readily to defend.

"Captain, look, the men are driving the natives back."

"My god, you're right. This might be the break we need to get out of here."

Ben and Seymour watched the sailors reinforce their position behind the lifeboats with the additional guns and ammunition they had stored on their fighting the natives into a hasty retreat back into the jungle.

Chapter 24

Battle on the Beach

Seymour got to his feet and prepared to join his mates at the lifeboats. "Here's our chance, Ben, let's go."

Ben not having to be told twice also got to his feet and makes ready.

"There, it's clear." All the warning Seymour gave Ben before busting from cover and onto the bright open beach. Ben with his much shorter legs compared to the captain, struggled to keep pace with the man racing with all his might to safety. The distance from the protection of the jungle and the freedom of the lifeboats seemed miles apart.

"Come on, Ben. Keep up boy, we're almost there."

The two can practically feel the wet sand under their feet when Seymour lets out a cry in pain. Ben turned to see an arrow pierce his friend's shoulder.

"Captain!"

One of the remaining sailors still alive spotted the two stumbling toward him and ran up to help.

"Take it easy, captain, I got ya," the sailor said, throwing the captain's arm over his shoulder. Ben did his best to help support the rest of the captain's weight.

"The captain caught an arrow in the shoulder. Get 'im in the boat." the sailor told, the men standing by their guns.

Ben got himself into the lifeboat next to the captain who is lying motionless across the boat's seat. "Is, is he going to be…"

"Well, we'll know better after we get him back to the ship and get the damn arrow out of him," the sailor said.

The men busy themselves with setting the oars and working the boats back into the tide.

"We ain't got much time til them natives decide to come back," the sailor said when his attention is drawn by the sound of gunfire a ways up the beach.

"What the bloody hell…?"

"It's Edgar," one of the sailors standing in the water next to the boat said, "He made it. Men give him cover fire."

The men sitting in the lifeboats stood and raised their guns and began firing over Edgar's head. The sound of the guns at this close range caused Ben to jump every time one fired. Ben held his hands tightly over his ears. Edgar's figure grew larger until he is almost upon them. The men stop firing when the boat picked up a wave and started to float out to sea.

Edgar with his arms raised splashed his way to the lifeboat that is carrying Ben and the captain. He tossed in his gun and with the water rising fast on him. He jumped into the boat and tumbled onto the floor wet and exhausted.

Edgar didn't realize with the force of the impact between his body and the wooden floor the jewel he so carefully kept hidden from his mates has fallen from his pocket and rolled across the boat deck to come to rest at the captain's feet. The captain regaining some of his strength noticed the glimmering object, leaned over with great effort and picked it up.

Ben too watched with surprise at what the captain has found as Seymour raised it up to come in line with his eyes. The afternoon sun bounced off the jewel causing it to glimmer with a radiant red.

After a moment, the captain's view fell to Edgar, who is still lying on the deck talking with his eyes closed about how many of the dirty natives he killed, unaware that the captain now possessed the only small treasure of the expedition the crew paid for with their dearest blood.

Finally making an effort Edgar sat up. "Uh, any of the canteens have wat...," He stopped speaking the second he focused on what the captain is now holding.

A cold silence washed over the boat. The expression of pure loathing and anger streaked across Seymour's face, he closed his hand around the jewel and put it in his pocket. Completely, at a loss for words, Edgar turned and pretended to look out over the ocean.

Ben sat next to Seymour, who is all but ignoring the blood still pouring from his wounded shoulder. Ben didn't have time to worry about another of Edgar's schemes to further himself, at the expense of his friends or how his laziness might have finally caught up with him. The captain's shoulder occupied Ben's mind now. He wasn't there when Jacob was wounded and resented the fact nothing more was done to save him. However, this time he has no intention of surrendering to losing any more of his friends.

"My God, look at them all." came from the sailor's lips with the action of a deflating balloon, his words reflecting the malée lea sprawled out in front of him. Tears trickled from his eyes and the overwhelming scenes of loss filled his heart; for among the dead were some of his oldest and dearest mates.

Not much more is said on the journey back to the Alexandria when the battered and weary party finally makes it to the port side. Abe and Daniel are there to greet them.

"Give us a hand. The captain has been hurt," Edgar said, standing up.

"Tarnation what happened? How come the captain got an arrow stickin' out of him?"

Edgar scampered out of the lifeboat. "Never mind that, help me get him below."

Ben followed what was left of the crew to the deck in the hopes of being more of a use than when Jacob met with a similar fate.

"Okay. One, two three, lift," Edgar said, to Abe and a few other men assisting them.

Daniel had come up from working on the engine when he heard the away party had returned.

Ben moved to go with them to the captain's cabin. Seeing Ben's intentions, Abe gave Daniel a nod to stop him.

"Daniel, what are you doing? I want to go with them. I want to help."

Daniel held Ben back out of the way of the men carrying Seymour. "No, Ben, there's nothing you can do right now."

The captain held out his hand. "Ben."

"Come here, boy."

Ben moved to join Seymour's side.

"Listen to Daniel, that's an order," Seymour said, pushing a small object into Ben's hand.

His eyes fixed on Ben's sending him the message that he couldn't say. Only when he was sure Ben understood him did he release the object and give Abe the okay to proceed. Ben is confused to the reason why he is made to remain out of the captain's care, compounding his confusion is why the captain placed the care of the jewel with him.

Without looking in fear of prying eyes from the few crew members still on deck securing the lifeboats, Ben slipped the jewel into his pocket where he rolled it through his fingers. All the while, he tries to sort out what it all meant.

Did the captain give him the jewel for the sake of denying Edgar his prize? Or was it to punish Edgar for his dishonesty? Or was he merely made its keeper until the captain himself could take proper possession of it?

Ben paused from his thoughts to notice the spots of blood on the deck from Seymour's injury trailing to the passageway below. His innards did a kind of flip-flop as they did so many months ago when he took his first steps on the deck of the Alexandria. Daniel looked from Ben to the bloodstained deck. "Ben, you alright?"

"Uh," Ben answered, afraid to say too much at the risk of succumbing to the force welling up inside him to be sick right there. Sweat trickled down his pasty white face accompanied by his mouth beginning to water.

"You don't look so good. You best get to the galley and eat something," Daniel said, nudging Ben with his shoulder. "Go on now. I'll get this cleaned up."

Without a word or a look, Ben moved toward the direction of the galley. The evening almost upon them the sunset colors of red, yellow, and orange dance across the deck and the sea is calm.

Ben grabbed for the doorknob when Admiral Tibbs gave him a welcomed rubbing against his leg. Ben bent over to pet the cat when he saw sparkly flashes of light dancing in front of his eyes, like something a person would see before losing consciousness. His head floated around like a balloon.

"Wow, I don't feel so good Tibbs," Ben said, as saliva gathered in his mouth.

"Maybe, maybe, I'll sit down here for a minute."

Ben sat in front of the galley doors, working to compose himself. He closed his eyes and rested his head against the door. Tibbs jumped into his lap and pressed his nose to Ben's.

"What is it, boy? Did someone forget to feed you today? Alright, come on." Unsteady on his feet Ben caught himself against the door before reaching for the knob again.

The room is dark and hot. Ben began to sweat immediately. The odor of yeast and lingering traces of musty wood intruded his nostrils. Ben groped for the light switch on his left side inside the doorway. The light snapped on and a room full of wooden tables, and benches appeared out of nowhere. The two entered the back of the kitchen, Abraham's sacred domain.

Opening the cabinets and drawers Ben warned Tibbs how it would not be best to make a mess in their efforts for support or Abe would be right cross with them. Ben remembered the last painful time he worked in the kitchen with Abe. He rubbed his hand, the damaged tissue from his burn still not completely healed.

Ben opening a door found saltine crackers and peanut butter stuffed in one of the many cabinets hung along the sidewall. He held up the jar of peanut butter to the Admiral, but the cat showed no interest.

"No?" The cat just stared up at him from the floor. "Na, me either," he said, putting the jar back and continuing his search.

Finally, the trauma of the events of his day started to catch up with him, and he is too tired to continue his search much longer. He tried one more cabinet and settled on a can of dried meat and bread. Ben and Tibbs sat down at a table facing the door and ate their cold supper.

Ben is not sure if eating the dried meat made him feel better or not. He is happy to give his last piece to Tibbs who doesn't seem to mind the taste at all. Venturing back out on the deck Ben saw Daniel pacing a bit up and down the port side of the ship with the captain's binoculars.

"Daniel, have you heard how the captain is doing?"

"What? Uh, no, I haven't heard," Daniel said, wishing he had some bit of reassuring news about the captain. With nothing more to add, he returned to watching out over the ocean.

"What are you looking at?"

"Nothing you know just looking around. I have to call down to check the engines," Daniel said, before heading in the direction of the wheelhouse.

Baffled by Daniel's behavior Ben looked out over the ocean again and then to the dark figure of Daniel peering out the wheelhouse window with the binoculars. Deciding to take his chances of being turned away by Abe, and to take a moment to go below and put the jewel in a safe place, Ben headed off.

In his cabin, rather the one he has inherited from his good friend Jacob, whom he is missing more now than ever, Ben sought out the perfect place to hide the treasure. After a few minutes, Ben remembered a hiding place once used by his comic strip hero Dick Tracy.

"Perfect," he said aloud.

Taking a book off the shelf built into the cabin's wall Ben read the cover, "Sea Monsters of the Deep."

I don't think anybody will miss this one. Ben thought taking out a stubby knife from the nightstand drawer. Taking out the jewel, Ben placed it on the first page of the book and outlined it with the knife then placed it on the bunk. Ben proceeded to carve the outline.

Paper parts flew everywhere as Ben dug deeper into the book's body, like a mad surgeon cutting out some needless part from his (victim) patient. After many minutes, Ben stopped digging and placed the jewel into the newly carved hole to check the fit.

"Perfect," he said, again.

Ben closed the book cover and placed it back onto the shelf next to the title, "Ten Ways to Beat Sea Sickness."

He tossed the last of the paper pieces out the porthole and into the ocean before hurrying to check on his friend. Abe standing sentry over the captain's cabin door spotted him as he came down the corridor.

"How is he," Ben asked, standing in front of Abe looking up into his large brown eyes.

Abe sighed before taking in the breath to answer in a tone he thought would be the less frightening to Ben. "Well, they got the arrow out and decided to thank god, it wasn't poisonous. So, iffin' he keeps it clean, he should pull out fine."

"The captain is a tough old sea dog; it'll take more than an ol' arrow to put him down," Abe concluded by giving Ben a toothy smile.

His words came to Ben as a welcomed relief. Ben fought the visions of Jacob lying in his bunk wounded and dying all the way down to see the captain. The two could hear murmured talking coming from inside the cabin.

"You're very lucky Seymour," the sailor said, "A few more inches and…"

The captain cut the man off mid-sentence to ask a question. "How many?"

Seymour put his eyes on the man who has busied himself washing his hands. "How many men did we lose?"

The man's eyes moved to connect with Edgar's who has remained silent.

"Well, I'm not sure of the exact count."

"How many damn it," Seymour said, making an effort to sit up, but falling back in pain.

"Let's just say there won't be two shifts running on the ship for a while."

"It's all my fault. I made them go," the captain said, in a low voice void of any emotion.

"You did nothing. They're grown, men. They decided for themselves."

"Yes, but I knew there could be trouble."

"There's always trouble Seymour, if they want to play it safe, they would have stayed home," the man said, checking Seymour's dressing already soaked with blood.

"Seymour," the kind man said. "Look at me."

Seymour turned his head to catch the smallest glimpse to satisfy the man.

"Seymour, they knew the life. You understand."

"What do you suppose they're talking about," Ben asked, Abe, trying to listen.

"Never you mind. It's none of our business no how."

Ben didn't hear Daniel come up behind him.

"How is the old bird?"

"I don't know, but they's talking, so that's a good sign," Abe said.

Daniel stopped asking questions long enough to look at his shoes and rub his chin before asking the next question. "Did you have a chance to tell 'em yet what happened while they were gone?"

"Tell him what," Ben asked, looking between the two.

"Boy, you ask too many dang questions," Abe protested.

"This doesn't really concern you right now Ben, best you make yourself scarce," Daniel said.

"But." Ben knowing to argue would be hopeless, turned and headed back the way he came.

Chapter 25

Enemies All-Around

"No," Abe replied

"Well, I have been tracking our shadow, and they're getting closer. They haven't spotted us yet, but, well, we shouldn't delay leaving," Daniel said, his voice riddled with worry.

Without a reply to Daniel's news, Abe knocked on the door and waited for a reply. The hushed voices inside the cabin went silent before giving Abe permission to enter. Abe's eyes fell on the pale face of Seymour, then to Edgar, sitting in the chair opposite of the door.

"What is it guys," the sailor asked.

"Well, we need to talk to the captain. It's important," Daniel answered.

"This isn't a good time. The captain needs his rest now maybe later when he feels better," the sailor said, stepping forward to shut the door on the two.

"Hold on there, let them in. It's alright I can still listen without doin' anything."

Reluctantly, the sailor stepped out of the way and let the two men in.

"Captain," Daniel started, "Since you were on the island, we picked up a strange ship off the horizon. At first, we couldn't make her out."

Daniel paused, hoping Abe would take it as a sign to jump in. When Abe didn't Daniel started again giving Abe a look of disgust. Abe's attention squarely on the captain's face took no notice.

"We think it's a German vessel," Daniel said.

The captain's surprised widened his eyes in anticipation of the rest of Daniel's news.

"And?"

Edgar not paying too much attention didn't say a word, preoccupied with the loss of his jewel.

"I've... we've been tracking her speed and pattern of travel. It's not on patrol; she's looking for something. I thought once maybe she was trying to signal us, but it was just water reflection." The room went quiet for a moment before Seymour spoke, "How far out are they?"

Daniel without looking at him said, "Can't tell; they're not cruising in a straight line."

"Has there been any more radio contact?"

"No."

139

"Captain," Abe said, "We best not be in this place tomorrow cause it's sure to bring trouble."

"But we haven't found the treasure yet," Seymour said.

"The treasure! We can't even get close enough to get the bodies for a proper burial, and you're worried about the treasure," the sailor said, completely overwhelmed by the captain's comment. Throwing up his hands he began to pace around the room mumbling to himself.

"How's the shoulder?" Daniel asked, trying to steer the conversation away from the treasure.

"Oh, better. I'll be okay thanks to his handy work."

"Did ya even see any treasure before the natives got all worked up?" Abe asked, completely sabotaging Daniel's efforts.

The captain turned to put Edgar in view, before answering, causing Edgar to squirm in his chair.

"No, I didn't see any treasure. But it's there I can feel it."

The sailor, a bit calmer now, returned to the captain's bunk side. "Forget the treasure, Seymour; you're lucky to be alive. The rest of you... get out. The captain needs some rest."

Out in the hall, Edgar passed the two before turning down the corridor toward the hold.

"What's up with him," Daniel asked.

Abe and Daniel proceed up on deck where they find Ben hanging around the steps leading to the wheelhouse.

"What are you doing, Ben," Daniel asked.

"Oh, nothing... Abe."

"Yeah."

"Oh, nothing."

"It's getting late, Ben, and you've had a long day. Why don't you go and get some rest? One of us will be by later to get you for watch duty."

"Okay."

Once Ben had left their sight, Daniel began. "You know, Abe, this is terrible, what's happened. A lot of good men died for nothing."

"Abe, I have served with the captain a long time, and I've never seen him like this," Daniel said, hoping his confession about the change in Seymour would get back to the captain's ear.

"What do you mean?"

"I don't really know but Jacob dying and all. It did more to him than we think. They were close, shared everything."

"Yeah, but in the end, I think the captain needed Jacob to step up and tell him not to do it, but he wasn't here," Abe said.

"Now, the captain blames himself."

"But the men voted."

"Don't matter."

"Well, we've got bigger problems right now."

"Them engines givin' you trouble?"

Daniel gave him a distressing nod.

"If that ship is the Germans looking for some payback, we're sitting ducks out here," Daniel said.

"Iffin' you ask me? The sooner we leave the better." Abe said, bidding Daniel a good night.

Turning his attention once again to the horizon Daniel peered out over the black water through the binoculars as the last of the twilight disappeared into the night.

His eyes adjusted to the darkness, searching for the running lights of their shadow ship. Across the bow, he searched, until his view caught the reddish-yellow smoldering from the volcano, rumbling across the night sky from the Island. Daniel looked further down the jungle. He saw something, which gave his spine a tingle of panic.

At the jungle's edge, a giant fire burned. The silhouette of figures dancing around it can be made out against the flickering flames roaring into the air.

"Seymour, what have you done?" Daniel spoke aloud, transfixed on the restless natives on the beach.

Ben rolled around in his bunk too tired to sleep, watching the fire's glow from his porthole window. He too wished to leave this terrible place and finally make the journey home.

Without even a picture of his mother, Ben replayed their last conversation over and over in his head. Her face is vivid in his mind. He rested against the porthole window frame, wondering what she's doing.

It is late he thought. She's probably gone to bed. How lonely the apartment must feel without him. No one to fuss over or talk to.

Stop it! He told himself, this wasn't helping. You'll get home when you get there and not a moment sooner.

Go to sleep, his final words to himself before closing his eyes and wishing his mother good night.

(Knock, knock, knock) "Are you awake?" a voice called.

"What? What is it?" the captain answered, from the darkness.

"I need to talk to you."

Seymour worked to regain his wits. "What time is it? Who is it? What's wrong??"

Without further conversation or invitation, the person belonging to the voice entered the cabin.

The figure moved toward Seymour's bunk and turned on the light.

Shading his eyes from the brightness Seymour spied through his fingers at the figure.

"Edgar? What do you want?"

Edgar hovered over the tired and injured man; the pale light of Seymour's desk lamp cast over Edgar's whiskey sunken features as if death had already come to him.

The first mate's breath was heavy, through clenched teeth he said, "I want my jewel."

"What?" Seymour said, trying to buy time to think of something better to say.

"You heard me, I found it, and I want it back. It's mine." Edgar leaned over slightly to appear more intimidating,

"You best be on your way mister," the captain snarled back.

"I'm not leaving without my jewel, I want it."

Edgar raised his hand as if to strike and ran his pudgy fingers through his greasy hair to brush it from his eyes.

"You've been drinking. I can smell it on you," the captain said.

Edgar started to scan the room with his glassy, blood-shot eyes for possible hiding places. "Where is it?"

"You touch one thing and you'll be spending the rest of the trip in the brig mister now get the hell out of here, and I'll forget it ever happened."

"This isn't over," Edgar said, before slamming the door behind him.

Seymour rested back on his bunk, his shoulder throbbing with pain.

Chapter 26

Alexandria under Attack

"Ben. Ben, time to get up, you'll be late for school."

"Mother, is that you? I… I had a bad dream, I."

"Ben, wake up. It's Daniel. You're dreaming. It's time for your watch."

"Oh, sorry. I thought."

A little ashamed Ben got out of his bunk without looking at Daniel. He rubbed the sleep from his eyes and took the flashlight and whistle from his friend.

"Remember, if you see anything at all; don't be afraid to blow that thing you understand?"

"I understand."

With Daniel off to his own bunk for some well-earned shuteye, Ben headed off for his watch. On deck, the ship seemed completely deserted, cold, and uninviting like some long-dead ghost ship. Following his usual pattern, Ben started his rounds at the bow of the ship.

The predawn air is crisp, and he is chilled. He yawned and stretched his arms over his head. He doesn't know how it's possible his body could ache from lack of sleep worse now than it did before he slept. The sun peeked over the horizon.

Not yet, awake itself. This place between night and dawn cast shadows across the protruding surfaces of the deck playing tricks on Ben's eyes. Twice so far during his trek around the deck, he positioned the whistle in his lips ready to cry for help. Only to be relieved at the sight under further investigation that the intruder to be only ordinary objects of the ship. Ben paused by the rail to look out over the water toward the island.

Bits and pieces of the following day trickled back into the front of his mind. None pleasant enough for Ben to want to dwell on. Ben picked up the binoculars hanging on a hook behind him and put them up to his eyes.

He swept the beach. All that remained was the smoldering ash from the native's fire from the night before. Scanning further down the beach Ben's attention is drawn to the unhappy noises his stomach is making. He ignored his stomach's complaints and continued his search. Ben took no notice to the sound in the water off the port side of the ship.

Placing the binoculars back on the hook, Ben wondered how much longer before he is relieved, so he could take care of the hunger pains growing in his middle. Ben turned to retrace his steps around the deck when he paused to take a second listen to something he thought he heard from the water. Not satisfied with the explanation for the noise his mind is coming up with, Ben ventured to the railing.

He doesn't get another step when he is startled off his feet by a colorfully dressed dark-skinned man miraculously appearing before him. The native's eyes are cold, empty, and penetrating, fixed squarely on Ben.

Ben hardly able to believe his own eyes scrabbled backward to his feet before turning to run. Up over the cargo covers and back onto the deck his hand groped for the silver whistle bouncing around his neck. He clumsily put the whistle to his lips and blew it with all the air in his lungs. Ben glanced over his shoulder to see if the native warrior is following.

 However, Ben lost him in the sheer numbers of men spilling onto the ship. He raced around the funnel and to the coned shaped stack sticking out of the deck, used to carry fresh air to the floors below. Sticking his head in the cone as far as it will go; Ben blew his whistle with every-last effort and breath. The sound echoed down through the ship alerting everyone within earshot.

 Ben with his own ears ringing pulled his head out of the cone, in time to hear the natives pounding down the deck in his direction. A few of the natives broke off from the group and burst through the wheelhouse door, over-powering the helmsmen before he could blow the ship's whistle.

Seymour woken by Ben's whistle, yelled at the sailors darting past his doorway, demanding to know what was going on. But none bothered to answer. Abe was busy in the galley preparing breakfast for the crew when he heard Ben's call for help. He raced to the deck, branding his meat cleaver. An explosion of the brightly painted, bloodthirsty natives continued to board the Alexandria. The crew busted onto the deck to greet them.

The two armies collided. The horrible sound of gunfire and fury and native battle cries rang out. Ben tucked out of sight behind the steps leading to the wheelhouse.

He spied around the corner of the wall to see a large and hairy native swinging what looked like a hatchet over his head. Ben pulled back and closed his eyes all his muscles quivered in panic and terror of being discovered.

Ben heard the savage's hatchet bury into something. He gathered all his courage and peered around the corner again. The native began hacking away at the cabinet containing the rest of the ship's arsenal of weapons and ammunition mounted on the wall below the steel steps.

 With a sound of cracking and breaking wood, the doors to the cabinet flew open, almost striking Ben in the forehead.

If the natives knew, how the guns worked or not, they would at least take possession of them leaving the ship even further defenseless against their attack. Ben desperate to stop the man looked around for any way to defend the ship.

He turned to see an angry native who was waving his arms and legs being thrown overboard by one of the sailors. Ben yelled for the sailor but the volume of the battle raging around him masked his pleas. Then he spotted his chance. He would have to time it right if he were to be successful.

The young boy counted in his head "1, 2," On three Ben ran across the deck to the railing where his answer hung to stopping the thieves. If he could get it to work before, he too is struck down by one of the arrows flying up and down the deck.

With all his strength, Ben pulled at the valve handle. To his surprise, he felt the cold smooth steel turn in his hand, then again. With the last turn, he watched the hose spring to life like a giant serpent lashing out to attack anyone who is near. Ben is momentarily caught off guard as to what to do next.

The thrashing fire hose has its own ideas getting caught in one of the supports of the steel steps and fired its attack of water directly at the unsuspecting native; bashing him off his feet and down the deck in a tidal wave of water.

 Surprised at how well his plan had worked Ben paused for a second to see that not only did it work better than he hoped, but the thrashing hose is preventing anyone else from getting anywhere near the gun cabinet.

"Shoot them," Edgar screamed, from the body-cluttered deck, fighting his way back down the deck. Armed with only his rod and his wits, he fought through the wave of natives. Ben turned to see Daniel racing around the corner and collide with an attacking native, knocking the native off his feet.

"Oh my god, there are too many of them," Daniel yelled, to Edgar.

"Forget that. Call the engine room," Edgar ordered, "We need steam."

Ben darted and weaved for cover across the deck.

"Get below," Daniel said, to Ben.

"No, you need me."

The engineer hollered to one of the sailors fighting off the savages to take charge of Ben before he made his way up the steel steps to the wheelhouse to follow Edgar's orders to call for steam.

The sailor grabbed Ben by the collar and dragged him to the doorway leading to the corridors below.

Ben struggled against the sailor's grip. "No, I don't want to go!"

Ben felt the sailor's grip loosen. He looked up to see the sailor's face wash of all color and expression.

."Help me," Robert moaned, falling forward into Ben's arms.

"No," Ben cried out. His eyes dropped to see the arrows sticking out of Robert's back.

Unable to support his friend's limp body Ben collapsed.

"Help, help, help over here."

Ben lying on his back watched arrows whiz overhead and splinter against the back wall of the entryway the weight of the man beginning to crush him.

"Help!" Ben forced out of his body.

Running frantically down the deck, Abe heard Ben's cry. "Ben, where you at?"

"I am over here."

Reaching the two, Abe grabbed Ben and pulled him free.

"Come on, we gots to go," Abe said, pushing Ben's head down. "In through here."

Ben looked back at the sailor lying on the cold steel floor, bleeding, motionless.

"But what about Robert? We can't just leave him there!"

"Hurry, we can't help him now. He's dead," Abe said, dragging Ben away from the scene.

Ben pulled his arm free from Abe's fingers. "Where are we going?"

"To get you safe," Abe peaked out a porthole window. "And that's the kitchen on this ship."

"The kitchen?" Ben said, in surprise.

"That's right now come on before somebody uses you for a pincushion."

"But." realizing he'd been overpowered, he complied.

The sound of the steam whistle carried out across the deck from the wheelhouse. The natives scattered from the deck into the water. Daniel turned to see the injured man standing behind him on the bridge, with his hand on the pull cord of the whistle.

"Captain, you should be in bed."

"Thought you could use some help," the captain said, leaving go of the cord.

Daniel released the phone receiver to assist the captain, but the captain gestured for him to return to the phone.

The captain dropped himself into his chair. "That won't scare them off for long. Make ready to get underway. We need steam now, Daniel."

The deck is stained with fresh blood puddled around the bodies of sailors and natives alike, lying everywhere bleeding, dying, or dead. The advancing sailors chase the remaining natives off the ship. When all is quiet on deck, Ben and Abe appear from the galley, Abe branding his cleaver. The sailors still standing to see to committing all the bodies to the sea. The moans of the injured are heard in every direction.

"Lord have mercy." is all Abe can think to say as he shook his head at the carnage before them.

Edgar took no notice to the suffering going on around him, his attention fixed on the ship approaching them from the starboard side. He waved his arms and yelled at the men on the bridge, pointing out over the water.

"What's he going on about," Abe said, leaning over one of the injured men. The two stood slowly to better view the source of Edgar's excitement.

Chapter 27

The Ship is Lost

"Colonel, we have a steamer insight: it must be the one we're looking for," the sergeant said.

Giving the binoculars to his Colonel the soldier resumed his post.

The Colonel lifted the binoculars to his eyes. "Yes, we have them. Set course to intercept."

Abe pointed in the direction of the approaching ship. "This ain't good, Ben, see there."

"What do we do?" Ben looked from the fallen sailor to Abe.

"We gots to tell the captain. He'll know what to do."

"Hey, what about these guys?"

"Ben, we can't save them. They're hurt too bad and iffin' we don't hurry; we'll end up just like 'em. Now come on."

The two friends stepped over the bodies of the fellow shipmates to make their way to the wheelhouse followed by Edgar, who is worked up to almost a panic.

"Engine room, hello, engine room full pressure to the turbines. We need speed now!" Daniel yelled, to be heard over the running machinery.

"Sir, we. . . the. . . isn't." a voice on the other end of the line pleaded.

"I don't care. Do it." With his last word, Daniel slammed the receiver onto the cradle and took the wheelhouse engine controls, pushing them forward into the full position.

The ship groaned as if she were in great pain. "She's gonna blow," a sailor screamed, after watching the pressure gauge glass shatter. The ship's main boiler began to blow rivets from its joints, gushing boiling hot steam everywhere before finally giving way to the magnitude of stress put on it from the building pressure.

The boiler exploded with fury, sending shards of red-hot steel in all directions; ripping through the freshwater pipes and the flesh of the sailors. The concussion from the explosion tore a ten-foot hole into the side of the Alexandria's hull. In a matter of seconds, the ship leaned hard to the right sending sailors in the engine room flying against the scorching pipes. The burning steam chased the sailors lucky enough to get to the door up the steel steps.

"Is everyone alright?" Daniel said, from the floor of the wheelhouse.

"They're attacking! They're attacking, the Germans are attacking. It's a torpedo. Help," Abe, yelled, from the top of his lungs, his hands gripping Ben's upper body for dear life, squeezing the air out of him.

"Get a grip on yourself," Edgar yelled, from his spot at the railing where he was thrown from the explosion.

"What was it?" Ben asked.

Edgar straightened his hat before answering Ben, "The boiler. It exploded."

Abe and Ben never making as far as the wheelhouse laid among the bodies of the injured and dying on the deck which was further scattered apart, with some washed overboard completely. Abe and Ben were stunned at the news.

"You two there," Daniel said, from the wheelhouse door, "Get up and go see who needs help. Hurry up."

Ben and Abe are snapped out of the shock and get to their feet. As they do, Ben beheld the sight of the deck boards that run along the center of the ship, splintered and broken. The two struggled up the deck leaning at an odd angle to the right and the stern lowering into the water. The two make it to the doorway leading below the survivors from the engine room staggered on-deck blackened and burned.

Coughing and gasping for air they attempt to speak. "No more…"

"What? What are you trying to say," Ben asked, the man who collapsed to his knees.

"No more survivors. We sealed the hatch."

Ben and Abe once again sport the stunned look they had a few minutes earlier.

"There were eight men in there and only three got out?" Abe muttered, from his quivering lips.

Daniel joining the men on deck insisted they must go below and be sure there are no more survivors.

"Now look, we don't know how much time we have so nobody messes around," Daniel said.

The corridors are dim with the lights running on only the ship's batteries giving the faded green peeling paint and dingy floors an uninviting appearance. They break the shadows with the beams of light coming from their flashlights. The ship moaned and creaked from the mortal wound inflicted upon her by the explosion. Doors from the cabins banged open and closed with every rise and fall of the tide.

"Keep going, search down there," Daniel ordered, to Ben and Abe.

"Ok, but ain't nobody down here," Abe answered.

Ben and Abe start down another corridor leading past the captain's and Edgar's cabin.

"Hello, anybody down here?" Ben yelled. His words reverberate back to him off the steel walls.

"Geez, Ben you nearly scared the pa'gee-bee's out of me," Abe said.

"Sorry."

Shining the beam of light in and out of each room, the two make progress but finding nothing. The ship lets out another long painful grown, and Abe decides it's time to rejoin Daniel and head topside. They meet up with him on the steel steps leading to the upper deck. Out of breath from running up and down the steps, Daniel asked the two if they found anybody. After listening to their report, Daniel added, he too had not found anyone else, and it would be best to be topside. On their way up, the ship shifted crashing the group into the railing of the steps.

"That don't sound good," Abe added.

"No, not good, we have to go," Daniel pushed forward up the steps.

Out on deck the captain is helping the engine-room crew. A few men from the battle with the island locals have regained consciousness and are sitting with the captain. Edgar is at the railing watching the German ship steam closer. Daniel too is concerned with the ship.

"Captain," Daniel said, his voice shaken as the impact of what happened began to filter into his mind.

"The ship it's... I'm sorry it's sinking, and we don't have much time."

Daniel stopped talking and watched the captain finish bandaging a man's burned arm.

"Did you hear me, Seymour? The ship-"

"I heard you, Daniel. We must prepare to abandon ship. Gather what you need, get Ben to help and get to the lifeboats." He told him in a calm and reassuring voice.

"Well, that's the problem, Seymour. We don't have the lifeboats anymore."

Seymour stood up to face Daniel. "What? They were tied up alongside. Where are they?"

"They were taken out by the explosion."

"Captain, you better take a look at this," Edgar called, from the railing.

"What is it?"

Pointing out over the water, Edgar directed the captain's attention to the approaching ship. He took the binoculars from Edgar and focused on the ship's flag.

"Oh no," the captain murmured to himself.

"We don't have much time. We need a plan," Edgar said.

"What are we going to do? We can't fight, and we can't run."

Seymour looked back at the injured and beaten men then back to Edgar.

"I, I don't know."

"If they catch us, you know what's going to happen. Don't you?"

In a moment of silence, as the two men ponder their situation, the ship rocks again as another storage tank exploded from somewhere in the belly of the ship. The concussion sent a wave over the deck.

"Come we have to tell them," The captain said, to Edgar, who is once again looking at the ship on approach.

"Is everyone okay? I never thought it would come to this," Seymour said, looking out over the water to escape the confused and terrified looks plastered on the men's faces.

"Look," the captain said, with his raised hand and pointed out to sea.

"What? What is it," Daniel asked.

"The ship is getting closer."

A silence fell over the men. Ben's body became heavy at the sound of the captain's words. His mind flooded with thoughts of how once again, he had put his shipmates in danger with no escape. If he had seen the natives sooner, they might have stood a better chance.

"We can't run, the ship's sinking. Even if we had the lifeboats where would we go? Daniel said, his voice becoming more desperate with each word.

"The natives are just waiting, waiting to finish us off."

"The lifeboats are gone," Ben asked, completely surprised, as were the rest of the men at this horrible addition to the already dismal chain of events.

"How?"

He had thought all along no matter what happened the lifeboats would be their last hope for survival. Thoughts of home and never seeing his mother invade his mind making his stomach turn. He saw his own expression on the faces of his mates.

"Edgar what are we going to do? I don't want to die, don't want to die you hear me," a sailor cried out, on the brink of panic. The other sailors pulled him back from grabbing onto Edgar's shirt. Edgar angered by the man's lack of courage scolded him.

"Well, unless you can swim 1, 500 miles home I don't see wh..."

"That's it!" Ben said.

"What? What's it," Seymour surprised by Ben's outburst.

"Captain, can I speak to you privately?"

Without reply, Seymour walked ways up the broken deck and bent over so Ben could whisper into his ear. After a few exchanges between Seymour and Ben, the captain returned to where the men are standing.

"Quickly, there may still be a chance. Go and get whatever things you need and meet back here. Hurry," the captain said. "You have two minutes."

"But what are you planning?" Daniel is cut off by the captain.

"Hurry, Daniel, hurry."

After what seemed a long time, the men started to appear on the deck again, all chattering to each other, none able to see any hope of escape.

"Ruddy waste of time. Them German dogs aren't givin' us a chance," a sailor said.

Daniel looked around the deck. "Is everyone here?"

"No, where's the captain and the boy," a sailor said.

"What are they up to?"

"There, there he is." A sailor pointed out watching the captain come down from the wheelhouse stuffing charts into his pocket.

Ben raced down the steps to his cabin to gather the jewel before it is lost forever to the sea along with the rest of the ship. Ben returned to the deck out of breath but there.

"Ben, where the hell? Oh, there you are," Abe said, stowing his own possessions in his pocket.

"Daniel, help the men over to the railing. Abe get a rope," the captain ordered.

"But." Daniel tried again to get some clue out of the captain to what he had planned.

"Don't ask questions hurry."

"Oh, no, I am not swimmin' home. I'll take my chances with the Germans," Edgar protested.

The captain turned to Edgar. "Look you're going to have to trust me."

"Trust you or trust the boy? Are you taking orders from him now?" Edgar peered into Seymour's eyes without a blink.

The captain's face contorted into a shape and color Ben had never seen on a man's face before. His fists closed tight. Without a word, Seymour turned to help the last man over to the railing. Before turning back to Edgar, "You'll need a sidearm and get one for Daniel, Ben, and Abe."

Edgar turned and walked away. Seymour faced the men to give them the details of the plan he hoped would save their lives.

Chapter 28

By the Skin of Their Teeth

Edgar returned from the gun cabinet and handed out the arms without a word.

"Okay everyone ties yourselves into the rope and on the count of three, everyone is going to jump into the water."

"What," Daniel asked, confused by the events unfolding in front of him.

"Some of these men can't swim."

"I know. That's why you're all tied together, to help each other," Seymour said, his words growing quicker and closer together.

"But where are we going to go," a sailor asked, from the far end of the row of men standing on the seaside of the railing.

Seymour didn't answer the man but turned his attention to Ben, who had been standing at his side the whole time.

Seymour put his hand on his shoulder. "You ready to do this?"

"Yeah, I think so," Ben said, after taking a deep breath and releasing it.

"Good, good everything's going to be fine. You'll see."

With those words, Seymour struggled to climb over the railing with his injured shoulder, letting out a moan in pain.

Edgar who already found a spot along the railing stood on his tiptoes to look across the deck to bring the approaching danger into view.

"They're almost on us. We best get on with whatever it is the captain's got up his sleeve."

"Everyone stay together," Seymour said, as the group of men prepared to plunge on the count of three into the dark freezing water below.

"Stop!" Ben said, lifting his leg over the railing and rolling to the deck. "I forgot something I'll be right back." Seymour watched Ben race across the deck.

"Come back, Ben, there's no time. Damn kid."

A second later Ben popped into sight running back to the railing carrying an angry orange cat unwilling to get near the water.

"I'm here," Ben said, out of breath from the sprint.

"Admiral Tibbs, I forgot all about him in all the excitement," Seymour said, touched by Ben's thoughtfulness.

"Let me have him and you get ready to go."

For a moment, Ben remembered his fear of the water. "Well, I was going to have to learn how to swim sooner or later."

In seconds, Ben is in the cold water with the rest of his mates.

"I don't like it either Tibbs." Seymour let go of the rail and plunged into the water.

The small party bobbed up and down hearing shouts coming from the Colonel as the German ship came alongside the Alexandria.

"Stay quiet, pass it on," Seymour whispered, to the men.

The party swam alongside the Alexandria's hull until the German ship came into sight.

"What if there's a guard on deck," The captain asked, through chattering teeth.

"Captain?" Ben too tired to form words through the uncontrollable shaking. His body jerked from the frigid temperatures of the water.

"Did you set the thing?" Ben finally is able to get out.

"Yeah, wait for it. Then we'll make our move."

The men could hear the sound of boots as the German crew boarded their beloved ship.

"If we don't get out of the water soon it won't matter," a sailor said to Ben.

"Look below. They're hiding! Find them," the Colonel said, from the deck of the Alexandria.

(Boom!) "Lookout," a man said.

Glass and wood splintered across the deck and the men go running.

"That's the signal, let's go," Seymour said.

The group watched as the guards on deck boarded the sinking ship in the attempt to assist the Colonel. Stroke by stroke the party made its way around to the opposite side of the German ship and began to board. Seymour hoisted Ben up to the ship's railing telling him to stay put as he himself boarded the vessel. Gesturing to Edgar and Daniel to follow, Seymour disappeared around the corner. A moment later, a thud is heard followed by a second.

Seymour whispered to the men. "Come on. It's safe."

Without a sound, the men and boy followed Seymour to the hatch that led inside.

"Ben," Seymour said. "The bridge is empty now thanks to Edgar. Take Abe with you and get us the hell out of here."

Ben stood up straight and saluted his captain, "Aye captain."

"What do you know about drivin' a German boat," Abe asked, Ben, coming alongside him.

"Nothing, but how much different can it be, right?"

In the ship's interior, the captain gave Daniel orders to take the engine room and to throw anybody he found overboard.

"Take Edgar with you."

"What about you?"

"I figure as soon as Ben throws the levers forward the jigs up, so we're going to give cover while we pull away."

"Cover from where?"

"Go! We only got a…"

Before Seymour could finish his sentence, the ship lunged forward when the engines fired to life.

Ben pulled away hard from the Alexandria's side, shouts from her deck rang out in German.

The captain positioned himself behind a door leading below. "Jig's up."

Gunshots whizzed by, contacting with the wooden frame around the door.

"Why you! Shoot at me, will ya?"

The captain pulled his revolver and returned fire. The soldiers on the deck of the Alexandria dove for cover.

"What's that? Gunshots?" Ben looked in the direction of the noise.

"Yeah, get down. Ya wanna get shot," Abe questioned, pulling him below the window by his wet shirt.

"Stop, I can't see where I am going."

Abe paid him no mind and covered his own head with a dry spittoon sitting next to him. After a brief scuffle, Seymour heard Edgar yelling and shouting followed by a couple of splashes, then a few more.

Ben is startled for a second by a clamor. "What's that ringing?"

"It's the phone, silly. Answer it," Abe said.

"Why me?"

"Well, I sure ain't expecting no calls."

"Me either," he said.

Reaching up Ben lifted the receiver and put it to his ear. "Hello," all the while trying to hang on to the wheel.

"Ben, you alright up there?" You have the bridge, right? Abe with you?"

"Who is this?"

"It's me, Daniel. We've taken the engine room, and I am sending all the steam she's got. It's crazy everything is in German. I can't understand a thing. Let me speak to Abe."

Lowering the phone, Ben handed it over. "It's for you."

With his face, looking a bit more confused than usual Abe took the phone. "Hello?"

"Abe, we've taken the engine room. You'll have full power in a second. Keep an eye on Ben."

"What did he say?"

Hanging up the phone Abe looked up at Ben. "You never mind. Just get us out of here."

Ben peaked over the window ledge and pulled hard on the wheel. The ship responded to Ben's command and moved out into the open water.

"Captain, I think we're out of firing range. They can't hit us," one of the sailors said, to Seymour, who is still slouching behind the doorway.

"I think you're right, listen to them," Seymour said. "They sound awfully mad."

The commandeered ship continued to pull away from the damaged and sinking Alexandria. A few minutes later, the remaining crew gathered on the deck to say their last farewells to their proud boat.

"She was a fine ship," Seymour said, taking off his hat and giving her a wave goodbye.

"She was one of the fastest ships I ever worked," Daniel added.

"I'll sure miss her. She was a fine lady," Abe said.

A silence fell over the crew, the same silence that crept into their presence the day they gave up one of their own to the sea. The kind of loss you can't fill or replace, but have to somehow go on without.

"Hey look!" a sailor said, pointing out over the deck railing to the boats approaching the Alexandra.

"Why, it's those natives. They must have regrouped for another run at us," Seymour said.

"Well, what do you know? I guess the Colonel's going to have something new to worry about besides shooting at us now," Daniel said, with a chuckle.

Seymour looked around the deck at what remained of his crew. "Anyway, is everyone alright? Anybody shot?"

With a few mumbles from the men about the state of their well-being, the captain took to handing out duties.

"Abe, take the injured to cabins and see them comfortable."

"Ben, get back to the wheel and turn us north, northwest."

"North, northwest, captain?" Ben a bit confused by the heading.

"Yes, that's the heading for home," Seymour said, with a warm smile growing across his whiskery face.

The men all gave their approval of Seymour's announcement. All but the first mate who still had other things on his mind.

Edgar slipped away before the captain has a chance to hand him a duty in pursuit of anything left behind by the former crew. A small consolation to losing his treasure and the ship he hoped to captain someday.

"Daniel, return to the engine room to see how set we are on fuel and then check to see what supplies we have," Seymour said, before moving to join Ben on the bridge.

On his way up the steps to the wheelhouse he stopped to give Daniel further instructions, "Get someone who can get the radio working, we'll need to know if anything is coming our way."

"Aye captain."

For a moment, Daniel stopped and in a slow turn, looked over his right shoulder and gazed up into the sky far beyond the horizon. He had only ever seen a sky look like that once in his life and hoped to never see one like it again. He fought back his instincts to sound the warning about what his eyes are seeing, and his heart is denying.

Chapter 29

Settling In

Ben stood at the wheel wet, tired and hungry, but glad to be alive and with his crew.

Seymour entered the wheelhouse. "Ben, you saw that soggy cat running around?"

"Yeah, I did a while ago. I think he is still trying to dry off."

"Well, that's good. He needed a bath anyway dirty old ship rat that he is." Seymour put his tired and injured body into his new captain's chair.

His eyes closed, and his breathing slowed. Ben looked away from the compass to check on his friend's condition.

"Uh, captain, you don't look so good. Maybe you should go rest?"

"No, no, I'll be alright; I want to stay with you for a while."

The room went quiet for more than a few long moments while Ben fished around for something to say to break the uncomfortable silence filling the room.

"You know captain at least the compass isn't in German. I heard Daniel is having a hard time reading the engine gauges."

Ben's comment went unanswered. He turned again to check on his friend only to find him asleep. Seymour's wound opening up again bled down onto his dark jacket a bit. His face expressed his suffering. Ben said nothing more and guided the ship on course that would with God's grace find them home soon. After Abe had made his shipmates as comfortable as possible, he set out to find the galley.

"I know I ain't gonna like what I find for a kitchen," Abe mumbled.

"Try and feed men with what? Sauerkraut and pork? That's no food."

After many turns and dead ends, Abe arrived at the galley. He opened the door and stepped in. The room is small and littered with dishes, pots, and spilled cups of coffee.

"Look at this mess. I see I got's to do all the cleanin' too."

Stepping over the mess, Abe got behind the counter and opened a cabinet. At that moment, a grey rat scampered across the floor behind him. Abe hearing the noise turned and threw a pot at the rat sending him racing out the door.

"Rats in my kitchen? I don't think so. You best not come back in here you old sea rat you hear me?"

Realizing he has been shouting to himself, Abe regained his composure and continued his search for some proper food. After many hours of hard work cleaning and cooking long into the night, Abe made his rounds to bring the injured a warm meal the best he could.

"Did you hear me, Ben? Time to get some supper," Abe yelled, into the wheelhouse. "Come on boy, let's go. Just pull back on the power and set the wheel."

"But the captain, he's asleep," Ben said, gesturing to the dark figure slumped over in the chair behind him.

Abe gave Ben a look of surprise. He hadn't noticed the captain. He stepped into the wheelhouse in the attempt to raise him. "Sir, wake up. Sir, it's time to eat." Abe pushed on Seymour's arm.

"Jacob, it's a hell of a storm. Cut back, cut back on the power, bring her about," Seymour called, out in his sleep.

Ben gave Abe a look of frightened confusion at the captain's words.

Abe started, "I remember that day, it was a terrible storm we hit about five years ago. The Alexandria nearly didn't make it."

Ben hung on Abe's every word daring not to interrupt.

"We were lucky we had the captain and Jacob that night. They saved us and the ship from getting busted up to pieces."

After he had finished his piece of the story, Abe tried to wake the captain again. "Sir, wake up."

Seymour flickered his eyes open and looking around. "What? Where am I?"

"We're on the ship, sir, the new ship," Abe said.

"Oh, yes, of course. I must've dozed off. Sorry about that mate."

The captain feeling more awake adjusted his hat.

"Sir, I made some food. I think you guys should come and eat. And we best look at that shoulder again too."

Seymour looked to Abe and then to Ben. "Well, that sounds good Abe. Ben could eat. Couldn't you boy?"

"But captain, who's going to steer the ship?"

"Pull her back two-thirds and lock the wheel. She'll be all right for a while; when the first man finishes, he can come up and take over. By the way, Abe have you seen Edgar?"

"Last I saw him; he was still rummaging around below deck."

Ben did as Seymour suggested and Abe moved to leave. Seymour remained.

"Captain, aren't you coming?"

"No, best I stay and keep a lookout. You go eat."

"But…"

"It's alright. You come back when you're done."

The captain told Ben as he stood up and gave Ben a nudge toward the door.

"Come on, the food is gettin' cold."

Abe and Ben left the captain and went to fill their aching stomachs. On deck, Ben glanced over his shoulder in the direction of where they had left the Alexandria in the hands of their enemies.

He couldn't help feeling the utter sense of loss and disappointment still lingering in him over the whole ordeal. His head is telling his soul that they're lucky to be alive, but his heart tells him the not so joyous truth. Abe put his arm around Ben's shoulder and led him to the galley. The smell of hot food came to Ben's senses. His nose is confused by the many aromas entering it at once. Ben doesn't recognize any of the smells but took them as a welcome relief to his hunger pains just the same.

"Here we go now. You grab a plate and dig in."

Ben plopped a thick grayish blob next to what he thought were mashed potatoes onto his plate. "What is it?"

"You don't worry about that now, eat it," Abe told, Ben while putting a piece of bread next to the blob.

Ben turned with his supper to join the few men who are speckled around the confined, poorly lighted room. He spied an open bench, sat down, and poked at the blob with his fork.

 Ben rubbed at his neck and scratched at his shoulder to relieve the tightness that raced under his shirt. The saltwater has dried and left him with the uncomfortableness of being dirty. Resolving to be salted and dirty, Ben put a portion of the grey mystery food in his mouth to appease his stomach.

He chewed it slowly; to his surprise, the unappetizing matter taking up space in his mouth isn't bad.

"Abe," Ben said, his mouth still full, "What is this anyway?"

Abe looked around the room for a moment before spotting Ben at the far end, "Dumplings and some kind of meat."

Ben quickly looked at his plate. He has had dumplings many times with his mother; never had they ever looked or smelled like this. Ben was still staring at his plate when a sailor who had been sitting in the middle of the table watching him leaned in.

"Best not ask too many questions about it lad. Best to just eat it."

Ben looked up from his plate to the man's face his eyebrows raised and a slight shaking came from his head. Finishing his plate, with his stomach full, Ben exited for the wheelhouse to relieve the captain.

On entering, Ben saw the captain was still sitting in the chair where Ben left him.

"Captain, you alright? I can take over so you can go and eat. But be careful of Abe's dumplings."

"Maybe I will. I could use some coffee if there is any."

Benjamin watched as Seymour moved to leave no longer able to conceal his pain, which manifested itself on Seymour's face.

"Captain? You alright?"

"Don't worry Ben, it hurts, but I have had worse."

Admiral Tibbs rubbed Ben's leg. Ben extended his hand to give him a stroke over his now dry and clean orange coat. Alone on the bridge, Ben looked out over the twilight sea. The sound of the engine murmured a subduing rhythm. His thoughts turned to his mother and how he wished more than anything to see her these long months.

He wondered what she would be doing at this moment if he were home sitting in his own kitchen perhaps telling him about her day as she prepared his dinner. Her eyes always full of joy to see him. For the first time since his journey began, he is finally on his way home and back to the person he loved. Ben broke from his daydream to check his heading and pulled hard right to correct his course.

"Best not be doing that too much. If I spill the captain's coffee, I'll have to hear about it," Ben told Tibbs, who didn't care to be skidded across the wheelhouse floor.

Daniel entered the galley, gathered his share of Abe's mystery blob, and joined the captain. Seymour held his shoulder with one hand and made himself eat with the other.

Daniel saw Seymour's discomfort. "Here now best let me take a look at that."

Daniel pulled open the captain's jacket. The captain cried out in pain getting the attention of the few men sitting around the room.

"Stop, I am alright," Seymour told Daniel through gritted teeth. His breath is heavy. His fist gripped his fork with such force his knuckles were turning white.

Daniel attempted to open his coat again. "Seymour, you know what will happen if that gets infected."

"Stop, I said."

Daniel looked up at Abe, who was now standing in front of them. Abe looked around the room at the men watching the scene, giving them an elusive nod. All the men moved on the captain at the same moment.

"What... what are you doing?" the captain shouted. His face flushed, sweat trickled down his cheek.

The men grabbed the captain and held him firm.

The captain cried out again, "Leave me alone, I am the captain, I order you to..."

"Hold him, I know you're the captain Seymour and we're trying to see that you stay that way. So, stop fighting and let us help you," Daniel said.

Opening Seymour's jacket, Daniel and Abe got a good look at the captain's wound.

"That's kind of bad, I'll see what I can find to mend it," Abe said.

"Looks like we caught this just in time any longer and gang green might have set in you old fool!"

Abe returned with a first aid kit and a bottle of whiskey he found stashed in a cabinet in the kitchen.

"What are you going to do?"

"Here drink some of this," Daniel said, putting the bottle to Seymour's lips.

After the captain had his fill, Daniel poured some of the whiskey into Seymour's wound.

"Geesh! Ahh, that burns," Seymour wailed out, his face contorted to express the sheer pain and agony Daniel is inflicting on him.

"Let me go. I just want another drink before you stitch me up like an old shirt."

The men looked to Daniel before letting go of the captain. He gave the nod to let go.

"Now calm down. Let the whiskey work cause you aren't going to like the next part," Daniel said.

Seymour scowled at Daniel. "I'll get you for this," the captain told him with a low growl of a voice.

"You hate me all you want. At least, you'll be here to do it."

"Okay, boys hold him tight. This is going to pinch a bit."

"You ever done this before," Abe asked, Daniel as he held the captain by the shoulders.

Daniel knowing everyone waited his answer paused.

"Yeah, lots of times," Daniel said, smiling at Seymour.

Daniel took out the stitching needle from the kit and threaded it. His hand shaking, he turned away from the captain so not to let him see. His eyes met Abe's without a word, the two exchanged all that they were feeling about the condition of the captain, and what they were about to do, what it would mean to them if the captain had a turn for the worse.

Daniel turned back after taking his time with the needle. "Alright, boys hold. Here we go."

"Wait!" one of the men said.

"What?" Daniel said.

"Don't you have to sterilize the needle or something?"

"What's he talking about? Do you know what you're doing or not?" Seymour asked.

"No, and yes, I do and yes I do. It's sterilized already from being sealed in the kit. Now quit stalling, here we go."

Chapter 30

The Storm

With the captain resting comfortably in one of the empty cabins once occupied by the former crew. Daniel and Edgar go to the bridge and relieve Ben from duty. They poured over sea charts attempting to plot a course home. It's late, Ben met up with Abe and the two found an empty cabin to rest.

Abe's snoring from the lower bunk made it difficult for Ben to sleep. Moonlight flooded through the porthole window striking the tired young sailor across the face. He rolled over and pulled his blanket up tight around his neck. The room is cold, sterile, void of any remnants of personality.

No shelves filled with old, musty books, no pictures of sweethearts, no rugs on the floor or rocking chairs in the corner. This room is nothing like the makeshift home Ben came to know aboard the Alexandria. At last, morning arrived; Ben awoke to the cheerful hollers of Abe as he poured water into a basin sitting atop the built-in dresser against the wall.

"Get up sleepy head. It's mornin'."

Ben pulled his blanket over his head. "What? Morning already? It's still early. Let me sleep."

Not settling for Ben's resolve to remain in bed Abe proceeded to pull his blanket off from the foot of the bunk.

"No… Stop, let go."

Now cold and awake Ben got to his feet mumbling about Abe's snoring in a rather cross tone.

"How's the captain?" Ben asked, pulling on his boots.

"Don't know yet, but Edgar said he would keep an eye on him through the night."

"We best get down to the kitchen and get some breakfast going."

"First thing I'm doing after work is finding my own cabin," Ben said.

Abe and Ben head out to the galley. The sun is up, and the breeze is warm. Along the way, the two-pass a swastika painted on an outside wall. Abe stopped in his tracks.

"What is it, Abe? What's the matter?"

"This." Abe pointed toward the symbol. "This here's gots to go." Abe's face held a look of contempt and hatred.

"What is it? I mean why is it bad," Ben asked, concerned with the face Abe is now wearing.

An expression he has never seen on Abe before. Abe realizing when he turned and looked at Ben, he had frightened him, quickly pushed down the hatred welling up inside him before he tried to answer Ben.

"It's… it's not nice. That's all. Not nice at all," Abe said, before moving from the subject.

However, Ben sensed there is something more than Abe is not telling him.

"Abe, want me to find some paint and paint over it?" Ben said attempting to make Abe feel better.

Abe paused and smiled at Ben, "You know Ben that's a good idea, right after breakfast you do that."

With a sense of great accomplishment, Ben followed Abe into the galley.

On the bridge, Daniel and Edgar, tired from plotting, figuring, and re-figuring all night take a break. Daniel took his hat off and ran his slender fingers through his dirty brown hair. "I wish Jacob were here. He was better at this figuring business than me. Always was."

Edgar hearing every word that Daniel spoke said nothing but gave up an emotionless grunt.

"Well, what do ya think of the new course?"

"Sure, why not," Edgar said. "Sailor, here is the new course."

"Yes, sir," the sailor on the wheel said, turning the ship to the new heading.

"Hey, any news about us over the radio yet," Edgar asked, the sailor operating the radio stack in a corner of the bridge room.

"No, sir nothing."

"That's strange. Thought we'd heard something about it by now," Edgar said, as he turned to leave the room.

"Where you going?"

"To get some shut-eye."

Daniel watched Edgar leave before turning his attention back to his plan.

"Sir?" the sailor in the corner of the room asked, "Are we still a long way from home?"

Daniel turned to look at the man. He recognized him from working in his engine room.

"Where are you from sailor?"

"New York, sir, my mother lives there."

"That's what I thought; you're from the engine crew, you're a fine greaser."

"Do you know anything about running radios sailor?"

"No sir," the sailor said, with a sheepish voice trickling out of his throat.

"It's alright, just keep doing what you're doing and tell us if you hear anything."

"Yes, sir."

"I have to go and find some coffee; I want you to hold down the fort until someone comes to relieve you."

"Yes, sir... sir how long until we get back?"

"We'll be home soon, sailor. Don't worry," Daniel said, opening the door to step out.

Exhausted Daniel entered the galley. It's smaller than the Alexandria's and darker. A few sailors sat in small groups around the room. All eyes are on Daniel when he enters.

"Any coffee?"

"Having a hard time can't read any of the labels," Abe confessed, holding up one of the many cans lining a shelf.

Daniel gave a snicker before he turned to address Ben, who has been busy carrying out Abe's orders around the tiny kitchen.

"Ben, how you doing today?"

"Good. I guess," Ben said, rooting through a drawer for a spoon.

Daniel grabbed a tray and a fork. "What's to eat, anyway?"

Abe plopped a massive spoonful for sticky white grits onto Daniel's tray, causing it to drop several inches. "Grits and toast."

Daniel rolled his eyes. "My favorite." This gained him a sinful glare from the cook.

"Here, Ben, take this down to the captain. He's probably starvin' by now." Abe pushed a tray full of food into Ben's hands along with a steaming hot cup of black coffee.

"Go on now before it gets cold."

"But-" Ben started but is cut short by Abe's interruption.

"Don't worry you can eat when you get back." Abe turned him by the shoulders in the direction of the door.

"But..." Ben tried again to finish his sentence.

"What? What is it now boy?"

"I don't know which cabin is his?"

Daniel who had been watching the two started to laugh at Ben's question. Abe shook his head.

"Ben, it's down the corridor first door on the right," Daniel said.

"Thanks."

Ben struggled out the door spilling part of the captain's coffee. After great effort, he arrived at the captain's quarters and sat the tray on the floor to free up a hand for knocking. With three light raps on the door, a voice can be heard from the other side.

"Come in," the voice replied.

Ben opened the door and bent over to pick up the tray, temporarily taking him out of the captain's view. The captain leaned over the edge of the bunk to catch a glimpse of the visitor.

"Ben, it's you, didn't see ya there for a moment," the captain leaned back. "How are ya today?"

"Good, sir, I have some food and coffee for you?"

"Thanks, I'll take the coffee, just set the food over there on the stand." Seymour pointed to the wooden stand by his bunk.

"Thanks for the coffee, but I need to get up and…" Seymour grabbed his shoulder falling back.

"You need to rest and heal before you rip your stitches." Ben used the scolding tone his mother had so often used on him.

"Maybe you're right. How'd you get so tough?"

"From working on a tramp steamer, that's how."

Ben made Seymour smile through the pain of his shoulder.

"Sit down and visit for a minute, would ya?"

"But, Abe will be wanting me back to help."

"It's alright, he won't argue with the captain."

Ben complied and pulled up the chair that had been sitting in the corner of the room and positioned himself beside the captain's bunk. Seymour patted Ben on the hand and began to talk about the events of the last few weeks.

"Ben, you're a good boy. It has been a pleasure having you aboard. Your mother would be proud of you."

Ben listened, not sure what words would reach out and offer comfort to his friend.

"Sir." Ben broke in. "Are you alright?"

Seymour shrugged his good shoulder before, he answered. "Things haven't worked out that well, have they? Not the way I wanted, not even close." Seymour's gaze wandered around the room in deliberate avoidance of Ben's eyes.

"First losing Jacob and then the trouble in port followed the crazy notion about the treasure." Seymour stopped speaking abruptly taking a deep long breath before continuing. "I even managed to lose my ship, not bad for a month and half worth of work would ya say?"

Ben listened to the captain's words laced with painful regret and despair searching his own mind for some life preserver of hope to throw his drowning friend. However, there was none to offer, Ben sat quietly picking at the torn fabric of his chair.

"Well, I think I best be getting some shut-eye now," the captain said, shutting his eyes.

Signaling to Ben, he would like to stop talking and be left alone. Without opening his eyes, Seymour told Ben he best get back before someone thinks he fell overboard. Ben excused himself and closed the captain's door behind him. When Ben got to the deck, the sky is filled with ominous dark clouds.

An eerie feeling washed over him; Ben turned to look out over the water in a different direction to see they have been engulfed in growing darkness. Ben cried out from the top of his lungs; a figure joined him on deck moments later.

"Is everything alright," Daniel asked, with a sense of panic invoice. "What's going on?"

Ben pointed up to the swirling vortex of clouds gathering around the ship. "There's a storm coming."

"I need you to get to the bridge and relieve the fella there; I'll need him below, take the wheel. Hold the course best you can."

"Okay, hold the course. Got it," Ben said, having to shout over the wind striking across the deck.

Rain began to fall, carried in all directions by the rising wind. Ben entered the wheelhouse; he delivered Daniel's request and took his place at the wheel.

Ben thought of the advice his friend gave about the unpredictability of storms and how merciless a storm at sea could be.

Ben's thoughts flash out of him when the wheelhouse door flew open bashing against the wall. The storm taunting him to come out, Ben tied the wheel and fought his way to the banging door, and forced it closed.

Ben moved back to the wheel, taking some doing to hold the course. The wheel moved as if under its own power. Ben's heart fell to the pit of his stomach. The ship's phone ringing almost could not be heard over the raging storm. The young sailor struggled to control the ship and reached for the receiver.

"Ben!"

"I'm here."

"Ben, the storm is worsening. I'm sending help."

"What? Speak up, I can't hear."

"I'm sending some help!" Daniel said, again from the engine-room.

"Alright and hurry, I can't hold it."

Ben dropped the receiver and pulled hard on the wheel, feeling a bit relieved at the news. He watched a wave climb over the railing and crash on the deck with a horrifying thunder, like a hundred sledgehammers pounding the deck all at once. Ben's breath caught in his chest; he gripped the wheel for dear life.

"Boy, that was a good one," a voice said, from behind him.

Ben engulfed in his fear doesn't hear the man's voice.

"Ben, you alright," the man asked. "Gees, Ben, you're white as a sheet."

"Here let me..." the sailor grabbed Ben's arm, which is rigid like aboard.

"Ben, Ben! Let go of the wheel, Ben!" With great effort, the man pried Ben's hands from the wheel.

"Snap out of it, Ben. I've seen way worse storms than this."

"Sorry, I'm alright now."

"I got this. You go below and see if they need help."

Ben gave the man a nod and opened the door; the wind ripped it out of his hand and banged it against the wall again.

"Sorry." Ben grabbed for the door and pulled it closed behind him.

He is tossed about the deck against the fury of the storm. The wind-driven rain is cold and sharp against Ben's face, whipping him from all directions. Lightning flashed across the sky temporarily blinding Ben, compounding his difficulty across the heaving deck to the door leading below.

"Ben, why are you here," the captain asked, coming up the corridor.

Ben is alarmed by the sight of him, but glad to see him just the same.

"I, I was going down to see if I could help." With Ben's trailing word, he and the captain are thrown against the wall of the corridor.

"Looks like we're in for it tonight."

"In for it?"

Seymour holding his shoulder read the fear in Ben's face. He tried to walk back what he had said. "I mean it's going to be rainy all night, that's all."

Ben bracing himself against the wall said, "You need to get back to your cabin, captain before you start bleeding again. You can't do no good."

"But," the captain said.

Ben pretends not to hear him and moves himself under the captain's arm.

In the captain's cabin, Ben helped him back to his bunk.

"There, now you need to stay here sir," Ben said, through chattering teeth.

"You're a good boy. Ben, before you go, I could use something a little stronger than coffee. Please, could you find me some whiskey? Or whatever them damn German's have. Check over there." Seymour pointed in the direction of a set of wooden shelves along the wall.

Ben moved to investigate the shelving; there alongside some books was a bottle of what looked to be some kind of alcoholic beverage. Ben pulled the bottle from the shelf and opened it, putting it to his nose then pulled it away quickly.

"Yep, it's something alright." Ben moved back to the captain's side.

"Oh, it doesn't smell that good, but it does warm the bones," the captain said.

Ben poured the toxic liquid into a small glass resting on the end stand of Seymour's bunk and handed it to the captain who drank it down.

Ben remembering, he still had the jewel, reached into his pocket and held it out to Seymour. The jewel glimmered sending a spectrum of green and blue rays of light around the room. Ben moved closer to the captain.

"Here, captain, I saved it from the Alexandria."

Seymour looked at the jewel than to Ben's eyes. He reached out his hand; with his fingers closed Ben's hand around the jewel.

"You best hold on to that for safe keepin' boy. Don't let old Edgar find out you got it." the captain told Ben.

"But it should be yours. It's all the treasure we found."

"Ben, do as I say, keep a hold of it and keep it safe. Got it?"

"Got it, captain." Ben slipping the treasure back into his pocket. "Sounds like the storm is getting worse, I should go see if I can help."

"Ben, take my coat there."

Ben took the coat and raced out. On deck, things have gotten much worse, the sky roared like an angry beast. With lightning dancing across the sky as if hell itself released its ferocity upon the ship. Ben standing in the doorway watched Edgar yelling, his voice muted under the sound of the raging storm. Only bits and pieces of orders scattered through the air.

The sailors on deck complied with Edgar's orders and went below. Edgar pulled himself along the rail to the front of the ship to check the anchor. Ben is pushed out of the doorway by a sailor coming up behind him to deliver a message to Edgar. Leaving the relative safety of the doorway Ben moved down the deck a ways to listen to what was being said.

"Daniel said, 'We're taking on a lot of water,'" the man continued. "He is down there trying to help with the pumps, but they can't keep up. If we can't get the water out of the ship, we won't last long."

Edgar began his reply when the radio antenna mounted over the wheelhouse gave way crashing into the sailor next to Edgar, knocking the man unconscious. The wire still blowing around the deck caught Ben in the face opening up a small gash across his cheek.

Ben screamed in pain. Edgar helped to revive his friend and get him to his feet. Abe appeared on deck before he could question Ben, Edgar ordered him to help the injured man below.

"Ben, you be careful out here," Abe said, guiding the man to the doorway.

Ben gave Abe a wave of compliance inching his way out to the railing along the port side of the ship. The vessel groaned under the pressure from the pounding waves. Through a surge of rain and wind, Ben can make out Edgar's figure along the railing heading for the bow of the ship. For a moment, all is dark again. When the lightning returned, the place where Edgar had been standing is empty and Edgar is gone.

In a panic, Ben tried to pull himself along the railing to get to the spot, but as the ship heaved, he is knocked to the deck with a thud. He moved up the deck on his belly as if he is swimming.

He scrambled to his feet and lunged for the railing. In the water, he spotted a figure of a man bobbing up and down with the rise and fall of the waves. It is dark again, and the figure is gone.

Edgar, he's gone. He's really gone. For the smallest amount of a second, Ben is relieved the source of all his pain and trouble aboard the ship was gone. Oh no... he's gone.

"Edgar!" Ben yelled, to the black water. "Edgar, where are you!"

For a moment, Ben listened but heard nothing. Ben yelled again, his voice silenced by the rumbling thunder and crackling lightning. The young frightened boy kept calling; all his fear and panic erupted into a state of desperation.

"Ahoy, I'm here."

"Edgar!"

Ben turned and grabbed the life ring out of the survival box and threw it out to sea as hard as he could, hoping it was enough. Benjamin strained to hear Edgar's voice carrying on the wind.

"I, I got it."

Ben pulled hard on the rope. His feet slipped on the wet boards, and he fell again. Before he had time to gather himself, a wave pinned him to the deck causing Ben to swallow a mouth full of saltwater. When the wave pulled back to the sea, Ben lied motionless his body rocking back and forth with the rhythm of the ship.

 As if startled awake by a bad dream he jerked, coughing seawater out of his gut. His eyes burned making it hard to focus. Gathering his senses, he put his hands to his face. He was no longer holding the rope. Ben searched for the end, finally finding it stuck on a bolt holding the rail to the deck.

 Again getting to his feet, he pulled hard; suddenly the rope went limp sending Ben crashing against the survival box. Ben didn't stop, he kept pulling up the slack, more and more rope came on deck.

"There," Ben said, as the rope went taut again.

He slammed his foot against the railing and pulled with all his might, grunting against the terrible weight of pulling Edgar's body through the water.

"Hurry," Edgar said, from the angry sea. The rope cut into his hands and they began to bleed. After pulling and losing ground to the sea and gaining it back again, he is worn out, his arms ached, and his breathing is labored.

A little more, he told himself, why doesn't someone come?

Ben couldn't go on and stopped pulling.

"Help!" Ben started to yell. "Help, somebody help!"

"I can't... I can't hold on."

The sailor staffing the wheel doesn't hear Ben's cry but spotted him on deck waving one of his arms.

"Oh my..."

The sailor blew the ship's horn; it barely made a sound over the storm. The ship heaved and rocked violently with every swell compounding Ben's pain with every passing minute.

Two figures began to appear down the deck. Their shapes distorted and blundered against the ship's lights and the heavy wind-driven rain. The two struggled to remain on their feet, being thrown about the deck. They reached Ben. Each man grasped the rope and pulled until Edgar came alongside the ship.

"We need to get..," one of the men said.

"What? I can't hear you."

"We need to get him out of the water before he gets beat to death off the side."

The two strong men finished Edgar's rescue. "Hurry, we're running out of time."

A moment later, Edgar is on deck with the rest of the group. Ben, unable to offer any more help, slid down the railing post.

"You get the boy," the sailor said to the other.

The man latched onto Ben and picked him up in one motion. The group made it to the doorway leading below, the wheelmen seeing them clear the deck cut the horn. Along the corridor, their feet sloshed through a few inches of seawater accumulating. The water carried cups, clothing, and hats, which were bumping against their legs.

 They entered the sickbay where Abe after getting word, was waiting to offer his help. The sailors put Edgar on the table, and Abe put his ear to his chest. The men and Ben waited to learn about Edgar's condition.

"His breathin' is good, doesn't look like he drowned, just had too much water. He's lucky to be alive. Any longer, I don't know. I've seen men drown for less," Abe said, putting a blanket over Edgar.

"The ship is not rollin' so bad now, maybe the storm's lettin' up," Abe said.

"No, it's not the storm, it means we're taking on too much water," a sailor said.

Ben's head bobbed a little with each heave and roll of the ship. He looked up at Abe who was propping him up.

"Abe," Ben said, "I didn't even know it was you."

"Yeah, you're kind of out of it. Too much salt water I suspect. You're goin' to be alright after we get ya warmed up."

"Give me another blanket."

Ben can't keep his body from quivering uncontrollably.

"I'll take care of them, you get back down below and give Daniel a hand," Abe said, to the sailors.

Ben attempted to get up. "I have to go and help too."

"You never mind about that now. Here, take this and drink it."

Without question, Ben reached out his shaking hands and took the glass from Abe. This amber-colored liquid smelled like the toxic mix Ben gave the captain.

"Uhh, what is it," Ben asked, his face contorted to resemble that of a grumpy sea turtle.

Abe glared in Ben's direction, Ben said nothing further putting the glass to his lips. He turned his attention back to Edgar, who was still lying on the table lifeless, but breathing. Ben watched Abe's attempt to revive him.

Abe slapped Edgar across the face. "Come on now, wake up. Come on, spit it out."

This startled Ben, leading him to a newfound respect for Abe, who was demonstrating a hidden bravery Ben was unaware of. After a few more slaps, Edgar began to come around. His eyes flickered open, swirling around the room not fixing on any one object.

"That's right you're alive. See you're gonna be alright."

Edgar started to cough out the excess seawater from his body onto the floor; gasping for air, he righted himself.

"What the hell you lookin' at?" Edgar snarled at Ben, who had been watching.

Ben said nothing and looked away. The liquor taking effect Ben felt himself warming up from the inside out, filling him with the urge to sleep.

"You be nice to that boy you old sea dog, he saved your life," Abe said, to Edgar.

Abe's words re-alerted Ben to his surroundings.

"Me? He saved me?" Edgar questioned, wearing an expression Ben nor Abe had ever seen him with an expression of surprise and disbelief.

As hard, as Edgar tried he was unable to remember much of what happened after he was washed overboard.

"It's true. Ben was the only one that saw you go in. That boy almost joined you, too."

Ben under the influence of the tonic thought Abe's statement made him sound somewhat heroic.

Edgar staggering to his feet rocked back and forth with the ship. He took the whiskey bottle sitting next to Ben and gave himself a drink. Swallowing hard, Edgar stepped to the door and out of sight without a word.

Well, at least he didn't kill me for saving him, anyway.

Abe reached over and took the empty glass from Ben before he dropped it on the floor, "Boy, I think you have had enough of that."

"You stay here. I'm gonna look for something dry for ya to put on."

Ben gave Abe a nod. A moment later he watched Abe dart from cabin to cabin, pulling out drawers and looking in trunks.

A few minutes later Abe returned with something. "You put these on before you catch your death." Abe put the old clothes on the stool next to Ben.

"Now, stay put, I have to go and check on the captain and see what's goin' on."

"Alright."

Ben with some effort stripped himself of the salty, wet clothes. He shivered when the air of the cabin hit his bare skin. Without wasting time, he got dressed. Either he is still overly comfortable with himself from the effects of the whiskey or these clothes seemed to fit him a little better than the ones he had on. Ben looked up to see Abe wade past the doorway pointing his finger at Ben to continue to stay in the cabin.

After checking on the captain, Abe made his way to the engine room where he found Daniel and the men frantically working on a pump. The water rose to the men's waists. He joined the men.

"It's no use. It's seized up," Daniel told Abe. "If the water gets much higher, it'll dowse the fire in the boiler, and then we'll roll over and sink."

"No, no, I ain't losing two ships. I don't like to swim, and I ain't no fish."

"Gimme that," Abe said, taking the oversized wrench from one of the sailors standing by.

"I." Abe struck the side of the pump.

"Ain't." Abe struck the side of the pump again.

"Goin' swimmin' tonight."

With Abe's final blow, the pump fired to life. Astounded, Daniel stared at Abe with disbelief. Pleased with himself Abe handed the wrench back to the sailor who looked at it before his eyes fell back on Abe, who was treading water back to the steps.

"Nobody can do nothin'. I gots to do everything myself."

The men cheered him as he climbed the steps. The water in the engine room receded, and the men were able to get the leaks in the hull under control. The storm gave way to the morning dawn breaking over the horizon filling the porthole windows with a welcoming warm light. Tired himself, Abe returned to the cabin he left Ben in.

When he entered, he was surprised to the captain's cat curled up on Ben. The two-fast asleep on the table. With the seas calm, the water sloshing around the ship's decks found its way back to the sea, and objects laid at rest where the sea left them. Abe lay down on an empty bunk and closed his eyes.

It would be midday before either of the three would wake. Edgar who had been busying himself on the bridge since his rescue also surrendered to his own exhaustion and faded off in a chair. He was woken several times by his own snoring, annoying the poor sailor operating the wheel. It's only when the captain entered the wheelhouse and gave Edgar a kick to his boots does he wake.

"Where are we," the captain asked.

Not sure himself, Edgar looked to the sailor at the wheel.

"Coming up on the Islands of the Bahamas, we were blown off course quite a ways. We should be able to see the coast of Florida in a couple of hours off the port side."

The captain picked up the com phone and waited for the engine room to answer. Rubbing his face with his hands Edgar asked the captain if he's all right before he could answer the engine room picked up his call.

"Engine room." the voice on the other end of the line answered.

"It's the captain. What kind of shape are we in down there?"

"Morning captain, well we're low on fuel, but the boiler is running good, and we managed to get the leaks stopped."

"Where's Daniel?"

"He went to get some shuteye; I can go and get him if. . ."

The captain cut him off. "That's alright let him be a few more hours, captain out."

During the captain's conversation with the sailor, Edgar left the wheelhouse for the galley for some coffee.

The captain not satisfied with the information he is getting about the goings-on of the night before, left the bridge to further question the crew. Ben finally stirring from his sleep awoke with a thumping headache to find Abe had already gone. Ben exited to the galley.

On entering Ben saw Abe tending to breakfast while a sailor complained about not being able to recognize the food again.

Over against the wall, the captain is questioning Edgar and a few other sailors. Who are grumbling about the coffee between Seymour's questions.

Ben felt Edgar's eyes following him to the counter. Ben picked up a tray and offered it to Abe, who gave him a welcoming smile. Ben chose a table with his back to Edgar and the captain; he can't help but catch a few words between them. Ben hoped food would counteract the effects of Abe's tonic and the saltwater he consumed the night before. After finishing his food, he came to the conclusion it doesn't.

"Well, good morning, Ben." the captain said as he joined his table.

Ben looked up at the captain, the sunlight streaming through the porthole window over the captain's shoulder worsened the thumping in his head.

"I hear you had a busy night."

"Edgar tells me you didn't let him drown out there in the water. He also tells me you nearly drown yourself."

Surprised at the captain's words Ben turned to glance at Edgar over Seymour's shoulder. Edgar doesn't return the glance.

"He said that," Ben asked, having trouble bringing himself to believe it.

"That's what he said," the captain took a long sip of his coffee.

Ben felt uncomfortable about the thought of Edgar talking about him in any way. The two sat in silence for a long moment until finally, the captain excused himself to return to the bridge after reminding Ben of his duties later that night. Ben is again alone at his table. No longer distracted by his headache, he pondered the captain's words over and over again.

Could Edgar really have said that? Is this just another trick?

Ben figured Edgar must have hated the fact, of all the people on board, Ben is the one to save him. Ben decided to not mention this to anyone to see what happened next. He is getting too close to home, too close to seeing his mother; can't afford to make any mistakes that would ruin it for him. Ben watched Edgar stand up and leave without a word to anyone.

That evening Ben took his turn at the wheel relieving the day turn sailor. The captain stayed for a while with Ben.

"How's your shoulder," Ben queried, not taking his eyes off the horizon.

"Oh, much better. It's still sore and stiff but better."

"This old tub doesn't make wake, as well as the Alexandria, did." the captain paused.

"What is it?"

"Let's see, hold a heading of 350 degrees."

"Aye, captain. Captain? Where is Edgar from anyway?"

"I'm not quite sure, really. He told me one thing, but then I heard something else."

"Has he always been like this," Ben asked, cautiously.

The captain laughed at the way Ben put his question.

"Edgar is a different sort of fella that's for sure. I know of other ships he's served on. I can say one thing: He's a damn fine seaman. About the rest, well-"

Before Ben could ask another question, the bridge phone rang.

Seymour picked up the receiver, "Captain?"

"Yes, what is it?"

"Pressure's holding steady and the water level is at 18 inches."

"Good work, Daniel."

The captain hung up the phone and turned for the door, "Well Ben, the bridge is yours. I am turning in for the night. If you need anything, just use the phone and hold your heading."

"Yes, captain."

Alone with his thoughts, Ben's mind drifted from Jacob, his mother, stickball in the street and back again. Somewhere between getting beat up by a kid named Michael Ciardi and almost being trapped in the stone island tomb forever, Ben drifted to sleep. His body hung on the wheel, rocking him back and forth like a cradle. The ship began to sail its own course away from Ben's.

Ring! Ring! Ring!

Ben's eye popped open, his head darted around the room not sure what was happening. The ship's phone continued to ring. Ben picked up the receiver and said hello.

"Everything alright?" a sailor asked, "You took a while to answer. Are you sure you're alright up there by yourself?"

"YES."

Ben tried to stretch the phone cord the distance from the wall to the wheel and compass.

"What did you say took you so long to answer?"

"I'm trying to drive up here," Ben snapped back.

"Don't have to be cross, just checking in."

While the sailor continued to chatter on the other end of the phone, Ben's view caught the time on the clock hanging on the wheelhouse wall. It read 2:30. His heart fluttered as he hung up the phone while the man on the other end was still trying to question him.

"I started my shift at eleven, how long was I asleep?" Ben said aloud.

He checked the heading on the compass, 010 degrees.

"010 degrees! Oh, no!"

Without thinking, Ben pulled hard on the wheel to bring the ship back on course sending some of the sailors flying out of their bunks, including Edgar and the captain to the floor.

Ben looked from window to window into the blackness hoping that somehow he would be able to tell where they were. Minutes later the wheelhouse door busted open, first the captain then Edgar.

"What? What's wrong, Ben? What happened," the captain asked him.

Edgar stood next to the captain. Ben stuffed his hands into his pockets, too embarrassed to speak he stood silent at the wheel; his gaze pinned to the floor.

"I'll tell you what happened, he fell asleep," Edgar said.

"Ben- did you fall asleep on duty?"

Ben knowing full well to answer would feel the same as pulling the rope on the gallows.

Ben swallowed hard, looked at the captain, then at Edgar and, answered, "Yes. I did."

Ben's body quivered with every word, not from the fear of punishment, he rightly deserved but from the disappointment, he felt from letting the captain down. Expecting to hear from Edgar, the words of how he could have destroyed them or how a boy doesn't belong onboard, but Edgar offered none. The silence from the two is almost worse than punishment.

The captain picked up the sexton left behind by the former owners and stepped to the window. Edgar took over the wheel, awaiting a new heading from the captain. Ben stood there useless and in the way. The tension in the room became unbearable. Ben moved to the door.

"Ben," the captain said.

Ben turned to face him.

"You don't have permission to leave the bridge."

"You got us off course, you fix it. Come over here."

Edgar staring out the window said nothing. Puzzled by the captain's actions Ben jumped at the chance to make things right, to make this sick feeling in the pit of his stomach go away as soon as possible.

 For the next few hours, Ben worked with the captain learning and plotting his way back on course for home. Ben with a lesson learned is given permission to leave the bridge. The captain and Edgar remain. As Ben left, Edgar turned from the windows and gave Seymour a look.

"What?"

Edgar without saying a word returned to look out the window again. Word spread around the ship, first how Ben saved Edgar and then how he fell asleep on duty. Ben is getting some mixed glances from the crew making it hard to tell his friends from enemies. The men of the sea don't take kindly to someone being derelict in his duties. The crew became unsettled. Ben's supporters take argument with those who want to see him severely punished.

Chapter 31

The Journey Home

Later, that afternoon when the young sailor had awoken from a well-earned nap, he worked hard to avoid the crew altogether. He wandered around the deck playing with the Admiral. Ben was all the way to the stern when he heard the call.

"Land ho!"

"Look, there. I see it."

Sailors rushed to see for themselves what it is the man at the railing port side was pointing at. Out across the water, they saw the coast of Florida. The crew looked upon the coastline as if it were the most beautiful thing they had ever seen.

Ben ran to the railing to see, shading his eyes with his hand. "What is it?"

"It's the coastline of Florida."

One of the sailors who had been using binoculars gave Ben a look. The young New Yorker had never seen this part of America in his life. Ben took in the wondrous sights of the coast, the wonderful wild birds, and pearly beaches. His memory immediately bounced to when he first saw the coast of the dreaded Treasure Island.

"Wow," is the only word Ben could say over and over about this beautiful place.

"Here, now. Let's have a look," another impatient man said to Ben as he took the binoculars.

Ben ran to tell Abe about the discovery. Across the deck, through the door, Ben rattled down the steps running into him coming up the corridor.

"Abe, we can see Florida. Does that mean we are getting close to home?"

"Yep, won't be long now, up the coast a piece."

"Tomorrow? Will we be home tomorrow?"

"No," Abe answered, with a smile inching its way across his face, "but soon."

"Come with me, Ben. I have a little treat for ya."

"What? What is it? Come on tell me?"

"Ol' Abe made a pie. It ain't the best pie I ever made, but it'll do."

"A pie? I love pie. What kind of pie? What kind of pie is it? Is it apple? Apple is my favorite," Ben continued, to chatter to Abe all the way back to the galley about pie. Entering the galley, Ben knew Abe had made his favorite; the aroma was intoxicating, he could almost taste it. Abe cut Ben a large piece of his steaming apple pie and handed him a fork.

"Thank you, Abe, thank you," Ben said, seconds before stuffing a forkful of the wonderful surprise in his mouth. It had been such a long time since he had tasted anything so good. While Benjamin savored every mouthful, Abe mixed the boy a glass of powdered milk to wash it down.

"Abe? Where are you from? New York too," Ben asked, between bites.

Abe finished his own pie and said, "No, I'm not from the big apple."

Ben laughed at Abe's words. "You said apple, and we're eating apple pie. That's funny."

Abe not appreciating the humor sat and stared at Ben impatiently waiting to finish his story.

"Sorry."

"I come from a town north of the big city, a little town."

"How did you get here?"

"You mean on the ship?"

"Yeah."

"Oh, well things changed where I lived, there wasn't much work, and I come from a big family. Lots of mouths to feed. Thus, me and my brother left to find work."

"So, you like ships and became a sailor?"

"I don't know about that, but I can cook and the captain was in need of one. So, here I am."

Ben offered his plate for another piece of pie. "Do you ever go home?"

Abe took the plate, added another piece, and handed it back.

"It's hard, but me and my brother do get to go back sometimes, and we write."

"Is that pie for anyone," Seymour asked.

"Didn't hear you come in captain," Abe said.

"Here you go."

"Captain," Ben asked, "Are you from New York City?"

The captain looked at Abe and then back to Ben. "No, well, I stay there now, but I come from Ohio. Cleveland, Ohio."

"Did you need to come here like Abe to find work?"

"No, I was in the navy for a while, when my tour ended, I just stayed. And being a sailor, it is all I know."

"Why all the questions?" the captain said, tossing Ben a question of his own.

"Oh, no reason. I thought maybe after we get home you know I might run into you guys that's all," Ben said, pressing his fork into the crumbs on his plate.

Seymour finished his pie and turned to leave. "Boy, you have bridge duty tonight. Don't be late."

Ben perked up at the news. "I won't, and I won't fall asleep again neither."

"You must be pretty happy, Ben. Soon you'll get to see your Mama."

Ben's eyes lit up at the thought of seeing her after so long. He has so much to tell her about his adventures and the people he's met. He thought maybe he would leave out the dangerous parts of his story.

"I would swim home if I thought it was faster," Ben said.

"No, don't do that little fish. We'll be home soon enough."

"You best get goin' if you're going to stay awake tonight."

Knowing Abe is right Ben said goodbye and left to rest before his duty. Out on the deck, the sun is warm and bright, the smell of the salt air washed over him. Seagulls flew overhead as if puppets suspended on a wire.

"Now, I gotcha," a man exclaimed, picking Ben up from behind lifting him off his feet and giving him a good squeeze. "How are ya, Ben?"

Relieved to see it was Daniel, who had captured him and not another, Ben answered, "Good, good."

Daniel laughed dropping him to his feet and strolling away.

Ben composed himself before retiring to his bunk. After a bit of rest, Ben washed his face and readied himself to join the captain and Daniel on the bridge. Ben came through the wheelhouse door; the captain looked at the clock on the wall behind the radio station.

"Right on time," he said.

Daniel on the wheel greeted Ben as he came in.

"Here, it's all yours," Daniel said, stepping away from the wheel.

Daniel gathered his hat and said goodnight passing Edgar on the way out who is on his way in.

Edgar hung his hat on a hook behind the door. "Captain."

"Edgar," the captain replied.

"Here you'll find the heading; the engine room reported full power."

Seymour leaned into Ben to whisper, "I left some coffee if you need it. Good-luck boy."

"Goodnight, all." the captain excused himself from the bridge.

Ben is alone with Edgar.

Ben thought was he staying to be sure he didn't fall asleep on duty again or was it something else? The hours passed without a word between the two, and then Edgar joined Ben at the wheel. He checked Ben's heading and reached into his pocket, pulling out a wad of bills.

"Here," bumping Ben in the elbow with the bills.

Ben looked at the bills, unsure why Edgar is offering him money.

"What's this for?" his eyes still fixed on the cash.

"It's yours from your letter. They must have fallen out of the envelope. I just keep forgetting to get it to ya."

Ben reached out, took the bills, and stuffed them into his pocket. "You took my money?"

"No, no," Edgar said, "the letter fell out of the mailbag by accident. I found it later. Not much sense in saving the letter after that, couldn't send it, anyway."

"You threw away my letter?"

"My mother... she doesn't know."

"All this time, I thought-but you-"

Ben stood there in shock at what he was hearing. He didn't appreciate the depths of Edgar's malevolence until now. How could he invoke such malice against another human being and still be able to live with himself. Ben's body is overtaken by shock and disbelief. Never in his young life has he ever known such hatred and betrayal.

"Check your heading," Edgar muttered, to Ben.

Ben pulled hard on the wheel to bring the ship on course. His hands gripped the wooden wheel tightly. He thought of how he almost killed himself to save him, so he could give him the chance to rip his heart out. It dawned on Ben if he hadn't saved Edgar, he would never have learned the truth about his letter or about what kind of person Edgar really was. Ben's emotions churned in him until he could no longer contain his anger, and he erupted in a fury.

"You say you had nothing to do with Jacob dying either, suppose you lied about that too!"

The words spilled out of Ben's mouth before he could stop them.

Edgar turned away from Ben, stepping to the door. "I meant Jacob no harm. He was a good man and a fine sailor."

Ben further confused by Edgar's comment watched him exit the bridge. Stop it, Ben told himself. He's just trying to get you to feel sorry for him.

Ben stewed over the ordeal for the next few hours. Around 5:30 am, all of his adrenaline used up. His thinking cleared.

No point in trying to get word to Ma now. I never done nothin' to him, Ben continuing the conversation in his head.

Ben skipped breakfast and went straight to his bunk to figure out what happened on the bridge.

Edgar stole my money, threw away my letter, tried to get rid of me, and threatened me, Ben thought. Out of the blue, he decided to come clean. Why? Ben was finding it hard to stay mad as his anger was giving way to the effort of trying to understand what it was Edgar was trying to say. Ben sat up in his bunk and began to talk to Tibbs, who was taking up space at his feet.

He didn't have to say anything he was home free. He had my money and knew no one would have ever found out.

Ben scratched at his head with both hands. "Okay, has he ever been nice to me? No, has he ever tried to help me? No, so why tell me about the letter? To be nasty? If so, then why give back the money?"

Ben sat there for a while not thinking about anything, his body pushing him toward sleep when "I got it. He was thanking me for saving him. It must have made him feel guilty about taking my letter. Feeling? Edgar doesn't feel anything."

Ben got up and moved to look out the porthole window. "Tibbs, do you think Edgar would feel like a normal person?"

"Listen," Ben told Tibbs, who is concerning himself with a cleaning. "Here's my problem, what Edgar did was really mean, but giving it back was a nice thing to do."

"So, is Edgar a somewhat nice person doing mean things or a mean person doing one nice thing?"

Ben sat back down and petted Tibbs. "I don't know, but it was a nice thing to do, anyway."

Ben put his boots back on and decided it was time to get some food. He picked Tibbs up and carried him on his way out the door.

"Has anybody seen Abe," Ben asked, popping his head in the galley door.

Two sailors sitting at a far table nodded in Ben's direction a no. Ben went to Abe's cabin and proceeded to knock on the door. However, Ben could hear him snoring so loudly he knew Abe would never hear his knock. Ben slowly opened Abe's door to find him asleep in his bunk.

"Abe," Ben yelled, "Abe, wake up. You know what time it is?"

"What?" Abe mumbled in his sleep.

"Wake up."

"What!" Abe barked, kicking off his blanket, "I am late, gots to go."

"Wait a second," Ben said.

"I have something to tell you."

"Ben? What are you doing here? Is everything all right? Are we sinking again?"

"No, I wanted to tell you something."

"Can it wait?"

"No," Ben pleading for Abe's attention.

"Well, hurry up."

Ben as quickly as he can without leaving out any of the details filled Abe in on what happened on the bridge. Abe is astounded by the speed in which Ben was able to tell the story.

"Well?" Ben asked his hands raised.

"Well, what?"

"Well, what I'm I supposed to think now?"

"That sounds pretty bad even for Edgar, Ben."

"You don't believe me?"

"Ben, you got any proof?"

Ben slow to answer knew where this was going. "No."

"Well, then it's his word against yours, and he did give back your money."

"That's what I mean, he didn't have to, and no one would ever know the difference. Why'd he do that?" Ben looked at Abe with an expression of total confusion.

"I don't know, Ben. You did just save his life, maybe that's his way of saying thanks."

"Thanks, would have been not to have taken my letter in the first place."

"I know it was bad, but he did the right thing in the end. That's what counts. You hear me boy?"

Ben returned to his cabin, tired and more confused he spread out on his bunk. He must have slept longer than he had intended because when he awoke the sun was setting in the westward sky. Streams of yellow, orange and red shined through the porthole window on to the floor.

Slow to wake Ben righted himself, rubbed his eyes, and rose to look out the window. Far off in the distance, he could make out the coast where exactly they were he's not sure. Ben straightened himself out the best he could and went on deck. He returned a friendly hello from one of the sailors roaming around.

 Still half-asleep and hungry, he set out to tame the rumbling in his stomach. The twilight cast shadows across the deck. Ben doesn't like this new ship much, he wished he and the rest of them were still aboard the Alexandria. The galley is half-full of sailors chattering away, some talking about plans they've made for when they arrive home.

Abe put a full plate of food in Ben's hands. "Good to see ya up."

Ben doesn't say anything, still sore at Abe for his comments from before. Ben put his fork in his pocket and sought out an empty table. In one corner sat a group of men talking, in the other sat Edgar. Ben sat in the middle.

"You know it ain't right, a fella falling asleep on duty," a sailor said, in a volume sure to catch Ben's ear.

"Put in the brig that's what they should do with him," another sailor said.

Slamming his fist on the table Edgar got up from his seat. "That's enough, no more, you hear? Drop it. The next man opens his mouth about it will be pullin' double duty."

At the conclusion of Edgar's speech, the men departed the galley with Edgar on their heels. Everyone in the proximity of Edgar's blast went silent. They have all seen his anger before, but never in the defense of anyone, and especially not Ben. Embarrassed Ben picked at the food on his plate not moving an inch until the last man has left.

"Well, what do you know?" Abe joined Ben at his table.

"Alright, don't you start," Ben said, without looking from his plate.

"I think maybe you have affected him."

"No, he just feels guilty."

"People can change you know."

"Yeah, and you can teach an old dog new tricks."

Wishing to change the subject Ben questioned Abe about where they were.

"The tides hold, we should be home in a day or two."

This news made Ben feel better.

"Abe, any of that pie left back there?"

"Sorry, Ben."

Disappointed Ben left stopping by the bridge on his way. The captain is listening to the radio with no time for Ben. On deck, twilight has slipped into night. The full moon is embedded in a sky of a thousand twinkling stars. A furry figure scampered out of a shadow. Ben is greeted by Tibbs.

 He began to stroke the fluffy orange coat. The cat's purring is soothing. Ben picked up the captain's cat and went below. Later in evening after Ben had had his fill of doing nothing in his cabin the boy decided to go back on deck for some fresh air.

 Coming up the corridor, Ben saw Edgar; he appeared to have been drinking. He moved from doorway to doorway his arms stretched out to steady himself. Ben watched him travel down the corridor. Edgar stopped and pounded on the captain's door.

 A moment later, the captain answered and Edgar entered shutting the door behind him. Ben moved to investigate.

"I want what's mine," Edgar said.

The captain attempted to lead Edgar to a chair. "What's yours? What are you talking about?" Edgar pushed Seymour's hand away and tipped back onto the captain's bunk.

Edgar closed one eye to better focus on Seymour. "The jewel you took from me, it's mine. I want it."

"Oh, that's what this is about."

"I don't have it."

"Liar," dribbled out of Edgar's mouth.

"No, I don't have it."

"Then who does?"

Seymour doesn't answer him.

"Doesn't matter. I'll find out."

"Forget about the jewel, I have something bigger and more valuable than any jewel. Something any man aboard this ship would kill for."

Ben is unable to catch anything of what's being said in Seymour's cabin. The steel walls don't transmit sound as well as the plaster ones in his apartment. Ben abandoned his mission, reported to the bridge, put in his shift and retired to his bunk.

Ben woke to a raining morning, the sky is grey, and the air is cool. Ben went about his business keeping an eye out for Edgar when at last he saw the captain on deck, clamoring away with Daniel. Benjamin joined the two.

"I swear, Ben, you've grown a foot these last few months. I bet your Ma won't even recognize ya," Daniel said.

Ben looked around the deck. It took Daniel a second to realize what he had said and how it may upset Ben to think about his mother.

"I mean…"

"Ben, you sleep alright," the captain asked.

"Yes, good."

"You have duty tonight."

"Yes, sir. Sir?"

"You'll be going to see Jacob's wife? I mean when we get back?"

"Yes, Ben. Daniel and I both are going."

The captain patted Ben on the shoulder. "But, I'll be seeing you home first."

"We should be in port soon. Right captain," Daniel said, attempting to change the subject.

"Yes."

Ben stepped to the rail; the fog made it hard to make out any coastline.

"You can't see New York yet, Ben," Seymour said.

"Well, we best not miss it. We ain't got the fuel to be wandering around lookin' for it," Daniel said.

The captain adjusted his cap and left the two.

Ben pushed his hands in his pockets. "I can't wait to get home and see my Ma."

"I know it's been far too long of a journey just to get back to where you started," Daniel said, turning and walking away.

Ben watched him go, then turned to look over the water. The rain came again, and Ben went indoors. The ship is quieter, men's minds preoccupied with thoughts of home.

Others dwell on the thought of returning home empty-handed. Some blame the captain, some plain bad luck. Seymour 's treasure hunting has never cost them so dearly before.

"There's always our wage to count on, we did deliver our cargo," a sailor said.

Toward evening, the fog cleared and Ben can see the coast. Other ships are also starting to appear.

Ben's ready to jump ship the moment they dock then thought about what the captain said, "I'll be seeing you home first."

Why would he take me home? Why? Maybe to smooth things over with Ma? Or to see I get there?

He doesn't think about it long; his mind is on something else.

Ben saw his friend coming down the deck. "Abe, could you give me a haircut, so I can look better for my Ma?"

"I suspect. Come with me."

The two go to Abe's cabin. Abe put Ben in a chair and rummaged around until he found a straight-edge razor.

"You're not using that, are ya?" Ben becoming concerned at the sight of the shiny blade.

"Do ya want a haircut or not?"

"Yeah, but I'd like to have my ears when you're done."

Abe positioned himself behind the frightened boy and shaved bits of Ben's brown hair away. The clumps fall to the floor.

"Abe, is the captain going to keep this ship or get another one?"

Abe turned Ben's head to get a better angle. "Well, I don't know what his plans are? He doesn't share nothin' with me."

"Maybe?"

"Ouch."

"Why? Why you want to know that?"

"Oh, what if I want to find you someday to say hello or something. If he gets a different ship, I won't know what it looks like."

"Don't you worry so much."

Abe continued to cut as the amount of hair falling to the floor began to worry Ben what he might be looking like.

"Can I see?"

"Sure, you go see."

Ben looked at his reflection in the mirror. "Wow, looks better, thanks."

"Now get something and clean up this mess," Abe said.

After dinner, Ben reported to the bridge as ordered. The captain, Edgar, and a sailor operating the radios are already there.

"There she is New York City!" A sailor called.

Ben rushed to the window to see what all the noise was about; then he saw it. The lights of New York City, sailors spilled onto the deck hollering and patting each other on the back.

"Unidentified vessel slow to one third," a voice over the radio ordered.

The captain gave a nod to comply.

"The city looks bigger," Ben said.

As the ship grew closer, the lights cast a sparkly reflection on the harbor.

The moment Ben had been dreaming about for months is finally here, it doesn't feel the way he thought it would. It felt good to be home but changed.

"It looks so different from what I remember."

"It's because you're not the same boy you were when you left," Seymour said.

"What do you mean?"

"You've done a lot of growing up, Ben. You're a young man now."

Ben waved at the other ships in the harbor as they went by. Ben spotted the Statue of Liberty; the lights gave her a green glow. He ran to the next window as they passed. He has never seen her from the harbor before.

"This is the harbormaster Identity yourself," the voice said over the radio again.

"This is the crew of the..."

"Best let me have it," the captain said.

"This is Captain Seymour Salinger of the lost U. S. S. Alexandria.

The radio went silent, Edgar watched the captain.

"Captain, make for dock six."

"Aye, dock six."

"Do not leave the ship harbor, master out."

"Here, let me have it," Edgar said, taking the wheel.

"There's our escort," Edgar said, watching a tugboat come alongside.

The captain lit a pipe he managed to find and began to tap his fingers on the radio box. Minutes later, the ship came to a stop alongside the dock. Dockworkers were already waiting to tie her up.

"All stop, cast the bowlines," Edgar shouted, from the bridge door.

"Well, best go see what's what," Seymour said, leaving the bridge, Edgar and Ben trailing after him. Daniel and Abe are already waiting at the railing. Coming up the gangplank is the harbormaster, a short, round man wearing a heavy blue coat and sailor's cap, along with a sharply dressed policeman.

"Captain Salinger," the man asked.

"Yes."

"You and your men are not permitted to leave this ship until I can see your manifest."

"I told you our ship was lost."

"Then you have some explaining to do. Officer, see no one leaves this ship," the harbormaster told the sharply dressed policeman standing by.

"Yes, sir."

The cop posted himself at the entry of the gangplank. Seymour led the harbormaster away to discuss the matter. Ben looked to the dock; he knew it well. His mind followed the path that led to his home. He is within running distance to his mother.

"How long is this going to take," Ben asked, with frustration in his voice.

"I got no idea."

Given Ben's last encounter with the cops, he's not keen on the fact that after his long journey home, they would be the first people he'd see. Ben moved himself away from the cop and to the bow of the ship where he watched the faces of the men working on the dock, passersby, and more cops posted there by the harbormaster in case anyone tried to make a run for it. The smells and noise of the city begin to be familiar to him again.

 The city almost seemed to be alive with itself like a magical creature of light and sound being attended to by its subjects. Abe joined Ben at the railing and looked at Ben, "See anything?"

"No. When can we get off?"

"I don't know; no one said. I don't like the docks, nothing but smelly fish."

"Ma, doesn't let me down here. She says, 'It's no place for a respectable boy.'"

"Sounds like she's a right-smart lady, your Mama."

"I can't believe we're stuck here."

"Why don't you, me, and the admiral go and get somethin' to eat?"

Ben transferred his view from the dock to his boots. "I am not hungry."

"Well, standing here ain't going to get us off this ship no faster."

Abe grabbed Ben by the shoulders and guided him away from the railing and into the direction of the galley. They find several other sailors sitting around also waiting.

"Abe, how about making us up some grub?"

"Sorry, boys the kitchen's self-serve today."

The sailor threw up his arms at Abe's comment. Ben and Abe head to the back of the kitchen and help themselves to sandwiches of jelly on bread. The day slipped into evening. The dock has gone quiet as the men wait to leave the ship.

"Look at the time. We have been sittin' here for hours." Abe said, his words giving way to a yawn.

Ben fought off the signs of fatigue setting in on him.

"Come on, Ben, nothin happening tonight."

"No, I'm alright. I can wait," Ben argued, his eyes half-closed with his chin resting on his hand to keep his head up.

"No, sir, you're goin' to hit your bunk mister," Abe said, to Ben getting up from his seat.

Ben does not argue a second time. Tired and disappointed Ben dropped on his bunk and fell asleep. He dreamed of losing Jacob and of their time on the island. Ben woke several times because of his own restlessness. The next morning Ben slept in while Abe is up and ready to start his day. Abe burst through Ben's cabin door. He shook Ben in an attempt to roust the boy from his slumber. "Come on sleepy head."

"I'm up, I'm up," Ben muttered, his eyes still closed.

Ben sat up and threw his legs over his bunk.

"Get up boy and get ready. We need to get up on deck."

Ben reluctantly readied himself and trailed behind Abe out the cabin door. Up on-deck, sailors have already gathered to observe the profanity and name-calling coming from the wheelhouse.

"Have they been at it all night," Ben asked, a sailor standing by.

"I don't know?"

The harbormaster exited the wheelhouse in an uproar yelling back at Seymour with every step toward the gangplank.

"Ah, go on with ya. Get off my ship," Seymour said, to the red-faced harbormaster.

From the wheelhouse door, Seymour paused to look at the sailors gathered on deck than to Abe and Ben.

"Well, you boys ready to get off this tub?"

The men let out a joyful hooray and scattered in all directions.

"Ben!" You meet me right here in half an hour and I'll take ya home," Seymour exclaimed.

"Aye, captain."

Home he said to himself all the way to his cabin. The word brought back images of his mother and the times they've spent together. It's the word Ben has longed to hear since his adventure had begun. Ben returned to his cabin to retrieve the few things he had left.

He is careful not to let anyone see where it is he has stashed his secret prize. Abe attended to his duties as did some of the other sailors who had to remain aboard. A half-hour later Ben waited impatiently on deck for Seymour until finally, he spotted him coming.

Seymour observing Ben's impatience waved his hand in understanding. "I'm coming, keep your shirt on."

"Well? You ready to go home," the captain asked, in jest of Ben's annoyance.

"Am I ready?"

Accompanying Seymour on deck is Daniel, Abe and a few others who have come to see Ben off.

Smiling, Daniel stepped up to Ben to say his goodbye. "You be a good boy and mind your Ma."

Daniel stretched out his hand and gave Ben a hardy shake.

"Daniel, thanks... you know for not letting the engine eat me."

Ben turned to face Abe. "Abe thanks, for everything. I am gonna miss ya."

Abe pulled an old handkerchief from his pocket and blew his nose. "You ain't been nothin' but trouble since the first day I set eyes on ya. Always needin' savin'."

Abe reached out for Ben and grabbed him for a hug. "You remember what ol' Abe taught ya, and you'll be fine."

Tears trickled down Ben's face. "I'm going to miss you, Abe. Come and see me sometime?"

"There, there now you best be goin', your Ma's worried sick about ya."

Abe pushed Ben back and walked away to hide his own tears.

Seymour placed his hand on Ben's shoulder and guided him to the gangplank. Ben looked one last time at the people that have become his family all smiling back at him and waving. One sailor stood at the ship's rail wiping his own tears and sobbing, "I can't wait to see my ol', dear muther; she's..."

"Shut up already," another sailor standing next to him said.

Ben even saw Edgar watching them leave. He gave them all a final wave goodbye and he and the captain stepped off the plank.

Seymour followed Ben down the dock, past the many crates and boxes making navigating in the right direction a little tricky. The friends finally reached the fruit market, which will lead them to the street Ben called home.

Ben's excitement grows; he is tempted to race as fast as his feet will carry him to the one he has missed the most. Ben and Seymour pass through the crowded market when Ben took notice of the street cop that had given him chase so many months before. The cop looked at Ben.

He doesn't recognize him and turned his attention back to watch the crowd of people. Ben and Seymour turn the corner leading to Ben's street, bustling with people of all shapes and sizes heading in all directions.

The captain struggled to keep pace with Ben's dashing and darting between the mass of bodies. He is a rather large man making his navigation into the surge more challenging than for the smaller boy leading.

"Watch it." one fellow barked at Seymour.

"Slow down, Ben."

"Come on! Keep up!" Benjamin called back to his captain, who was noticeably becoming out of breath.

Midway up the street, the noise level grew as so did Seymour's frustration.

"How can anyone live here like this," he said, getting drug back a few steps by some rather rude passersby.

"Ben!" a voice called out from the middle of the street.

It's one of Ben's schoolmates who is caught up in a game of stickball. Ben smiled and waved at the boy. A few steps later another boy shouted Ben's name.

"Are we almost there," Seymour asked, with one hand on Ben's shoulder.

"Yes, we are almost..."

"Ben!" A female voice cried out from somewhere above them.

Ben and Seymour stopped in their tracks and looked for the source of the voice.

Ben blurted out, "Ma!"

Ben's mother hearing his shout from the street waved her arms at her son from her window. Overexcited about what to do next, she darted into the apartment and back out again. Ben raced to the double doors of his apartment building, which led to the steps leading to his mother.

 The little, chubby woman with grey-hair waited for him at the top of the steps with tears streaming down her face. He embraced her; they hugged for a long moment followed by many kisses from his mother. Mrs. Holt pushed her son away and held him at arm's length to get a proper look at him.

"My boy I have prayed and prayed you would come back to me," Ben's mother said, through sobs of joy.

"Oh, Ben, how you've grown, you're so skinny. What have you been eating?"

"I'm okay Ma. I'm good."

"Ma, there's someone I would like you to meet," Ben said, turning sideways to reveal Seymour standing by the double doors.

Nervously, Seymour removed his cap and tried combing his hair with his fingers.

"Mrs. Holt." Seymour offered his salutations with the greatest respect and honor.

Ben's mother glared at him, like a dangerous lioness preparing to pounce on her prey. She started down the steps toward him. Ben attempted to pull his mother back, but it was too late, she was on her way. Mrs. Holt walked up to Seymour and put her finger in Seymour's face causing him to lean back.

"You, you're responsible for taking my son. I have a mind to call the cops, but I want you all to myself. They can have what's left."

Her eyes are wide and her cheeks are puffed out and rosy red. Ben leaped the steps to join his mother and Seymour who is now leaning so far back he almost toppled over.

"Ma, Ma stop," Ben shouted. "It's not like that; he saved me and got me home safe."

"I got stuck on his ship by accident and Captain Salinger saved me."

Ben hoped throwing Seymour's title out there would somehow impress his mother into backing down. However, it didn't. Seymour became completely frightened of Ben's mother, wishing he had said goodbye to Ben on the street. Seymour looked from Ben's beet-red face to the double doors several times. Ben's mother became wise to this.

"Oh, no, you're not going anywhere, mister. You're going to tell me everything."

Seymour raised his eyebrows in a confusion about what to do next.

"That's a good idea, Ma. Captain Salinger can stay for dinner," Ben said.

It isn't until Ben told his mother how much he loved and missed her did her expression soften again, turning her attention back to Ben. She took him by the arm and led him into the apartment door.

Ben turned to look at Seymour. The young man beckoned him to come. Seymour joyfully shook his head no. Ben gave him another forceful gesture to follow.

"Come in, captain."

Reluctantly, Seymour trailed behind them. For the next few hours, Ben ate his mother's home-cooked food and told her all about his great adventures, minus the scary parts. Moms don't always need to hear about the scary parts.

 When Ben and Seymour ate their fill and tired themselves out from talking, Seymour decided it was time to go.

"Thank you, Mrs. Holt, for everything. That's a great boy you have there."

"You're welcome captain," Ben's mother said. "Thank you for taking care of my son; he's all I got in this world."

Ben blushed at his mother's comment.

"Well, I'll see ya to the door, captain," Ben said.

He opened the door, and Seymour put his hat back on.

"Well, Ben this is it, you're home, come by and see me some time. I have enjoyed having you around. You're going to make a fine captain someday."

Ben overwhelmed grabbed the captain around his middle and gave him a hug. Unprepared for such a show of emotion, Seymour awkwardly patted Ben on the back. After releasing the captain, Ben reached into his pocket and pulled out the jewel.

Ben whispered to Seymour, "I still have it. I...I want you to give it to Jacob's wife."

"But, Ben, you need...," Seymour started to say.

"Please, I want her to have it. He was my friend."

Seymour didn't argue with Ben, took the jewel, put it in his pocket. While giving Ben a lasting smile and left the apartment.

"You make sure you take care of that shoulder and don't forget to feed Admiral Tibbs."

He watched his captain make his way down the rickety stairs. Ben stood there in the doorway a moment before he closed the door.

"Oh, Ben, it's so good to have you home," Ben's mother said, grabbing him and giving him another rib-breaking hug.

"Ma, Ma too tight."

"Sorry, dear."

The two entered the small living room. His mother sat in her chair and looked at Ben.

"Ma," Ben started. "I have something for ya."

Ben reached into his other pocket and removed some folded up bills and handed them to his mother. She took the money and looked with astonishment at her son.

"I earned it working on the ship," Ben said. "You don't have to worry so much now."

His mother welled up with tears of joy and pride for her son. She grabbed Ben again and pulled him into her bosom.

"Oh, Ben, I love you. I know your father would be so proud of you, what a fine man you have become, the man of the house."

Ben's heart filled with pride at his mother's words.

Chapter 32

The Adjustment

As weeks have passed since Ben has returned, he couldn't help feeling that somehow things were different. He was different. Somehow, his old life was gone, replaced with a new one based on a greater understanding of the world and himself.

"Ben, time to get up, you'll be late," Ben's mother shouted from down the hall.

Ben opened his eyes. The morning sun streaked through his window and struck his mirror over the dresser, filling his room with a bright and warm light. His excitement of what awaited chased away his sleepiness.

Ben threw on his worn and faded trousers along with his favorite worn-out shirt. His mother's voice traveled down the hallway again in search of Ben's ears. This time the sounds moved Ben to a smile. The sound of his mother humming to herself in the morning is something Ben had forgotten he missed so much while away.

The melody took him back, back to before he was swept away on his adventure many months ago. To a time when his greatest worry in life was getting enough of the gang together for a game of stickball.

He sat on his bed for a moment, rolling over in his mind how those memories seemed like a lifetime ago.

He was no longer the young boy struggling to find himself. Ben pulled on his holey socks and went to join his mother.

He pulled up his suspenders as he entered the dingy kitchen. The smell of his mother's cooking quickens his steps to his chair at the table. The smell of scrambled eggs and toast filled the room enticing his hunger.

"Here now, they're hot so eat slowly," Ben's mother said

Setting the plate of steaming eggs in front of him.

Fork in hand Ben dove into his plate of eggs, making weird breathing sounds. As he tried to cool the eggs in his mouth.

Ben's mother observing his impatience in waiting for his eggs to cool, and handed him a glass of milk, which Ben drank down full.

"Ah, thanks Ma," Ben said before he shoveled more eggs into his mouth.

Ben's mother joined him at the table not eating but watching her son as if it was the first time she had ever laid eyes on him.

After a minute or two, Ben looked up from his nearly empty plate with egg fragments clinging to his face. The noise of his fork clinking off his plate made him aware of the vigor in which he was devouring his breakfast. Ben dowsed with embarrassment set his fork down and wiped his mouth on his sleeve.

His eyes slowly moved from his plate to his mother's face. "What?"

"My, you sure have grown into a fine young man."

"Ah Ma."

"You're not my little boy anymore." Tears began to streak down her plump, rosy cheeks.

Ben got up from his chair and moved to put his arms around her. "It's okay, Ma."

Ben's mother squeezed him so tight he lost the ability to speak for a moment.

"I love ya, Ma. You know that always will."

Ben's words of love and comfort caused his mother to squeeze him even tighter.

"But, you're choking me, Ma." His face now various shades of red.

Releasing him, Ben's mother wiped her eyes on her apron and began clearing the dishes in an effort to compose herself.

"You best get ready; you don't want to be late."

Ben washed his face at the sink and pulled his semi-toothless comb through his dark hair.

"Brush your teeth mister, you don't want them falling out of your head like your Uncle Elmer." Ben's mother ordered. "Poor man could only eat bread and soup up 'til the day he died."

"Yes, Ma."

"I think I'm ready Ma."

"Do you have everything," she asked, inspecting her son from head to toe.

Not finding anything apparently wrong, she fussed with his hair, anyway.

"You be a good boy and do as you're told, and you'll be just fine. I love you, and I'll see you when you get home."

"Ma, I don't...," Ben started.

"Not another word, I made my decision. You're a grown man now," she said, putting on a firm face. Ben had come to know when she meant business.

Ben picked up the bag that his mother has prepared for him and flung it over his shoulder. Ben taller now, looked at his mother square in the eye, I love you and I'll miss you while I am gone.

"I love and will miss you too. Now go before I change my mind."

With a last look at his mother and his home, Ben closed the door behind him.

Down the rickety steps, he went. Out on the street, the sidewalk is full of people, and the noise of the city is everywhere. Ben dodged and weaved between passerby's stopping in front of the shoeshine stand. To see a man holding up a newspaper. The front-page read, "Germany Declares War."

The man in the chair looked over his paper to see Ben standing like a statue frozen to the spot. The man slowly folded back the paper to read the front page.

"Can you believe that? Germans always starting trouble. They're claiming some Americans made off with a ship right out from under them."

After recovering from the front-page news, Ben turned and continued down the street. His mind preoccupied with the memories of his own run-in with the Germans.

 It's not until Ben reached the turn that led to the fruit market. And onto the waterfront did he become aware of his surroundings. Ben saw the fat little man in the dirty apron arguing with a woman over the price of tomatoes. The market is busy as it always is on a Saturday morning. A few moments later Ben broke out of the crowded alley and onto the waterfront dock.

Chapter 33

The Reunion

The dock is lined with crates and baskets and barrels smelling of fish and wet rope. Ben made his way through the maze of goods waiting to be loaded onto the ships. He found himself standing alongside one ship that he has come to know so well. Onboard, the men take no notice of him right away, running about, following orders and making things ready.

"All right now don't be foolin' around there. Get to it," a man shouted, across the deck. He knew this voice. Ben noticed the name painted across the bow of the ship "The Alexandria II." A wide smile grew across his face.

He walked to the foot of the gangplank that led to the ship's deck. Ben threw his bag on deck at the feet of his old friend giving him a startle. The man turned ready to give him the what for when he broke into a laugh.

"Ben!" Abe yelled out.

On hearing Ben's name, the men stop what they are doing and turn to get a look. Ben gave them all a happy wave.

"Permission to come aboard?" Ben shouted.

Edgar who had been watching the men work turned as well to bring Ben into full view. He walked to the ship railing and looked down the plank at the young man waiting for an answer.

The crew stood silent, Abe looked from Edgar to Ben and back.

Edgar took a slow breath and replied, "permission granted," a piece of a smile hung on the corner of his mouth.

He turned and walked away to look as if needing to attend to something. Ben raced up the plank and gave his friend a hug.

"How you doin' boy?" Abe pushed Ben away to get a proper look at him. "I swear you've grown a foot taller since I've seen ya."

Ben stood there for everyone's inspection. Daniel approached him, grabbed hold of his hand, and gave it a hardy shake.

"Where's the captain?"

The group stood for a moment without saying a word looking between each other.

"What, what's going on?"

Abe spoke up. "Well, Ben, the captain… I mean Seymour… well, he retired and… well, Edgar is the new captain."

"Uh?"

"What are ya doing here anyway," Daniel asked, trying to recover Ben to his senses.

"Ma said it would be okay… you know do me good to be with you guys for a while longer."

Abe butted in, "Well, I'm glad to see ya boy. We could always use the help and I even still have your cabin open."

Edgar overhearing the conversation caught Ben's eye and gave him a salute off the rim of his cap.

"Well, come on now boy. We gots lots to do before we leave," Abe said, guiding Ben down the deck.

"Where are we going this time?"

"You don't worry about that now, we gots lots to do, Ben. Ol' Abe is glad you're back."

"Me too."

The two friends strolled down the deck with Tibbs trailing behind them.

The End